# THE WITCH FINDER

Tracy Whitwell was born, brought up and educated in the North-East of England. She wrote plays and short stories from an early age, then in the nineties moved to London where she became a busy actress on stage and screen.

After having her son, she wound down the acting to concentrate on writing full time. Many projects followed until she finally found the courage to write her first novel, *The Accidental Medium* – a work of fiction based on a whole heap of crazy truth.

Today, Tracy lives in North London with her son, and has written quite a stack of novels. She is nothing like her lead character Tanz in the Accidental Medium series. (This is a lie.)

**More by the author**

*Adventures of an Accidental Medium series*
The Accidental Medium
Gin Palace
Cross Bones
The Hidden Dead

# THE WITCH FINDER

## TRACY WHITWELL

PAN BOOKS

First published 2026 by Pan Books
an imprint of Pan Macmillan
The Smithson, 6 Briset Street, London EC1M 5NR
*EU representative:* Macmillan Publishers Ireland Ltd, 1st Floor,
The Liffey Trust Centre, 117–126 Sheriff Street Upper,
Dublin 1 D01 YC43
Associated companies throughout the world

ISBN 978-1-0350-3702-5

Copyright © Tracy Whitwell 2026

The right of Tracy Whitwell to be identified as the
author of this work has been asserted in accordance
with the Copyright, Designs and Patents Act 1988.

All rights reserved. No part of this publication may be reproduced,
stored in a retrieval system, or transmitted, in any form, or by any means
(including, without limitation, electronic, mechanical,
photocopying, recording or otherwise)
without the prior written permission of the publisher.

Pan Macmillan does not have any control over, or any responsibility for,
any author or third-party websites (including, without limitation, URLs,
emails and QR codes) referred to in or on this book.

1 3 5 7 9 8 6 4 2

A CIP catalogue record for this book is available from the British Library

Typeset in Stempel Garamond by Jouve (UK), Milton Keynes
Printed and bound in the UK using 100% Renewable Electricity by CPI Group (UK) Ltd

This book is sold subject to the condition that it shall not, by way of trade or
otherwise, be lent, hired out, or otherwise circulated without the publisher's
prior consent in any form of binding or cover other than that in which it is
published and without a similar condition including this condition being imposed
on the subsequent purchaser. The publisher does not authorize the use or
reproduction of any part of this book in any manner for the purpose of
training artificial intelligence technologies or systems. The publisher expressly
reserves this book from the Text and Data Mining exception in accordance with
Article 4(3) of the European Union Digital Single Market Directive 2019/790.

Visit **www.panmacmillan.com** to read more
about all our books and to buy them.

To all my beautiful witches. You know who you are.
And to a wondrous diva, Evelyn Mary Butler
(1935–2025). Rest in peace.

# PROLOGUE

Wyllam looks around him, eyes darting with fear and mistrust.

'There be more witches in this region than we can hang.'

Ivan looks terrified. 'Maybe they know the ones you're 'anging be not witches.'

'Halt that mouth of yours, you fool. Of course they be witches. Truth be, all of 'em are witches – these sly cows with their lies and their "ways". Once they've bred, we should hang 'em all. More peace for us. And that damned turncoat, a man who wants to defend these ugly crones – only right that he be dying with 'em. We're doing God's work.'

Ivan smiles. 'Well, if it be right with God, it be right with me. But I be thinking to get a new pricker. That one is obvious, Wyllam. Folk are getting wiser, not believing so 'ard.'

'When we reach Hawkshead I'll look for a craftsman who can make a cunning bodkin. One that no pryin' eye can suspect.'

As he speaks, he's still casting glances about him, obviously rattled. I'm absolutely stoked that I managed to smack Wyllam, but also scandalized by what he said. Bullshit misogyny as always, stretching back and back in time. It's so upsetting, as I've also seen love back then too – real love – and it feels like there are two kinds of men and they're almost a different species from one another. Just like there are different kinds of women, and the spiteful, manipulative ones seem to have had a ball going along with the murder of other innocent lasses, for material gain or to wipe out a rival.

The annoyance of it makes me try again for one last clout. I decide it will have more effect if I aim for Ivan this time, so I hold my palms up and, launching myself forward, clap him on his ears as hard as I can. Well, you've never heard a yelp like it as Ivan jumps in the air in fear, then falls on his backside. This time all the workers on the gallows stop what they're doing as Ivan continues to make terrified noises from the ground. Wyllam is absolutely infuriated by this display and crouches down by his 'friend'.

*'Get up. Get up now and don't be squawking like this.'*

Ivan turns to him and suddenly he looks only half-solid as the vision slides and I hear him, in the distance now, cry out tearfully, *'The witches be not happy with us!'*

That's when my vision goes and I pass out.

When I wake up, my duvet is in a bunch mostly to the side of me, and I'm lucky that I'm wearing my fleecy winter pyjamas or I'd be freezing now, as the heating's off and the chill in the air is bracing, to say the least. Inka is standing on the pillow next to mine, illuminated by my little glowing

Frida Kahlo night-light, which is kitsch but oddly comforting, staring at me with her big, wise cat-eyes. Goodness knows what I was doing in my sleep, but she's looking rather perplexed.

The clock says it's half-past five and I pull the duvet back around me, cooing at Inka until she snuggles into my chest and begins to purr. I can't remember all of my dream, but I know Thor was in it: my saviour, my Icelandic pocket rocket, who rescued me from being marooned and made it his quest to give me the beautiful time that he felt his best friend had denied me. I try not to dwell on his smile, his red-brown beard and his kiss. It's been three days and I've cried about my trip a lot. I've adjusted to my new friend Birta being dead as best I can, and I've accepted that I met an incredible man who is basically a gorgeous little wizard, but that he's a wizard with a girlfriend who lives in another country. As intense as everything was in those few days, I can't keep making these mistakes, swapping man for man and chaos for more chaos. I need to stabilize my head. But fuck me, I miss Thor so much, it's almost a physical pain.

I close my eyes again and sniff Inka's silky little head, feeling her pointy ears twitch against my face. She gives a tiny squeak of contentment and I whisper a little lullaby to her, comforting myself with the vision of a far-off cave filled with fire and ancient songs, and with the knowledge that in a dainty wooden box in my bedside drawer there is an exquisite little bell, gifted to me by the most precious of beings. A Hidden One from the land of deep drums and soaring eagles.

These calmer thoughts begin to weave their spell and

soon everything goes black. Then it swiftly occurs to me that if I was actually asleep, I wouldn't know everything had gone black, would I? And I sigh warily, as all at once I feel rough hemp over my face, with the smell of something fetid from the fabric choking me. The hemp envelops my whole skull and makes it hot and uncomfortable to breathe. Why is there a bag over my head? I can hear voices, some laughing and jeering, some sobbing, and my wrists hurt from being tied behind my back with a rough rope. I can also feel sore points all over my body. What the shitting hell have they been doing to this person? My heart races faster as I try to work out what's going on. I know this is me, but at the same time it's not me – I'm feeling someone else's pain. I also know that I'd like to wake up pronto. The bag is about to be pulled from my head, I know it is, and I truly dread seeing what happens next. I close my eyes tightly and will myself to wake up, now fully sure that I'm inside someone else's head. I call out to my dead bestie and will him to reply. This really is the fucking limit.

'Frank, I've had enough excitement recently to last me a lifetime. You let me wake up now or I'm going to kill myself, then come and find you and punch your lights out.'

Just as the bag is being pulled from me and bright light is piercing my closed eyes, I flicker them open and find myself back in bed, Inka still snuggled in and my nightlight shining right in my face. I shouldn't have it on really, as I like to sleep in complete darkness, but after my latest adventures I'm still too unsettled to remain in the absolute dark.

'Frank, for God's sake, you come here now and tell me

what all that was about. I'm trying to sleep here – I can do without more nightmares.'

Frank is a law unto himself when it comes to showing up in my head. He's been especially flaky lately, disappearing for ages at a time and leaving other 'voices' to help me work out what's happening in the world of spookiness. Thankfully this time he obliges me.

'*Hello, Tanz, nice pyjamas.*'

'Bugger off, they're very cosy.'

'*I actually mean it, you touchy cow.*'

'What was that horrible vision I just had? I'm absolutely not being dramatic when I tell you that I'm still processing what went on in Iceland and I can't cope with more darkness and drama.'

'*Oh, come on, you live for the drama – that's why you're an actress. Anyway, as I told you on your flight back, a bit of catch-up on sleep and then it would be showtime.*'

I feel absolute panic when he says this. 'Please, Frank. Please, please let me recover for a bit. I'm not feeling right at all. I've felt floaty and "not in myself" for three days. I'm dizzy and tired, and I think I'm coming down with something.'

Frank's voice is unaccustomedly gentle when he replies, '*Tanz, I don't make the rules. If it was up to me, I'd let you snuggle in bed for a month. But things "come up", certain energies are attracted to you like a beacon, and you use your magic to help whoever is calling for aid. That's what you're wonderful at. But if it makes you feel any better, you have a lot of support from this side right now, and we will do everything we can to make this as gentle as possible.*'

'Why do I need fucking reinforcements, Frank? Usually I don't need a legion of helpers; you and the odd soft-voiced lass or healing angel can do the trick. What's going on?'

*'Nothing you can't handle. You'll never be sent something you can't handle. Now get some sleep. No more weird dreams tonight, I promise.'*

'Frank.'

*'Yes?'*

'I feel so fucking odd. I think I'm scared.'

*'Don't be. You're in safe hands.'*

Thinking back to how many times I've been in mortal danger since Frank reappeared in my life, that isn't as comforting as he thinks it is.

# LONDON EYES

Sheila and I are on the London Eye. This huge wheel, with its pods made mostly of glass, moves very, very slowly. Annoyingly so, as it happens. I know it's meant to turn at a sedate pace so that we can look over the whole of London, but come on: I at least want to feel some motion – this is like a massive circular stairlift.

I called Sheila as soon as I woke up this morning and said I really needed to chat, to get my head straight. I mean how many people can you talk to about ghosts, dead mates who you think are alive, portents of doom while you're trying to get your beauty sleep, and little Icelandic sex gods that you only knew for a few days but can't dislodge from your every waking thought? Sheila's just glad I'm home in one piece after I disappeared to Reykjavik without a word, so she inexplicably suggested that we have a little day-trip around the River Thames. We don't do touristy things as a rule, but it seemed like a nice idea at the time, so I said yes.

After we arrived at Waterloo station, coming on this

big glass wheel was an impulse decision and now we're trapped in this fish bowl in the sky, with cold sunshine streaming in through the windows. Luckily it's only us in this pod; the one before us had a gaggle of very animated young Japanese tourists boarding it, and I really don't have the bandwidth for that kind of noise at the moment.

Sheila is wearing green velvet trousers with a silky black jumper and her customary gemstone silver rings and jingling bangles. I'm very happy to see her and to smell the Samsara perfume that surrounds her in a sexy fog.

'So, Tanz, without wishing to sound like your mum, what the hell were you thinking: jumping on a plane like that?'

I sip at a can of Diet Coke that I'm not supposed to carry on here, as there's a no-food policy and the only drink allowed is water, but my tolerance for rules seems to be wafer-thin right now.

'I don't know, Sheils. I'm pretty sure I've been having a bit of a breakdown since the whole business at Cross Bones Graveyard. That's the second time someone has tried to murder me in cold blood. Plus, I don't know, the rest of the time when I'm not being subjected to mortal danger I find life really, well, dull. I don't seem to have a middle ground. Nothing makes me feel just happy.'

Sheila's laugh is welcome and infectious. 'Of course you feel bored by ordinary life – you're a witch, you need something deeper than the norm. And you do get very caught up when you're attracted to someone. But I must say, it was dangerous running off like that and not telling me where you were . . . You could have disappeared for ever; that idiot Einar could have been a killer, and no one would have known how to find you.'

'Sorry, Sheils, I know it was crazy, but it turns out I was there for more than snogging a nutter. My instincts weren't wrong – I needed to be there. Einar was just the lure, then everything changed when I got there and the true purpose was revealed. As Birta said, it was a kindred soul calling out for help, and I answered.'

Sheila sits on the bench in the centre of the pod and I join her. She pats my arm.

'Well, I can't argue with that, sweetheart, I suppose. And I do feel I need to say something about what happened with your friend Birta. We know, from your experience with Nelly and her family at Cross Bones, that you are no ordinary medium. In your dreamworld you basically time-travelled and haunted generations of a family. I've never met such a highly developed dream warrior.'

Fuck, what a great term! I'm absolutely delighted to be a dream warrior; it certainly sits better with me than some of the names I've been called in my lifetime.

'But the thing is, Tanz, you've now gone higher up in frequency again, since you met Birta and communed with the Hidden Ones in Iceland. I can feel it coming off you in waves. What happened with you and Birta was something I'd not even heard of anyone doing before – not in real life – so to be honest, you're the teacher and I'm the student here. You hung out with a ghost in their own lifetime, like they were solid and real right now. It's like you met in a twilight world between the living and the dead. Birta wasn't lying to you; she was solid and alive where you met, and you eventually set her free without her prompting you at all. I don't have a clue what you'd even call that; it's a beautiful thing, but it's also so far up the evolutionary scale of being a "seer" that you're lucky you don't fall off the top. I think you probably feel dizzy at the moment because you aren't quite settled back into your body. Some may say you dreamed your experiences with Birta, but I'd say you linked in so hard that your spirit-self took over.' Sheila reaches out now and pushes a strand of hair away that's got caught on my clear lip gloss. 'I'm so proud of you for handling all of that on your own. It's amazing.'

Right on cue, I feel tears begin to form at the corners of my eyes.

'She was my friend, Sheils, she felt so important to me. Like I'd known her for ever.'

'I think you probably have known her for ever. Or for a few lifetimes at least. And I reckon the greatest comfort you can take is that it hurts now, but that you will be seeing her again. Birta needed your help and you gave it; you were there when she called on you, like all true pals are. We all know that proper friends can go for ages without seeing each other and it's just as comfortable and easy the next time you see them; that's you and Birta, but spanning lifetimes instead of decades.'

'Thank you, lovely lass. Just think: that probably means you're stuck with me over several lifetimes, you poor sod.'

'I think I'll cope, Tanz. I'm also pretty sure there's more to this grief than what happened with Birta.'

Bloody hell, there's no hiding anything from this woman – she's got laser eyes for other people's troubles.

'This is the bit I'm embarrassed about, Sheila. My love life makes me cringe, so goodness knows how ridiculous and trite it sounds to other people. I know you liked Neil the policeman. I *liked* him, but I realized after a while that that's all I did. I *liked* him and he was building a future in his head with me. It couldn't work and I had to nip it in the bud before I really hurt him. Then I flew out to Iceland out of the blue, to be with that fucking idiot Einar, who you actually told me was an arsehole, but did I listen? So how can I expect you to take me seriously when I talk about Thor? Thor, who came along and showed me how it really should be with a man. His energy, his caring nature, his natural love and, well, his beautiful sexuality. We fitted. I didn't want to sleep with someone new, you know. I didn't want to confuse myself, and I didn't want to get attached. Now the whole thing is a head-fuck.'

'We feel what we feel.'

'I know. But it really is a bit too intense, all of this, even for me. It feels like another close friend just died, even though Birta wasn't alive in the first place; plus I've met a man who I truly connect with, but can't be with. Doesn't it make sense that I feel so lost? My spookiness doesn't really feel like a "gift" if I have to be living in grief half of the time.'

'Of course it makes sense, but that's because the earthly human you clings to stuff. The truth is that you're not being *punished* – spiritual you is actually being given lessons. Fast-tracked lessons that seem very intense and emotional, but they're heightening your understanding and healing abilities in a short time. The secret is to breathe through what happens, enjoy the amazing bits that others wouldn't ever get the chance to experience, and accept that, conversely, you'll be sad sometimes. Really sad. Eventually you won't take life so personally any more, you'll just marvel at how the puzzle pieces always fit together and make sense in the end. Plus, on a sidenote, many, many people would love to have as much amazing sex with varied, interesting blokes as you do. Maybe you've needed a sexual wake-up and not a proper boyfriend. Maybe it wasn't the right time yet.'

I wipe my eyes with some scrunched up loo-roll from my bag and nod miserably.

'I still feel lost, though.'

'Well, let's do something to ground you again.'

'Okay. It would be very nice not to have nightmares for a bit and to actually feel safe in my own life. And to stop bloody moaning. I don't want to be the whinging Geordie who depresses all her mates.'

'You're not that, you daft bint – you're just getting it off your chest. That's what mates are for!' Sheila checks something in her little pocket diary. 'Right, tomorrow afternoon I'm going to treat you to something different that might help.'

I nod and give a big sniff. Thank goodness for spooky mates who 'get it'.

# THE SINGING BOWLS

When Sheila said she was going to help, I didn't expect to be driving to a stranger's house in Enfield for a 'sound bath'. I'm not a great fan of airy-fairy stuff – Sheila knows this. We've already agreed that retreats and all that business would probably have my toes curling so hard they'd snap off, so she doesn't invite me to any of the woo-woo weekends that she sometimes attends, where they spin in circles or breathe with each other, and do group activities. I will literally do anything in my power to avoid any kind of group activity, so trusting that she's taking me somewhere I won't hate is a leap of faith. As we sit in my knackered tin-can of a car, in yet another traffic jam on the A406, Sheila winks at me.

'This is something else, Tanz. Erikah is a special one. Have some bloody faith, will you?'

It's not that I don't have 'faith'. It's just that the world of spookiness attracts so many charlatans and people who are trying to be gurus and show off their 'power', and I'm not one of them, nor do I want to be in their company. I'm a 'one or two'-at-a-time kind of girl, and I like to know the 'one or two' personally. Everything else is overwhelming, and overwhelm makes everything so much worse. But after another restless night, when I'm absolutely sure I woke up to the sound of a panicked woman being tortured horribly, I'm willing to try anything.

The lady who opens the green front door is mixed-race and has her hair tied up in a black, gold and green scarf. She looks at me intently, then gives the biggest smile and welcomes us both in. Sheila gives her a warm hug and we walk up the hallway into a bright kitchen-diner area with yoga mats on the floor, embroidered cushions ranged around them, and a bunch of beautiful glass or crystal bowls – I'm not sure which – in a range of sizes, plus other interesting-looking instruments, on a teak table. There's no one else here.

Erikah indicates that we should choose a mat each and makes sure that we have a cushion to sit on, then puts another one at the top of our mats. She also hands us both a warm patterned blanket, which I hug to myself like a snuggly friend.

'Welcome, both. Nice to meet you, Tanz.' Her voice is honey and stones. 'Usually I'll have five people here on the floor, but after speaking with Sheila, I decided to dedicate this one just to the two of you. Sheila has helped me many times in the past, Tanz, so I wanted to do something lovely in return. Plus, what you've been through recently would be a lot for anyone to cope with, let alone someone who's still young on their spiritual path, but developing so rapidly. It's an honour to meet you.'

I don't know how much Sheila has told this luminous woman, but her words are like a balm.

'Thank you, Erikah.'

She stares at me a little too hard again, not with malice, but rather with curiosity. She's completely grounded and peaceful, and I know how paranoid I get, so I take it as part of the experience. Quietly she motions that we should begin, so Sheila and I lie back on the mats. I get as comfortable as I can, and Erikah lays my blanket over me, smoothing it with hands that leave a trail of warmth on my arms and all down my legs. For a moment I feel my reluctance rise and I slowly breathe it away, knowing there's a natural cynicism within me that attempts to fight anything that takes away my control.

Then Erikah tells us to close our eyes and, after a little while, the most extraordinary sound fills the room. It starts low and soft, then builds until the inside of my head is absolutely vibrating with the notes, like she's thrumming those bowls right inside my brain. Sound-wave after sound-wave comes through and I find that I couldn't move even if I wanted to; I'm pinned to the floor, hands resting, with no feeling at all, on my tummy. I lose all grasp of time, as noises like birds and a tumbling waterfall add to the soundscape. It's while this is happening that I hear the voice. It's Alfvin, my beautiful guide from Iceland. Supposedly a fucking elf, he's actually a tall, beautiful man-like creature with stars for eyes, who gifted me a tiny bell when I was trapped alone in a dark cabin, and brought me absolute faith that there really is more to heaven and earth than what the dickheads on this planet would have you believe.

I feel a tear form as he speaks, his voice clear, like a beloved friend confiding in my ear only.

'*Chosen.*'

'Alfvin?'

'*The witch comes. Much love and much danger. I am with you. Always with you.*'

'Much danger?'

'*I am with you.*'

'Whoa. Am I going to die?'

There's a cough-cough sound, which I know is Alfvin laughing. He seems to find me intensely amusing. The warmth that generates when he speaks to me and the joy that he is still communicating, despite me leaving his 'home', generates such a well of emotion that I have to swallow hard to keep myself in check.

'*All must die, Chosen. But I am here.*'

The sound bath is finishing, and the notes that made the walls vibrate have died down to almost nothing. The incense that fills the room smells of forests and deep lakes. Despite my best efforts, I'm crying. Proper fat tears, dissolving into gigantic, uncontrollable sobs. My body shakes with them and I feel a presence drop down to the right of me, and a hand – a warm, kind hand – on my forehead, then whispered words from Erikah.

'Let it come, Tanz. Let it purge you. You've been through a lot. Excuse me for staring when you arrived. I could feel an energy so strong coming out of you that I was actually questioning whether you were human at all. You're evolving very quickly, and recently something has sped up your lessons and also sent your frequency through the roof.

Your guides are helping this to integrate, but it must be quite the trip for you. It will take a little while yet.'

She's so clever and understanding. I lift my left hand and put it over hers as Erikah gently cradles my forehead. This woman smells of cinnamon and oud, and her energy pulsates like her healing bowls. I open my eyes and stare up into hers. They are dark and searching and radiate kindness.

'I don't know what you just did to me, but I can't thank you enough. You took me out of myself. I think that's the trick in life, isn't it? To see everything that's happening from the outside.'

'That's right: observe the feeling, don't *be* the feeling.'

I nod. 'Also your instincts were bang on. I'm not human at the moment, I'm a shipwreck with a pulse. This helped a lot.'

Erikah smiles so widely it stretches her cheeks to the limit.

'That's what we're here for, Tanz, we wise women. We're here to help each other through this journey. I'm a healer's healer, and so are you. What a pleasure to meet you.'

Sheila suddenly sits up and, after a stretch and a yawn, gives me such a smug look that I burst out laughing. Sheila sticks her tongue out, then laughs too. Erikah looks from one of us to the other, then joins in, and soon we're all convulsed with the giggles. I already know that Sheila is going to be insufferable on the way home. But in this instance she has every right to be. She scored a winner. And to think I didn't even want to come here. What an idiot!

# SHADOW-PLACE

I have to rest when I get home from the sound bath. It's only five o'clock, but my limbs are as heavy as wet logs and I'm utterly exhausted. In the past, Sheila and I would have had cocktails or shared a bottle of wine in Purple Haze or Minnie's and had a debrief, but to my absolute amazement I don't want booze at all. I want to lie down and not get up again for a week.

I fill Inka's food bowl when I get in; she's not here and is probably prowling the gardens for gifts to bring me, like muddy dead voles or a freshly murdered bluetit, but she'll be yowling for dinner once she plops back through the cat flap. I also make myself a herbal tea and, moving to the living room, I put it on the coffee table, meaning to sit on the sofa and watch a gentle movie. Instead I slump sideways, then stretch out on my back, too knackered to do anything else. It's not the newest, my sofa, but it's comfortable and wide enough to sleep on, so I move a cushion under my head and breathe deeply, trying not to think of anything.

As I stare at the ceiling I hear the tiniest tinkling. I listen hard, wondering if I just fell asleep for a second and dreamed it. Then it happens again. A tiny bell. I've put the bell that Alfvin gave me in a safe place because I have a terror of losing it, but it sounds exactly the same. I try to move my arm and find that I can't. Then I hear his voice again, soft, in my ear.

'*Chosen. Eyes closed.*'

I do as I'm told. I feel the air around me change, grow cooler, and I hear voices whispering in a language I don't understand. An ancient tongue that sounds familiar and yet completely alien.

'*You are with us. In the shadow-place. I will give you strength. Tomorrow is a new path.*'

I crack my eyes open a fraction and see the guttering fire first, then the distant walls of the cave interior and misty, cloaked figures. Finally I shift my focus to the outline of Alfvin, by my side. I'm lying on some kind of simple bed. There's hay-stuffed rough fabric for a mattress. The air is heavy with the scent of herbs and woody, leafy mulch. Earthy and wet. I'm with the Hidden Ones. I feel incredibly lucky to be with them, and also scared that it might change at any moment and I'll be catapulted back to my barren 'real' life.

I feel a touch to my nose. Alfvin just booped me. He's done this before. Nose-booped by a mythical creature; it could only happen to me, and I can't help but smile. Being near him gives me such a sense of belonging and of sacred connection. He then puts his hand over my eyes. It feels like warm feathers at first, then lightning. The energy crackles. I feel other beings draw close. Soon the chanting begins. I don't recognize the words, but I recognize the feeling. They are singing a harmony that reminds me of breaking waves in the distance, of a love that ebbs and flows, and of life after loss.

Alfvin takes away his hand, but I don't reopen my eyes. I feel him draw close to my cheek and blow gently on my skin, then he speaks a torrent of ancient words, like a stream bubbling downhill. I suddenly smell Birta's Icelandic moss tea, then I get that feather-and-lightning feeling on my chest and the strangest sensation of something being 'pulled' from me. Now many gentle hands rest on different parts of my body, as they all join in with this incantation that my soul seems to recognize. The crescendo is gentle and ebbs, rather than getting louder. I smell something musky and dark, and what feels like a thumb presses into my forehead while oil lightly trickles down, almost into my ear. I've been 'anointed', it seems. Finally Alfvin breathes near my ear – in, out, in, out – until my breathing synchronizes with his. My love for him is infinite in this moment, and the peace inside me absolute.

As I'm about to drop into sleep, now back in my living room and sinking into the sofa cushions, I feel an itch on my forehead between my eyes and rub it with my middle finger. It comes away with a thin film of oil on it. The last thing I remember is pressing this finger to my nostrils and inhaling the scent of hidden caves and deep magic, before I black out.

# PHONE SEX SWERVE

It's midnight when I open my eyes again. Amazingly, instead of climbing on me and waking me, Inka is curled up on my reading chair and is also sparko. The heating timer switched off about half an hour ago, but the room is still cosy enough and is lit by the street lamp outside streaming through the half-open blinds. I can't believe how long I've slept, but I must have needed it. I hear the ping of a text from my phone, in my bag on the floor. I sit up and am amazed that not one bit of me aches, despite having been in one position on the sofa for hours.

I feel about in the dark, and slightly moist, recesses of my day-bag until I find my phone, then look at my messages. There's one from Sheila, checking that I'm okay; and one that arrived two minutes ago, from Thor:

**I miss you so much I feel sick. Can we talk?**

This is what I've been avoiding since I came back. I thanked Thor via text for the painting, which I've not hung up yet because it makes me cry. And I've kept any other replies to his messages short. I've done this for self-preservation reasons, and because I have a big mouth with no filter and I can't control what I might say to him. But now I decide that this may be the time to be brave and hear his voice again. I'm not tipsy, so at least the wine won't take over and start telling Thor things without my consent. I take a sip of stone-cold peppermint tea, which isn't that bad actually, and reply:

**Yes. I'm around now.**

Within seconds my phone is buzzing and I take a breath, then answer.
'Hello.'
'Tanz! You exist. Thank GOD.'
Immediately I'm laughing and so is he.
'Thank the Goddess, you mean.'
'Yes. Thank the Goddess. I thought maybe it was all a crazy dream. It's so good to hear your voice. How are you? You've seemed distant – are you okay?'
'I am, but it's been a bit intense, trying to adjust.'
'You try being in Reykjavik after the Geordie witch has gone. It's like someone dimmed all the lights. My eyes don't work properly.'
He doesn't have that strong an accent, as his English is ridiculously good, but I relish Thor's voice, the gentle way he pronounces his words.
'How has it been since I left? Did you make up with Einar?'

'Oh, Einar won't talk about you or what he did. Not yet. He's very jealous, in actual fact. I know it sounds crazy, but just because he messed up doesn't mean he wanted you and me to get close. He knows how badly he fucked up, and he knows that I care about you, so he's been hiding from me ever since.'

'Oh dear.'

'It won't last long. I'm the nearest Einar has to a brother. I'm not worried about him.'

There's something in the way Thor says 'him' that alerts me to the fact that something else might not be well.

'So who *are* you worried about then?'

'Oh, it's nothing. One good thing I do have to tell you is that the story of the dug-up bodies has been big news here. It's had a lot of coverage, and Ernest has become quite the celebrity. He did an interview for the evening news before he flew back to England, and he came off well. Every inch the eccentric older guy with the clever eyes – plus he's a private investigator! I think he could get married six times over if he decided to live here.'

This tickles me no end.

'Wow! I love that. I'll have to call him soon, thank him for taking the heat off me.'

'You're such a strange woman. I think that's why I love you so much.'

I don't know what to say. Any flippant comment I might have had ready dries up in my throat. It's an impossible situation, but at the same time the joy that comes from hearing those words . . .

'Thor, I . . . You have a girlfriend.'
'That's not the absolute case.'
'What do you mean?'
'I told her – I had to tell her that I slept with you. We said we had an "open" relationship, but that we'd always admit who else we'd been with. Well, I told her, though I kept all the details to myself, tried to make sure it wasn't hurtful. I thought she wouldn't mind; she's been with lots of others, mostly women. Anyway she must have sensed that I cared about you more than I was admitting, because she didn't react the way I expected at all.'
'Uh-oh.'
'Uh-oh indeed. I was about to tell her that maybe we should just be friends. We don't live together, we're not in love – it shouldn't be that hard. But she went crazy, Tanz. Absolutely batshit, I think is how the Brits say it. She was crying and wrapping herself around me and saying she only wanted an open relationship because she's scared of getting hurt, but that I'd hurt her anyway, and she doesn't want other people any more and only wants to be with me. She even hinted that she'd hurt herself if I left her.'
'Holy FUCK.'
'I know.
I'm scared to ask the next question, but I ask it anyway.
'So what did you tell her?'
'I told her to give me my space, as she demanded that I do for her, before this. I don't know what to do, Tanz. I've fallen in love with an English girl who changed my life in three days. But I don't know if she feels the same, and how

it would work. What do you think that mad Geordie woman would tell me, if I asked her?'

I put my fingers to my lips, remembering that last incredibly intimate night together and our goodbye kiss at the airport, which felt like someone ripping a piece of my soul away and taking it with them.

'I think she'd say that she keeps making great big mistakes, when it comes to men, and that you should do what you feel is right for you and not rest it on her shoulders. You both live in different countries, and long-distance relationships are a ball-ache. Saying that, she would also tell you that kissing you felt like coming home.'

Thor breathes at the other end of the phone for a few seconds before he speaks again.

'I miss how your skin smells.'

I know where this could go. I'd better nip it in the bud.

'Thor, let's talk another time, before this descends into rampant phone sex.'

He bursts into big Icelandic guffaws.

'Dammit, you sussed me out!'

'BUSTED!'

But we both know it's a lot more than Thor fishing for phone sex. Breaking the seriousness of the conversation tonight doesn't mean we've sorted this situation, by a long shot. I make my goodbyes and tell him I adore him, without bandying the love-word around again. Thor's so special to me, but whatever happens, we have to be clear-headed. Iceland is fucking miles away and I'm pretty terrified of getting hurt again, or of hurting him. He's too special for that.

Still, whatever Alfvin and the Hidden Ones did, I'm ready to go back to sleep already, and once I'm under the duvet a big smile spreads over my face. Thor cares, he really does. It's very nice to know.

# LITTLE MAM WITH A SACK OVER HER HEED

To my absolute surprise, I sleep hard until eight o'clock the next morning and only wake up because my phone is buzzing furiously. When I pick it up, it's my little mam and she's squawking like an angry goose. At first I can't make out what she's saying, then I hear, 'Bloody sack over my heed!' and all my senses spring to life.

'Mam, Mam, slow down, what's the matter?'

'Eeeh, Tanz, are you messing with them spirits again?'

'No, Mam, honest. I've only been back a few days and I've spent most of it asleep. What's wrong?'

'Well, I'm glad you've been getting sleep, because I certainly haven't. Terrible dreams I've had the past few days. About some woman – it was me, but it wasn't me; she had her hands tied behind her back and a sack over her head. It bloody stank, and there was all these people screaming and shouting and crying. Then I dreamed that she was being tortured. And she wasn't the only one; screaming blue murder, these poor women were. Then last night . . . well, last night it was the same again with the smelly sack over my head, but this time they pulled it off and it was the olden days, and there were all these people there in the daylight on a field in front of a bloody gallows with a LOT of nooses on it. I mean, what do you make of that? Who the bloody hell hanged a load of people at once?'

'I don't know, Mam, but it sounds really scary.'

'Well, it was, I tell you. I've had a cuppa and a few biscuits to calm down now, but half an hour ago I was up a height. I woke up in a right flutter. It felt real, pet, I'm telling you.'

'Is there anything you want me to do?'

'I don't know. But I can't keep dreaming this stuff. I'm not like you, I want peace and quiet, and no ghosts.'

'I don't think that's possible, Mam – you're at least as spooky as I am.'

'Don't you say that! I don't do that stuff. I need it to go away. I can take the odd dream, but this is ridiculous.' She then goes into a rant about how me messing with 'spirits' has brought her 'nowt but trouble' and, as she vents, I realize that I can't tell her I dreamed something similar two nights ago, because it'll freak her out. There's no way it can be a coincidence.

And just then Frank pops up in my head.

*'Aye-aye, your new mission.'*

'What do you mean, Frank?'

*'Time to take a trip to Gateshead.'*

'Really? Why?'

*'Remember what your pet elf said.'*

'DON'T CALL ALFVIN THAT.'

*'Well, whatever – you need to go north to sort this out, or your mam's going to have worse and worse dreams every night and you'll get the blame.'*

'Do you know what's going on?'

*'No, not this time. But you seem to have plenty of help these days.'*

'Are you jealous of Alfvin? Or Thor?'

*'Neither. Icelandic twits.'*

'Oh, you *so* are.'

I decide to cut my mam off before her venting turns into a screaming fit.

'Mam, I'm going to come home.'

'What? Why?'

'Moral support. Maybe you're having dreams because "someone" needs help. I know you hate all that stuff, but you're very tuned in, whether you like it or not. Plus, of course, I can see Dad, visit Nanna and have a coffee with Milo. It's a win-win.'

'Eeeh, well, if you're sure, pet.'

Of course Mam probably rang with this very outcome in mind.

'Yes, I'm sure. I'll have a shower, get some provisions, then jump in the car. You'll be trying to force a cup of tea on me by three o'clock!'

# WIND TUNNEL IN SPACE

The drive up is actually very informative. I've got my wired earphones and a new holder for my phone, so I can make phone calls without danger of arrest. First person I consult is my mate Gladys – she of the perpetual carrier bag full of sweeties, cottage full of crystals, owl-like giant specs and heart of a kindly lioness. What Gladys lacks in stature she makes up for in intelligence and witchiness and I bloody love her. The line, however, is absolutely flippin' atrocious.

'Well, Tanz, what a lovely coincidence. I was goin' to message you today.'

'Gladys, you sound like you're in a wind tunnel in space.'

'Sorry, love, I've gone away. This is the best reception there is.'

'Ohh, where are you?'

'A pilgrimage. On a very special anniversary. To be with my Andrew.'

Gladys's son drowned when he was four. I 'met' him

once while I was knocked out in hospital. He was the cutest thing ever. She cried so hard when I told her I'd seen him. She's never told me much about the time she lost him, as it still smashes her to pieces even to think about it. I imagine she must have had a bench erected, or something, where she can go and be with him. By the sound of the line, it's in Delhi.

'Anywhere nice?'

'Yes.'

I know not to push this. She's a private lady and I respect it.

'Well, I'm on my way up north for a bit, so can you let me know when you're back and I'll take you out for cake if I'm still there.'

'That would be lovely, pet. Now what's happenin'?'

'Well, me and my mam are having similar dreams – very similar – and I daren't tell her, because she's scared enough of spooky stuff and it'll set her off even more. You should've heard her this morning. She was like a rocket about to shoot into space.'

Gladys titters, then sounds like she takes a bite of something. I can imagine it's a Viennese whirl or a piece of Battenberg, as she practically lives on those two. I usually don't appreciate someone chomping down the phone, but the line's so wavery, it's not like I can really hear it.

'So come on,' she says, her voice suddenly clearer, 'what ya been dreamin'?'

'A woman with a hemp bag over her head. Lots of screaming and wailing. Plus pain like she's been tortured. Mam went a step further and stayed in the dream long enough for the sack to be pulled off. Said she was on some kind of field, with a lot of nooses set up.'

'Wey, do you not know about the trials?'

'The what?'

'The Newcastle witch trials. They hanged a load of lasses, and one man, at the same time. One of the biggest mass hangin's in the country, ever. And it all happened on the Town Moor.'

The Town Moor is a large bit of land in Newcastle that hasn't been built on. Once a year it is home to a massive travelling funfair called the Hoppings. It's been going since the late 1800s – my nanna told me that, which means that everyone you'll ever meet in the North-East of England was obsessed with the Hoppings at some point as a child. It was the Holy Grail of events for us. Different death-traps would arrive each time, which you could climb into and get thrown about in, as well as little diddy rides that were safe, where you could go round in circles and wave at whichever poor sod had been press-ganged into taking you. Plus, there was candy-floss, and live goldfish in bags that you won when you hooked a plastic duck. As I remember it, despite the funfair being in summer, it was always muddy there. I've not been for quite a few years, but I doubt it's changed much.

'A mass hanging in Newcastle? How the hell didn't I know about this?'

I don't know if Gladys has moved a bit, but even though she still sounds distant, I can hear what she's saying more clearly now.

'You'll have to really dig to get all the details. I reckon

they found out pretty quickly afterwards that the witch-finder fella they brought in had been a bloody psychopath and not an actual witch finder at all. A lot of the records disappeared. I mean, imagine: you hang a bunch of citizens, then find out it was all a load of hokum.'

'Bloody hell. That's horrific.'

'I know. It all started with that James the First; he was king then. Wrote a three-part book on how to identify witches. He was obsessed – absolutely bonkers, he was – and he caused total panic in the population. So many people died. The ones they killed up here, fourteen women and one man, I think it was, they were all normal innocent folk. I can't remember all the details, but you should look it up. It's very interesting.'

'Jesus! Thank you for enlightening me, I had no idea. Saying that, I wonder what it's got to do with me and my mam.'

'Well, pet, if it's both of you, maybe it's comin' down the family line. Maybe you're related to one of the so-called "witches". Maybe there's some kind of anniversary goin' on, or maybe you "wakin' up" more and more means that the ones who went before you are findin' it much easier to contact you. Either way, I reckon you'll figure it out pretty sharpish. You're a clever one and no mistake.'

'No, I'm not. I didn't know anything about these witch trials.'

'Just another warnin' about letting blokes run things. I'm tellin' you, that's why I stay as far away from them as I can.'

'God, you sound like Sheila.'

'It's amazin' how much good sense you collect as you get older, Tanz. I mean there's nowt wrong with havin' the odd sweetheart, if you like that sort of thing, but really men do cause a lot of trouble in this world.'

'And some of them are lovely.'

'I know, lass. But I haven't got the patience to be weedin' out the annoyin' ones any more. Anyway, listen to me: whatever you find out, you're as protected as you've ever been. You've got energy radiatin' off you like a nuclear reactor. So if you find things getting spookier, you'll have superpowers at the ready.'

'Well, let me know when you're back, please. I might need your help.'

'Okay, my darlin'. Hope you find out what's goin' on without too much hassle.' Her voice is getting wavery again.

'Yeah, because that usually happens. Never any trouble when I'm about.'

'Aye, you're certainly not boring!'

'Safe travels, Gladys. Look after yourself.'

'I will. See you soon, pet. And remember you're a special one.'

'So are you.'

# A CHINESE BUFFET IN BYKER

Okay, so I wonder if I'm imagining it when I get about half an hour from Gateshead. The sun has been crisply bright through the clouds, despite a strong chill in the air, but all at once it seems darker – not like night's approaching, but like there's a haze in front of my eyes. It's not as if I can't see to drive or anything like that; it's almost undefinable, but the atmosphere is definitely heavier and I feel weird. I'm very thankful for whatever Alfvin did for me last night, because one thing I am not now is exhausted. My vitality has returned somewhat; I pretty much jumped out of bed this morning and was happy at the prospect of a long drive with my music for company.

But now I can sense anxiety licking at the edges of my mind as I approach my place of birth, and I have to breathe deeply and slowly to resist any dark thoughts. In my bag on the passenger seat is a packet of paracetamol, so I grab them to ward off a potential headache. I manage to liberate two from the foils with my left hand, because I'm basically a genius, then wash them down with the last of the large skinny cappuccino that I bought from the service station in York. That's exactly when Milo, my best friend in Gateshead, decides to call me back after not answering at the start of my drive.

'Tanz! Just listened to your message – sorry to miss the call. You're coming home? Yay.'

'Hello, cheeky. Yes, I'm pretty close to my mam and dad's right now.'

'Okay, you sound a bit odd. Are you okay? Has Iceland broken you? You want me to go and find that giant fucking idiot and set his hair on fire?'

'God, no, Milo. I don't even care about Einar, he's completely gone from my mind. But I've got a bit of a sore head. I've taken some tablets, so I'll be right as rain soon.'

'Oh, that's good. Can't wait to see you, so you can fill me in on your full adventures, you mad cow.'

'You around later?'

'I am this afternoon, but I'm out tonight,' Milo replies.

'You're going out? Tonight? Is it a writing thing?'

'Erm, no. I've got a date with my lad.'

'You've got a WHAT with your WHAT?'

Milo laughs nervously. He never laughs nervously; what the actual fuck is happening?

'Oh my God, you have a BOYFRIEND?'

'Erm, yes, actually, I suppose I have.'

'Milo! When did this start? I know you: if you'd met this fella recently, you would never call him your boyfriend, so I can only assume you've been holding out on me.'

'I . . . well, I wasn't holding out on you. I just met this

lad at the uni when I was giving a talk to the writing students. He's a music teacher. I didn't know what to think – I always attract fucking imbeciles. But he was nice and bought me a cuppa in the canteen, and then the past couple of months we've chatted and all that. Then suddenly we had a snog and . . . here we are fixing to eat at a Chinese buffet tonight in Byker.'

'Holy fuck, Milo, I'm so happy for you. I wang on about my own chaotic bonfire of a love life so much that I forget to ask about yours. I'm so sorry. I'm a selfish dick and now here you are, dating a music teacher. How brilliant.'

And I do think it's brilliant. But I'm also a bit crestfallen that Milo didn't tell me before. We used to tell each other everything, but I've lived in London for a long time and it would stand to reason that his life is developing and changing independently, exactly as mine is.

'So what's he called, and what does he look like?'

'He's called Rob and he has a face with two eyes, a nose and a mouth.'

'That's a good start.'

'To be honest, Tanz, I'm in shock. I've been a total disaster on legs when it comes to men, so the ease of getting to know Rob has knocked me right off-kilter. And the truth is: he's beautiful.'

Milo sounds a touch scared as he says this.

'So are you, Milo. The most beautiful person anyone could meet. I'll bet he's had this exact same conversation about you.'

'Doubt it.'

'Look, I'm nearly there now. Let's meet up when you're

free. You can tell me about your date, and I can fill you in on little mam's latest drama. Have the best night.'

'Champion. See you soon!'

I know I cut off the call a bit briskly, but I am nearly at my mam and dad's, and I also suddenly have this strange feeling of time passing and me being left behind. It's like déjà vu, but more depressing. I want to use my time on this planet productively; I want to help people; I want passion, I want peace; I want to stay this age, because my neck is going crinkly. Most of all, right now, I want a wee.

Life's complicated, isn't it?

# BLAND BISCUIT

Little mam is wearing black leggings with stirrups on the bottom, pink trainers, a pink cardigan over her white sweatshirt and pearlized pink lipstick to match. She has her lightened hair lacquered into a perfect Geordie helmet. She's the antithesis of a storybook witch. But she knows stuff. She dreams it, she feels it, she even tunes into my dreams, and a few hundred years ago it would very possibly have been her, with some bastard bloke pointing an accusatory finger and sending her to her death. I look at her as I enter the kitchen, after quickly running to the loo. She's drying the dishes and humming. She's put little gold hoops in her ears and looks even shorter than usual. My mam has tiny feet. Imagine murdering a fragile woman who's scared of spiders and wears teensy shoes, just because she's wise.

'Eeeh, hiya, pet, it's nice to see you.'

She gives me one of her brittle hugs, which feels like clutching a pitchfork.

'Hiya, Mam, how you feeling?'

She begins to pour what looks like very stewed tea from the teapot, and for once she doesn't ask if I want one.

'Well, I don't mind telling you, I'm exhausted. I need a good night's sleep. Do you want anything?'

I shake my head and she perches on one of the wooden dining chairs at the tiny kitchen table. I sit on the other and produce my water bottle from my bag.

'Where's Dad?'

'He's walking Zorro, he'll be back in about half an hour.'

'Okay . . . So, Mam, have you heard of the Newcastle witch trials?'

'The what?'

'I rang my mate Gladys – she knows a lot about everything. She says a load of women and one man were hanged for witchcraft on the Town Moor. I'm wondering if that's got anything to do with our dreams.'

Oh shit, I didn't mean to say that. Mam's immediately on to me like a bloody missile – eyes like darts.

'"Our" dreams? What do you mean "our dreams"?'

'Nothing, sorry. Slip of the tongue. *Your* dreams.'

'No you don't. I wondered why you were so quick to say you were coming up here. What the hell have you been dreaming? I knew this was something to do with you.'

'That's nice, isn't it? It has to be my fault. If you must know, this doesn't come from me "dabbling". I don't know why it's happening, but I also had a dream where there was some kind of hessian bag over my head. I heard people screaming, and all that. Also people crying. And I felt pain all over my body.'

'Yes, pet, like you'd been burned and cut, and all sorts.'

Mam shudders, then delicately fishes a custard cream out of the conveniently placed biscuit barrel.

'Mam, did you feel like it was "you"?'

'Wey, now that you ask: no. I felt like I was experiencing someone else's pain. But I was inside her body, to feel it properly. And I'd be quite grateful if it didn't happen again. Why do you think it's happening at all? What did your Gladys say?'

'She suggested that we might be related to one of the people who died, but I want to start investigating, find out as much as I can. Finding out where they're buried will help – we can go there and "get a feel".'

Mam flinches in her seat. 'You can bugger off if you think I'm going anywhere to "feel" ghosts, Tanz. Are you mad?'

To be fair, trailing a little squawking woman who hardly likes leaving the house and is in absolute denial of her 'powers', around sites of potential paranormal activity, is almost definitely a terrible idea.

'Okay, Mam, that's fine. I can go on the detective trail and I'll report anything interesting back to you. How about that?'

'If it means I get a proper night's sleep again, that's perfect. Can't Gladys go with you?'

'Oh no, Gladys has gone away on a little trip. It's to do with her young son who died. I suspect it's his birthday, or the anniversary of losing him.'

'Eeeh, that poor woman – imagine.'

'Imagine, indeed; you'd have no crazy daughter chasing spooks around.'

'Don't, Tanz. What an awful cross to bear: your child dying before you.'

She nibbles at a malted-milk biscuit. I do not understand that woman; she could have something with chocolate on it, or a Gypsy Cream, but she goes for the blandest thing in the barrel.

'Luckily I'll never have to worry about that.'

'You might change your mind about having kids, pet.'

'No, Mam, I won't.'

# MAN-SIZED CAT

Sitting up the Octopus Tree in Saltwell Park, the place where I spent most of my time during my childhood, used to be how I got away from everything and went into my own head. And here I am again, almost thirty years later, and I still love it up here in the branches. The park will close soon, as it's growing dark, but I suddenly decided after my chat with little mam that I needed to stretch my legs and have a think, and this is where my feet brought me. The park is pretty much empty. I saw one dog walker five minutes ago and that's it. The parkie will ring the bell soon to let everyone know the gates are closing and it's time to leave.

As my legs dangle and I pull my coat more closely around me, I look to the branch opposite and remember Frank sitting there, looking handsome, the last day I ever saw him. His mam still lived in Gateshead then, and he was visiting her. We'd had one of our little rows, as usual, then Frank had told me that we should make a pact that if we were both single in a year's time we should actually get together. It's something I try not to think about too often. Especially as later that very day he drove off towards Scotland in his fucking revamped show-off car and crashed in the rain. Thinking about the last day I ever saw him alive still brings up such sadness, even though circumstances have rather changed since then.

I mean, between my first brush with Sheila and right now, Frank has become a lot more than just a memory; in fact he first popped up again in my head when I started working at Mystery Pot – his voice still alive, his cheekiness intact. As soon as Sheila helped me to 'open up', Frank was there, appearing in my head when he felt like it, and once or twice in human form in front of my shocked eyes, and he has got me into nothing but bother ever since. I recall him swinging his legs and looking awkward in that very branch in front of me, and I remember staring at him and seeing him in a way that I'd been trying to deny for ages. The boy was now a man. A clever, gorgeous man who could turn his hand to anything and, despite being an absolute goof, was always there for me when I needed him.

I sit here and remember our last hug, outside my mam and dad's house, and I feel a tear fall. Everything has been changing so fast, while nothing has changed at all. I make the same mistakes, I scrape a living in a terrifyingly expensive city, I occasionally see the small band of friends I've accrued, and I hug my cat close to me while denying how lonely everything is. Even Elsa – my most shallow, London-loving friend of many years – has moved away, to Scotland of all places, after realizing how empty her life felt.

'*Oh, shut up, will you?*' The voice in my head is warm, despite the insult.

'Hello, Frank.'

'*Why are you sitting up a tree in the cold, when it's getting dark? You're supposed to get more sensible as you age, not less.*'

'Stop talking about ageing, will you?'

'*Oh dear, someone's got the hump. There's no point still getting upset about me, you know. I can give you an insight here, if you want it.*'

'Go on.'

'*I fancied you for years – loved you even. You were my best mate and my favourite woman. But I also had other favourite women who'd come and go. I acted like I was ready, but I would have made a mistake and pissed you off, if we'd got together. Us ever "making it" is a romantic notion. I was still a wandering minstrel, and you were loving being a nomadic actress. Just be happy that we're still around one another. You'd probably think I was a complete wanker now, if I was still alive.*'

Maybe Frank has a point.

'Okay, Mr "Suddenly Emotionally Mature". I shall take that on board.'

'*Good; it's not like you've been short of romance since then. To be honest, it's been like the revolving door at John Lewis for you recently.*'

'OY. Fuck off.'

As I say this, I see something big run in front of me, then disappear. For a second I blink, trying to process what I think I witnessed.

'Frank, did you see that?'

*'See what?'*

'A fucking MASSIVE black cat. In fact not a cat – a panther, but fatter. No, wait a minute, that has to have been a costume, as it was on its hind legs. Is there some loon running about the park in a cat outfit? It was quick, but I definitely saw it.'

*'You saw someone in a cat costume run in front of you? I think you need some sleep.'*

'Stop it, Frank, I'm not joking. Now I'm going to have to climb down and leg it. That's so weird.'

Then I hear another voice. A woman, whispering close to my ear. *'They said he turned into a cat. Cat man of the Moor. Fools, all.'*

The back of my neck is prickling. Goosebumps are forming, despite me wearing layers. I climb carefully down from the tree and look around me. Dusk has fallen and darkness is pooling in the shadows of the old stone walls around Saltwell Towers. I don't feel safe now. Quickly I head for the gate. I walk down a tree-lined path that leads to the well in the wall, then the exit gate. Suddenly Frank's gone and I feel the vulnerability of being a woman alone in the dark, with no one else around me. The trees hem me in and, just as I'm turning a corner onto the path to the gate, I hear a noise behind me like a cat hissing, then a loud yowl. That's all it takes to turn my brisk walk into a solid gallop. I run like the absolute wind and don't slow down until I've exited the park, crossed the road and run down most of the length of Saltwell Cemetery – a place that I usually love and find peaceful, but right now it looks dark and full of dangerous nooks and crannies where danger can lurk.

By the time I reach my parents' house I'm boiling hot and as red as a beetroot. My mother's going to have some questions for me if she sees me in this state, so I sit on the wall outside to cool down, watching the cars and buses pass, feeling comforted that the house is on a main road. I'll probably be better off telling my mam that I saw a flasher – not uncommon in that park when I was a child – than admitting that I think I got chased by a giant demonic cat. I mean, come on, what the hell is happening here? Also, that voice. Not menacing or nasty, but conversational really. Couldn't place the accent, either. But still, conversational or not, if you get someone whispering in your ear in the dusk while a bloody man-cat is scuttling around behind you, it's going to spook you out.

I know one thing, though: there's someone who loves all this stuff, who probably wouldn't get spooked at all and who might be able to give me some insight. I'm going to go upstairs to my childhood bedroom with a cup of herbal tea, because the thought of booze is still messing with me, and call Sheila. She always puts things into perspective. Even yowling human cats.

# GHOST SONG

I manage to avoid any weird questions from little mam by telling her I'm shattered and that maybe walking to the park wasn't such a good idea, as I felt ill when I got there. She seems gratified by this, as she's always telling me that I 'do too much' and it'll eventually catch up with me. This is usually wrong and absolutely about her, but now she feels vindicated and gives me a big bowl of homemade pea-and-ham soup to make me feel better. She and my dad have already had theirs and Dad is dozing on the sofa, with his faithful shadow Zorro lolling on the floor beside him. I've noticed that Dad's lost more hair, and what he does have has gone a lighter silver, and I've resisted the urge several times to stroke his head, like he's the dog. Time is a bastard. Mam is watching a game show.

I sit in the kitchen, eating the actually very warming and tasty soup, and watch the trains pass by in the darkness. The sky is currently clouded over because of the drizzle, but every now and then a clear patch passes over the moon, and the distant hills become momentarily visible, bathed in the illuminating moonlight.

As soon as I get upstairs to 'my' bedroom I turn on the tiny globe lamp, leaving the curtains open, sit cross-legged on the single bed, pulling around me the comfy grey cardigan that always lives in the wardrobe, and call Sheila. She picks up quickly.

'Flippin heck, Tanz, I knew you were going to ring.'

'How?'

'Just felt it – you plopped into my head out of the blue. How was the journey?'

'It was okay, but there's definitely something "off" here.'

I explain about the strange feelings as I approached my home town in the car, and about the shadow of the 'human cat' that I saw in the park; and as I'm about to move on to the witch-trial stuff, there's an almost blinding flash of lightning from outside and a massive boom. I nearly fling the phone across the room, I get such a shock, and the gasp from Sheila is audible even from arm's length away, as I lean forward towards the window to make sure nothing exploded.

'What the bleeding hell was that, Tanz?'

There's another flash and another boom, slightly less ear-shattering, then sleet begins to hammer down. How is there a storm? It didn't feel stormy in the slightest before. Only miserable and drizzly.

'A bloody great thunderstorm just kicked off, with big, fat sleet hitting the window.'

'That's so mad. I love a good storm, but this really isn't the time of year for them, is it?'

As she speaks, the globe lamp flickers twice, then goes out. I can hear the TV is still on downstairs, so it's not a full power-cut. Maybe only the upstairs lights shorted.

'Bloody hell, Sheils, the lamp went out—'

I stop short. The room suddenly goes pitch-black and as I glance to the corner on my right, I see a woman standing there. I blink and look again. She doesn't go anywhere – she's as real as me. I can't see her face properly; I can only make out youngish features in this darkness, which is disconcerting in such a small room, but despite this I can 'feel' her and I don't think she wants me to be scared. She's about my height, wearing a long skirt and top, or dress, and I can smell a heady mix of cinnamon and sage, plus something else that I can't identify. It's almost overwhelming. She's humming. I don't know the tune, but I hear it coming from her, from the corner, not from inside my head, and I feel the top of my scalp contract with the strangeness of it all.

Then my phone shrieks to life and I see that I've accidentally killed the call and dropped the phone on the bed. Sheila is ringing me back. When I look back to the corner, the humming shadow-woman has gone. The storm stops abruptly, the sleet turning to a light drizzle and, with a flourish, my lamp switches itself back on. I stare at it. The phone stops ringing, then starts again. This time I answer it.

'What happened? You disappeared.'

'Sheila, a woman showed up in the room.'

'You what?'

'A woman just now, standing in the corner. She was all in shadow, there was a strong smell – a pleasant one actually – and she was humming a song. I don't know what it was. Then you rang me back and she was gone again. So has the storm. It stopped like it never started.'

'Wow. Who do you think the woman was?'

'No bloody idea.'

'You don't sound half as scared as I'd expect. Are you all right?'

'Yes, I'm fine, but a bit creeped out. To be honest, once you've been stuck in the middle of nowhere in Reykjavik with a ghost banging on all the walls, plus you find out that your new mate who's as solid as a chest of drawers actually died in 1976, you're kind of not surprised by anything supernatural any more.'

'That's my girl.'

'Better not tell my mam, though – she'll have three cows.'

'Look, before you called, I did get a message myself. No whistles and bells. I just heard the words "The witch is coming." Then you rang. You know what: I think I should come up there pronto. Something's happening, and I'd like to help you find out what. It'll be an adventure and I have a bit of time on my hands at the moment.'

*The witch is coming.* I recently heard something similar. Yes, Alfvin as he gave me his healing in the cave last night: *'The witch comes.'* 'I'm not sure how I feel about this – I thought I was the witch around here!'

Sheila laughs.

'When you say you have time on your hands, Sheila, is

that because your lover-boy has gone back to Jamaica for a month?'

Sheila has been 'secretly' seeing Troy, her Jamaican lover, who's a chef and is many years younger than her – like nearly thirty years – since he came for a reading at the New Age place that we worked at, and she put him back on the right path before a certain family member hurtled him any deeper into the world of serious crime. He's done very well for himself since then, and he obviously adores Sheila, as he nursed her through illness and still visits her as often as she'll let him. She tries to keep it 'open' and encourages him to find someone his own age to make children with, but honestly speaking, I think they have a stronger bond than Sheila wants to admit to herself; she even has a pet name for him: Pan, partly because he's always cooking, but by my reckoning more to do with his similarity to the lusty god of nature, which tells you everything you need to know. Also, from what I can gather, he totally considers her a goddess, and he's not wrong there.

'Will you stop calling him my lover-boy? Yes, Pan has gone away, but it's not only that; you know how much I love a good spooky mystery. And I'd love to visit your home town. Any idea what "The witch is coming" could mean?'

'Maybe you're the witch, seeing as you're now coming here. Please do. I'm not sure how it would work logistically, though, staying at my parents' – there's not really the space.'

'Oh no, I'd want to get myself a hotel room and experience the North-East without worrying about living in someone else's house. You know how much I like my space.'

'Yes, I do. And so does my mam, so it'll probably be much more fun for you that way. There are some fab places to stay.'

'Okay, I'm going to sort the train and find a hotel for as soon as possible. This is so exciting.'

'Yay! And just so you know: I spoke to Gladys today and she told me about the Newcastle witch trials. I won't tell you anything else, apart from it's mental how many people they hanged at once. She thinks I may be related to one of them. That would shed a bit of light on "The witch is coming." I'll try to hold off researching too much else, though, because maybe if we do it together we'll make some magic!'

'Maybe we will. I'll text you when I find a place and get the train times. I'm really looking forward to this now.'

Famous last words. I try not to get excited about anything these days, because when I do, it always goes wrong. But Sheila's not me, and 'wrong' is a relative term, I suppose. I mean, yes, absolutely insane things happen to me on a regular basis, but I'm still alive, aren't I? For now.

# WITCH PRICKER

Three a.m. and my eyes are the same size as the globe lamp by my bed. I should have put it on when I woke up, but I didn't, because the 'woman' is back and I don't want to move a muscle. She's humming that song again and I can't take my eyes off her. The room isn't completely blacked out, so I can 'see' her silhouette and I can smell her scent, which is earthy and imbued with sweat as well as those tantalizing herbs. It's intoxicating. Part of me wants to scream for my mam, but a bigger part of me is intrigued. Maybe Alfvin gave me a new strength, or maybe I've already been scared as much as anyone could be by ghosts and murderers, but I don't want to make the woman go away, I want to talk to her. I give it a go.

'Hello.'

Holy fuck, she stops humming and her shadowy self shoots across the room straight at me. I'm so shocked that I don't scream, but I do jump with fright. My heart jackhammers, as I feel and smell her next to my face. I can't see her now, but her presence is palpable. And my consciousness winks out as she takes me on a trip. I say 'trip', but it actually feels like passing through a pitch-black tunnel on a train. And now I'm awake and in some kind of prison. But not a prison from nowadays, with central heating, a single bed with a duvet, and plaster walls with pictures Blu-Tacked on. No, this is gaol – old-school gaol like you see in historical films. Damp stone walls with water running down them, a tiny high window with very little light coming through, an actual pot to piss in, and a musty stink that makes me gag.

There are people in here. Two women, chained to the walls. Their clothes are filthy and one is crying quietly to herself. Her skirt has been hitched up and there are sores on her legs. They look like burns. I can hear screaming and crying from another cell. Someone is being hurt and it's pitiful to hear. Two of these women are around forty, as far as I can tell, and the other is around sixty, and when I put out the 'feelers', they're normal family women. Nothing remarkable or bad about them, and definitely not criminals.

'*Innocent.*'

The voice I hear – presumably the humming woman's – is the one I heard talking about the cat man and has the strangest northern accent, not Geordie, not Scottish; it sounds like a hybrid, but is not really definable, which is quite something for me, as I usually consider myself a connoisseur of accents. I can't place this one at all.

'*They did nothing to anyone. Stuck in here for a whole year. Hurt and hurt, and hurt again.*'

I can't see her, but fuck me, I can sense her all around me. And the smell that she emanates is the only thing saving me from vomiting at the stench in this cell. She grabs my hand, which is the weirdest sensation when I can't even see her, but it's exactly what is needed, as my energy is being pulled towards the despair of these ladies. There are more of them, I can feel it. A group of innocent women are stuck in this terrible place; they have no hope and they're being tortured, which has broken their will more and more. I'm outraged for them, but could also go under with the depression of it all. I wonder if the lass holding my hand was one of them.

I don't get to ask her, because suddenly I'm hurtling through another black tunnel. The stench has gone, but it's replaced with fire and flesh. I'm in a field at twilight and a bunch of women are tied to stakes in the middle of a bonfire, which roars around them. There is screaming and hollering, from people watching this disgusting spectacle, but nothing from the women themselves. Their heads loll and they're unconscious.

'*Strangled first. Hundreds of them killed. Hundreds. Dead for no reason.*'

Her voice is so sad. I wonder where this is. We didn't burn witches in England, we hanged them – even I know that. As I stand here, watching this horrible event happen, I can tell there isn't a lot of cheering. Yes, there are shouts about killing the witches, but there seems to be a lot more despair in the emotions that I catch on the breeze. I squint through the smoke and make out a lot of dirty, solemn faces and sobbing families. They *knew* – wow, people knew this was bullshit. I always assumed that some kind of fervour convinced everyone that 'witches' were causing mayhem.

But no, these people knew. They just felt powerless to stop it. I can actually sense the helplessness coming off them in waves. What the actual fuck?

*'His face, there. Him.'*

A man steps forward into the glow from the fire. His face is serious, pious even, but there's a filthy look of glee in his eyes. He fucking knows as well; he knows these poor women are innocent of any wrongdoing. He did this, he caused this, and he's loving it.

*'Witch pricker.'*

She spits this with absolute disgust. I've no idea what a 'witch pricker' is, but I can make an educated guess that it's not a nice thing. As I stare at the man, he shifts his gaze in my direction. His glare is something else: hatred and lust, a terrifyingly potent mix. He is flanked by two other men, both with fake-serious looks on their faces, both built like brick shit-houses. He's smaller, puny even, but with a glint of dangerous cunning. I try to look away from those piercing eyes, but can't. As we have an unintentional stare-off, something else hits me and my heart drops like a stone. His eyes are now my eyes. His face shape is my face shape.

I try to shake off this vision, but I can't. 'She' is showing me this man for a reason. I'm seeing this to help me understand. I'm related to someone from those bad times. But not to a witch. I'm descended from that bastard. I'm from the family line of the fucking witch pricker.

# BLACKBIRDS AND BONFIRES

So I know I told Sheila I'd wait until she arrived before I did any proper digging, but once you've woken up yowling before 7 a.m. in your parents' house and your mam's run in wearing her nightie, waving a cat ornament as a makeshift weapon, the bags under her eyes like small suitcases because she dreamed all night about torture and a bunch of women on a bonfire, that goes out of the window. Research is needed immediately.

I'm actually so shaken up by my visions that I've done the absolute unthinkable and accepted a cup of tea from Mam's teapot, put some of Dad's UHT milk in it and am drinking it in the kitchen, after letting the dog out into the garden. Little mam has wrapped herself up in her pale-blue dressing gown, which looks like it's made of cotton wool, and has joined me with a big mug for herself, with the open biscuit barrel at the ready – 'for the shock'. (I have to admit that a few digestives definitely make breakfast tea more palatable.)

'Tanz, what the bloody hell do you think is going on?

And don't bother hiding anything, please. I think it's pretty obvious we're dreaming about the same things. What I want to know is: WHY?'

'Mam, I honestly don't know why. Something's woken up and it's come after both of us, not only me.'

Mam purses her lips. 'Well, that's marvellous. Do you know how many years I've spent trying to dodge this kind of trouble?'

'I honestly did nothing to cause this, Mam. But if you promise not to go crackers at me, I can tell you what I reckon so far . . .' I absolutely know that I need to miss out some stuff, but Mam's actually very tuned in and if I give her enough information, she might actually solve this before I do. She'll just not realize she did it. 'So you dreamed of women in a stone gaol, yes?'

Mam nibbles on her malted milk and nods. 'There were more there than I could see, Tanz, I know that. And I also know they'd been there a long time. "Too long" is the feeling I got. Like it wouldn't usually happen like that.'

'Yes, I felt that as well. And this one woman – her skirt was up, like they'd been messing with her, and her legs had horrible marks like burns.'

Little mam winces and pulls her dressing gown tighter around her. She's wearing old-lady slippers on her tiny feet, even though she isn't old. 'Oh, they were messed with all right. And that smell. Eeeh, it was horrible. Then next thing you know, though, I was in a fire.'

'In it?'

'Yes, I wasn't burning or anything, but I was in a fire, looking straight out at this man. Weak little bugger who loved to hurt women. Loved it, pet. He stared straight at me, you know. If I could have, I'd have kicked him in the whatsits, but then I woke up, because you were screaming your head off and I thought we had burglars. Now of course I realize that I wasn't thinking straight, because burglars don't usually come in the morning, do they? Anyway I picked up the first object I could find and came running in. Your dad didn't even stir; he could sleep through an earthquake . . .'

'Mam, I don't want to freak you out, but you know that man from the dream?'

'Yes.'

'I saw him as well and stared straight at him. But something else happened.'

'Eeeh, from the look on your face, I'm not sure I want to know.' Mam delicately dunks her biscuit and takes a nibble, her worry apparent.

'It's nothing too scary, it's just . . . Well, I know, from seeing those poor women who were hanged, that it feels like we're descended from one of them. But from what I saw in my dream, that bloke was the witch finder, and while I was staring him out, his face became my face, then turned back again. I mean, it doesn't take Einstein to work that one out: we're not descended from the poor sods who got killed. We're descended from him.'

'Are you bloody joking?'

'No, and don't go thinking I like it any more than you do. All this time trying to help spooks and people in general, and to reconnect with my spiritual side, and then I'm basically told that I'm descended from an evil shit who got his rocks off by torturing innocent women and getting loads of them killed.'

'Well, if that doesn't beat everything! But it doesn't really explain why we're dreaming about those women, does it? Surely we should be seeing everything through his eyes?'

'Yeah, that's where it gets strange.'

'*This* is where it gets strange?'

'You know what I mean. Relatively speaking, this is where it gets strange. There's a woman – I saw her.'

'Saw her where?'

No fucking way am I telling little mam there was an old-fashioned humming lady standing in the corner of my bedroom last night. At the very least, she'll feel compelled to march up there and hoover immediately.

'In my dreams. She seems friendly towards me, but is also angry at the bloke, and called him the "witch pricker". She's the one showing us stuff. I don't know who she is. Smells amazing, though.'

'Well, can you ask her to stop showing me, please? I didn't volunteer for this – I'm not a fan. Tell her that's enough.'

'I'll try, Mam, but you've got to remember something. If I'm descended from him, then so are you, and whatever happens to me is seemingly going to happen to you as well. I can't control that. Technically, this is all your fault. You came with the spooky family line and then gave birth to me. I didn't ask for this.'

'No, but you let it in!'

'I didn't have much choice. I was hearing voices, and I have things happen to me that I wouldn't even dare tell you,

Mam. They don't let me block it out; if I try, things only get worse. Anyway you can't ignore your birthright.'

'Well, I was managing quite nicely.' A piece of Mam's dunked biscuit topples into her tea and she frowns. I wonder if she's going to blame me for that too.

'No, you weren't. Having years of dreams about things that come true, one way or another, isn't exactly avoiding your birthright. It's just pretending not to acknowledge it.'

'All right, Miss Clever Pants. So what happens now?'

Her little face is pinched. She really does look freaked out, and I must have given her such a fright, screaming out in my room like that.

'Don't you worry, Mam. I'm off to the Lit & Phil in town. I get this feeling it's better if I go and do my research the old-fashioned way and that it'll bring unexpected bonuses. You never know what extra nuggets you can glean from books that were written around here, seeing as it's local history.'

'Try not to make it worse, pet. I need some sleep – I'm bushed.'

As she says this, something crashes into the window and Mam knocks the rest of her tea with melted biscuit in it onto the floor. It goes all over the fake parquet and I jump out of my seat, open the window and peep my head over the ledge. A perplexed and always un-violent Zorro is sniffing at a stunned bird that evidently smashed into the glass.

I look round at little mam, who's thrown a bunch of kitchen roll onto the spill. Luckily her mug survived the fall.

'What the bloody hell was that?'

'Looks like a blackbird thought the window was open and flew right at it.'

'Tanz, my nanna told me that blackbirds signify death and bad omens.' She looks terrified. Poor little mam. I need to find out what the spooks want from me or she's going to lose her shit.

'Don't worry, Mam, it's not dead – only stunned.'

A bit like me.

# BEEHIVE GLAMAZON

The ceilings of Newcastle's Literary and Philosophical Society are so high, I feel like I'm in a cathedral. One that worships knowledge and books. I love libraries anyway, but this one is absolutely fantastic and I always feel like I've stepped into another realm when I walk in. I speak to the lady on the desk about why I'm here, and she directs me to a seat in a corner and brings me a bunch of reading matter.

'It's not as well covered as you might think. You'd be surprised how little surviving original material there is about the hangings. It's not a part of history anyone's proud of.'

'Do you think information about that time was actually destroyed?'

She nods. 'Anything else as monumental as that, in an area's history, is usually reported on left, right and centre. You get accounts from all different points of view and it builds up a pretty solid picture of what went on. In this case, we haven't even heard of secret accounts that were found later on. I think the Church may have had a hand in wiping out the written information, plus ashamed councillors and the like. They accepted all kinds of bribes at the time, and shared the witch finders' fees. The corruption was all supposed to be hush-hush, but once it was found that the witch finders weren't qualified to be doing what they were doing, it was very embarrassing for the people who ran the towns and cities that were affected. And maybe even dangerous, from the point of view of citizens who saw family members being treated so terribly and, in many cases, put to death. Much better for them to hush everything up and not let it be recorded for posterity.'

I thank her and log into Google with my phone, to cross-reference stuff. I get stuck into the writings of a man called Ralph Gardiner from South Shields, who witnessed the mass hangings and was disgusted by the whole thing. Obviously they hadn't managed to shut him up. Apparently some bloke was summoned from Scotland as a witch finder and had shown up with his 'witch pricker', which he'd stick into people and, if they didn't bleed, they were guilty. Ah, so that's what a witch pricker was. The whole thing sounds pretty suspect, even from this little nugget of information. Ralph Gardiner's disgust at the entire spectacle only backs up my feeling that not everyone bought into this 'witch' shit, even at the time, and I decide to delve into the methods they used to extract confessions. I get the feeling these witch finders would now be called common-or-garden sadistic murderers – they just had a license for it then. And from what I've seen so far, they got paid per 'guilty' witch, which gave them an incentive to kill innocent people.

A shadow falls over me as I'm looking up torture methods, and all at once I am taking in a tall, broad, fulsome woman, with a very bleached pile of hair styled into a makeshift beehive on the top of her head, with a fringe and curly, wispy bits hanging down. She is wearing a navy shift dress with a biker jacket over. Doc Martens and a thick slick of cherry-red lipstick finish the look. She's huge and strangely impressive, with bleeding smoker's lines around her lips giving her an extra air of a 'couldn't give a fuck' mature woman. She stares at me and doesn't say anything, then sits opposite in the only other chair in this corner of the library. She smells of jasmine perfume and cigarette smoke. She's such a huge presence that I absolutely can't sit there and not acknowledge her.

'Hello. I've not taken your seat, have I?'

She sniffs, then shakes her head, craning to see what I'm reading. 'This one's fine. You reading about the witch trials?'

'I am.'

'I studied them for years. I still come in on my day off and read about all things witchy.' Her voice is deep and raspy and she's obviously bloody nosy, but I can't hate her because she's so different. I love different. She's also trying to keep her voice down, but failing quite miserably. Not that anyone is telling her off.

'Are you a witch then?' I say it lightly and laugh, but she doesn't laugh in return.

'Not quite, but I'm very interested. Terrible time in history, that. Those poor women.'

'I know.' I pull a sympathetic face. She's quite closed, I

can't get at her energy, but she comes across as an intelligent eccentric.

'There was a man an' all.'

'Yes, at least you can say they didn't discriminate in Newcastle.' Another attempt at a joke from me that falls flat.

'Oh yes, they did. One man, but fourteen women. And I'm pretty sure he got accused because the woman who said he'd bewitched her kids was mentally ill and fancied him. There's always sex at the root of these things. Or jealousy.'

'Yes. I'm pretty sure that's at the root of most negativity on this planet. As well as a love of power, obviously.'

She nods at this, her beehive not budging a millimetre. 'You know, the woman who accused the fella of being a witch, she said he turned into a black cat and got her kids to do his bidding. I mean, even that many years ago they *knew* that people weren't turning into cats – the bloody cowards.'

I get a little jolt at this, as I immediately think of the human-sized cat that I saw in the park. So the humming woman was actually showing me proof of what one of the 'witches' was accused of?

'And that's why they hanged him?'

'That's why they hanged him. The woman obviously had it in for him. I think every single one of those poor souls was just in the wrong place at the wrong time. Did you know the town crier used to walk around Newcastle asking people to report any woman they thought was a witch? Any *woman*. And you were much more likely to be believed to be a witch if you weren't young and pretty. An effective way to eliminate the crones, eh? Wise women were *not* appreciated in those days. Still aren't, really.'

'Well, I think older women are the absolute business, so I appreciate them. I'm pretty much one myself now.'

She smiles at me, a turned-down-at-the-sides smile that shows big square teeth with lipstick on them.

'Being an older woman has its advantages, I suppose, now that they're not allowed to kill us just for knowing stuff.' I smile back at her, lipstick and all. 'I think you're pretty magnificent.'

She actually flinches with surprise at this. 'Do you? Why?'

'I don't know. You're obviously clever, and your look is strong and you're into witches. That's a start,' I tell her.

'I'm descended from one of them.'

'Oh my God, really?'

'Yup. Jane Martin, the miller's wife. She was the only one held in Newcastle Keep. The place was falling down, with no roof, but she was from Northumberland and came from a different district from the rest, so that was the prison where she was kept, while the rest were in the gaol on Newgate Street. They were in prison for nearly a year, which meant that the gaolers got a year's pay for 'taking care' of them. But they didn't care for them. They tortured them and drove the women half-mad. Thirty were accused in all, but fifteen were hanged, and Jane was one of them. They were hanged along with other prisoners, so twenty-four were hanged in one day. Savages.'

'Holy shit, that's horrifying. How did you find out you were descended from her?'

'My mother did one of them family trees, and a relative that she found who was still alive had papers all about it. Like a family badge. I always felt something was 'off', because my life's not been the luckiest. I actually thought I was cursed. This convinced me that something had been passed down from that horrible event. Jane had done nothing wrong. It all came from a dispute about inheritance; once you dig in the few places where you can study it, the whole thing stinks to high heaven. The woman who accused her also accused Jane's sister. The sister had mental problems, I think, and confessed to stuff that wasn't true about both of them. Do you think that can happen – that horrible stuff like this can come down the family tree?'

'I think trauma can be passed down, yes. But also that it can be halted.'

'I'm not so sure. Let's just say that the more I dug, the more I realized that there have been – and still are – truly evil shits in the world who would kill for a few more coins in their pocket and for the fun of seeing others die. And they were, and are, never punished. Nobody pays. How can that be fair?'

'It isn't fair. I do wonder, though, if some people do receive karma and we just don't see it.'

'Well, my ancestor was murdered because someone was aggrieved about money. That makes me sad.'

'It's horrible. What's your name by the way?'

'I'm Lydia.'

I hold out my hand. 'I'm Tanz, and it's nice to meet you.'

'Nice to meet you, Tanz. I think I recognize you from somewhere.'

'I've got one of those faces.'

'What's your interest in witches, Tanz?'

'Oh, just research.'

'So you're not related to the poor sods who got hanged?'

'Not as far as I know. I'm scared that I might be related to the fucker who killed them.'

'Oh God.'

'Yup. Not sure – just working on a hunch. But I need to find out everything I can, and this seemed the best place to start.'

'It is. It's my sanctuary.'

'Well, I've only been looking for a teensy while, but it looks like the witch trials were basically a corrupt way of exploiting people who'd been through plague and civil war. Scaring them into believing stuff that made life even worse, and charging them for the benefit of seeing their neighbours murdered, for no reason. Some things are too horrific to take in. And it's always the women who have suffered. Always us.'

'You're right there,' Lydia concurs.

'What makes me mad is that wise women are the ones who can make life easier for everyone. Because they've been through a lot and understand how the world works. Plus, they have humility.'

'Try telling the men that. In their eyes, if you're not someone they want to have sex with, you're not deserving of life.' Lydia pronounces 'sex' as if it's in inverted commas, like my mam would.

'Holy shit, that's dark, but very true. My friend's coming up tomorrow to see the sights and she'd love this conversation; she's always telling me to steer clear of blokes. Obviously, I never do.'

Just then my phone beeps. It's a message from Thor.

'Oooh. It's a message from one of the good guys. There are definitely a few left on the planet. I'd better call him.'

'Okay.' Lydia's eyes are curious as I walk away.

# A MINOR MAIMING

'Thor, hi there. Everything okay?'

'Not really, but I feel much better just hearing you speak. I had the strangest feeling in the night. I dreamed you were in a dark room and I couldn't reach you.' He sounds upset, but even so, it's lovely to hear his voice again.

'What kind of room?'

'It was made of stone – it echoed. I told you to keep saying my name so that I could find you, but your voice got more distant instead of closer and I woke up crying.'

'Oh, Thor. I'm sorry. And at the same time, aw, that's so sweet. Please don't worry about me. I'm in Newcastle now, researching witch trials that happened well over three hundred years ago. I'm not in any danger from the living. It's the dead who are restless, and Sheila's arriving soon to help. We're the dynamic duo. All is well. How's your girlfriend?'

He sighs. 'She's crazy. I had no idea until I pulled away. She's a control freak. How do I attract these people? She said she wanted freedom and to date multiple people. Now she's stolen my mother's number from my iPhone and keeps leaving voicemails about how she wants to die. I'll figure it out, but wow, I've learned a lesson.'

'That sounds terrible.'

'It is, but it's good that I found out before it went on any longer. I miss you, my northern witch.'

'I'm not so sure I am a witch, Thor. I've had some things happen that have made me wonder if I'm one of the bad guys. A witch killer.'

'Don't be ridiculous. Bullshit! You're a magical woman. But I can feel something isn't right and it's really freaking me out. I'm so far away, I can't protect you. I know you can look after yourself, but sometimes we all need back-up and I want to be your wing-man.'

'Sorry for laughing. I've never had a wing-man, just wing-women, as in best mates. What does this job entail?'

'Well, mostly guarding from the rear and taking a bullet when needed. I mean, when you think about it, the wing-man is a temporary job, as you'll probably die pretty quickly. Or at least get maimed.'

'So you're willingly volunteering to get maimed for me?'

'Well, I'd rather get a kick to the thigh or be called some unkind names. But if maiming is called for, then yes, I'll take it. Though minor maiming would be preferable.'

I don't know if I'm laughing harder at his jokes or his outrageously good grasp of the English language.

'Right, thanks for volunteering for a minor maiming, but I'm okay for now. Though some rather freaky things have been occurring over the past few days, and I reckon my mother is going to have a nervous breakdown if I don't find out why we're dreaming about people who were put to death all those years ago. She blames me entirely, but it's not my fault we're spooky women. I mean she was spooky before me, but I always get the blame.'

'Just so you know, I heard my Hidden One in the dream. I'm sure it was her. She said, "The witch comes." I wondered if she meant you – that you were coming back to Iceland – but it didn't feel like that. It felt more scary and strong. Do you know what she meant?'

'Fuck. Not totally, but Alfvin said the same thing to me.'

'What the hell? I don't like this, Tanz. I want to fly over to your home town and guard you like a jumpy bear.'

'What the fuck is a jumpy bear?'

'A worried grizzly. An anxious koala?'

'You're ridiculous.'

'I'm a devoted fool – please be careful. There's something going on. You said I was a wizard. So listen to this magical bearded man. And come and see me soon.'

'I'll have to become a millionaire if I want to visit you more regularly.'

'So let me come to you.'

'It's not that I don't want you to, Thor. But you know how horrendous my track record with men is. I don't want to see you and realize we just had an intense holiday romance, with ghosts and murder included, and then we don't click in the normal world. Or we do click, then you bugger off back to Iceland and never contact me again. I'm so tired of getting it wrong, and I'm not sure my heart can take any more of a battering right now.'

'Just promise me this. You want me to fly over, message me. A couple of words even and I'll be there. I miss you too much.'

'I miss you too, but don't quote me on that.'

# WITCH BONES

Lydia was gone when I went back into the library. I didn't see her leave, but there are loads of specialized reading rooms upstairs and downstairs, so maybe she went to study something elsewhere. I read whatever I can for an hour or more, but it gets hard going, finding out precisely how innocent people were forced to admit things that weren't true about themselves. I defy anyone to enjoy reading about torture methods that wore people down sufficiently to sentence them to death – and a death in pain, because of what was done to them to extract a confession. An absolute circle of misery.

Luckily, out of the blue I suddenly get an irresistible urge to go to St Andrew's Church on Newgate Street. The prison where most of the women were kept was also on Newgate Street in the old days, and the graveyard of St Andrew's Church is apparently where the 'witches' were buried after they were hanged – on the shady side of the churchyard because it was less holy, according to some idiot or other. I mean consecrated ground is consecrated ground, isn't it, and all it makes me think is that absolutely everyone knew these witch trials were bullshit. They just didn't dare say it aloud. The walk to the church isn't long, as it's pretty close to the town centre and literally minutes from the library, so I reach it while the cold sun is still peering through the clouds.

Despite growing up in Gateshead and spending a huge amount of the first twenty years of my life in Newcastle, I've taken surprisingly little interest in historical buildings like this church until now. In the hazy winter light I stare up at its walls and take in exactly how old it looks. A small part of the grounds is actually connected by a wall dating from when the original castle was built, and that bit truly is ancient. But even the mucky, mossy church looks incredibly old. The graveyard isn't very big at all, and although there are some beautiful (and very weathered) gravestones, there are no stones marking where the victims of that shitty greed- and cruelty-driven cull are buried. I know roughly where they are, though, as I saw a photo of the place where 'witch bones' were found during a renovation; plus, it's mentioned in a few pamphlets and books which part of the cemetery holds them.

As I stand by the grave of a young schoolteacher who died when he was only twenty-six, it becomes apparent that I don't have to look that hard anyway. Because standing by the wall opposite is the lass from the corner of my bedroom, and my dream last night. I can see more of her face now. She's wearing a grey gown with a beetroot-red woollen shawl and she has pronounced cheekbones. I can't see her eye colour, as she's too far away, but she has dark hair and is staring straight at me, chewing something and humming at the same time. It's faint, but I know it's the song I heard before. She lifts her arm and points further up the wall. As she does so, a bunch of shadowy people begin to materialize.

As with transparent holograms, I can still see the wet, mossy stonework behind them, but I also feel the most chilling despair. It's absolutely heartbreaking. The women are silently weeping and the one man has no shoes, and from what I can make out there are bones protruding from his feet. I just read about torture methods, and one of them was making someone walk over stones for hours at a time, tied behind a horse. It was rumoured that's what they did to the man, and now I seem to be seeing the result. He looks destroyed and as I stare harder, taking in the mess he's in from the ankles down, he seems to morph into a black cat on its hind legs, then back to a man again. This doesn't scare me as much as it should, partly because he more resembles a projection from a silent movie than a solid person, but also because it's as if I'm being shown how preposterous it all was. Man becomes a cat – ludicrous nonsense.

Noting that the graveyard is absolutely empty right now, I edge closer to the humming lass and ask her name in my mind. She doesn't reply, but actually puts out her hand to me. I keep getting closer, my heart beginning to race at the proximity, until I can reach my own hand out to hers. She's transparent, but to my surprise, I feel warm fingers in mine. Like she's reaching through the past to touch me for real. I close my hand around hers and hear her voice in that strange but oddly soothing accent.

*'Close your eyes.'*

I do as I'm told and there's a vision in my head of the same graveyard, but looking different from the way it looks now. I can't see much further than the grounds, but there are certainly fewer buildings around, the birdsong is stronger and the gravestones appear dissimilar. I know the church was worked on and rebuilt about a hundred years after the witch trials, and I can see when I look up that the structure of the church looks different from the present one, but it also seems the gravestones from that time differed from the ones I was looking at in present-day Newcastle.

It's beginning to snow in the vision, and a large trench has just been filled in by the gravedigger. This makes me unaccountably sad. A fucking awful anonymous burial after a nasty, pointless bunch of deaths. I hate that these poor souls were treated so callously from start to finish. As I watch the gravedigger straighten up and massage his back then wander off towards the church, my humming friend appears. I can smell her distinctive scent, even as I watch her from inside my head. And now, all at once, I'm allowed to hear the song she's singing. Not all of it, but the first line.

*'Sleepe, sleepe, though greife torment,'* she sings, as she swings a little basket with something burning in it.

The unidentifiable herb that I smelled on her is even stronger here, as it casts its pungent smoke over the unmarked mass grave. She tosses handfuls of tiny stones or seeds, then suddenly stops at the edge of a long, rectangular grave, and her song turns into a chant.

*'Thou wilt be avenged, angels of innocence. Thou wilt*

*feel the sunshine of kindness through your line, as the accuser finds torment in the fires. Thou wilt be avenged, kind souls. Mag avows it on this day.'*

'Is that your name?'

Even as the vision fades, I see the humming woman turn and nod straight at me.

*'Aye, Mag. And Mag is with thee. Avenger of the innocent and friend to the witches.'*

I open my eyes, and now I'm standing in the empty present-day graveyard, with the scent of herbs around me and the song of Mag's growing more and more distant. Wow. Well, I know where I'm bringing Sheila as soon as humanly possible. She'll absolutely love it here, and with two of us standing together, who knows what extra information we might glean?

For now, though, I fancy wandering up to Blakes on Grey Street and asking if they'll do me a big hot chocolate. It's getting rather bloody nippy, and standing in this graveyard has turned my toes to ice. Next stop on the 'people who were murdered by liars' tour will be the Town Moor, where they did the mass hanging, but I think I'll need company for that one. Anyway, it's getting late and I don't fancy going there on my own in the twilight. Jotting a few notes down about what just happened, with a steaming mug of chocolate beside me, is a much better option than tramping my freezing feet across muddy fields. Besides, I'm supposed to be a writer now, aren't I, so this will be a good exercise in putting pen to paper.

As I exit the graveyard, I spy a blackbird sitting on the fence by the gate. It's watching me intently. I remember my mam saying they're portents of doom, so I give it a wink as I walk by, hoping he'll be my friend.

'Hello, lovely bird.'

He takes off at a lick as I say this and flies over my head, so close that I feel the backdraught of his wings. I also feel a splat on my foot. The absolute swine has dropped a gloopy poo on my shoe. Better than shitting in my hair, I suppose, but bloody hell, it'd better mean good luck and not 'I'll get you.'

# MOCHA MUSINGS

Sitting in Blakes, bird poo now decisively removed with a handful of binned paper napkins, I savour a very tasty mocha, with my notebook open before me, and remember the day I hung out with my friend Gladys in here, after meeting her for the first time on a ghost-walk on the quayside. Gladys had a carrier bag of snacks with her on that walk, and huge spectacles on her small face. Little did I know, when I saw this small, round, hilarious woman for the first time, that she'd become a friend – an ally in getting rid of an evil ghost and the biggest sugar-feeder I've ever met. No one can visit Gladys without eating several kinds of biscuit and at least two slices of cake. She also has so many crystals that you can hardly see the surfaces in her living room, and right now I'm wondering how she is. It seems sad that she's making a pilgrimage all on her own, but with her husband dead and no relatives left, it's also an intensely private thing to share with someone who isn't close family.

I shudder when I consider a time when I don't have my

parents any more and all of my relatives have gone, and I'm the old one. This is what many of those poor women must have faced when they were accused of witchcraft. I wonder how many of them were just defenceless older ladies who were easy to accuse, because their husband had died, or whatever, and they had tasty bits of land or dwellings to snatch away after they died.

I know this isn't the full story, though, because when I looked from face to face of all of those people in my dreams who were exterminated, many of them weren't that elderly and some of them didn't look much older than me. I make some lacklustre notes as I consider how easily I now accept visions of long-dead accused witches, plus the presence of Mag, with her distinctive scent and her humming. I'm not even scared of her, she feels so familiar to me. Obviously it's not ideal to see a shadowy ghost popping up in the corner of your bedroom at night, but after I got more of a daylight look at her today, my most pressing sensation was of feeling close to her. I mean there must have been a reason why Mag chose to attach herself to me when I got back to Gateshead, and there must also be a reason why I accept her presence so easily.

My mind skips back to my dream about the fire – people already strangled before they were burned. I did a bit of research today and it turned out I was right. England was not big on burning witches, but Scotland was. In fact Scotland was a 'hotbed' of witch burning (see what I did there?). Many hundreds were killed and, from what I saw, at least one of the 'witch finders' responsible was getting off on the senseless murder he wrought. And, horrifyingly, I'm pretty sure I'm descended from him.

That aside, I went to the graveyard again today and Mag showed me the poor sods who'd died and who still seemed to be rather upset. Considering how many times this has happened now – ghosts in distress showing themselves to me – I'm pretty convinced I have some kind of job to do here, but I'm bamboozled as to what that job can be. I'm sure a lot of people, local ones especially, like Lydia who I met today, know the history of the witch trials and have felt the injustice of it. I'd be willing to bet that plenty of people have visited that graveyard and done blessings and all sorts to make sure the dead there are honoured. But suddenly I've been 'called home' and am being haunted by someone who could have loomed at me in my childhood bedroom any number of times since 'I tuned in' at the Mystery Pot all that time ago. So why now?

Once Sheila arrives tomorrow, hopefully we can work together to find out what makes the current date significant enough for the dead to be crying, and for Mag to be on the warpath. I'm still wondering why she's telling me stuff and not attacking me, seeing as I'm descended from the nasty bastard who caused all this harm. She doesn't seem to be mad at me at all, and today she said I could help her.

So that's it: tomorrow I'll take Sheila to the graveyard and then we'll hit the Town Moor and see what we can sense there. She's getting here in the early afternoon, which means I can lounge in bed a bit, if I fancy. I'll also take Milo along, as he loves Sheila. He's actually got the day to himself tomorrow, which makes a change, as he's a total mover and shaker these days and always seems to be busy.

When I wake up, I find that my dreams have been pretty gentle. Gravestones and blackbirds, but nothing terrifying. And seeing as I've not been woken up by Mam squawking anything at Dad about nightmares and 'messin' with them ghosts', she must have had a peaceful night too. It's still quite early, so I put my earplugs in and elect to lounge in bed as long as is humanly possible before driving Milo and me over to Newcastle to meet Sheila in her hotel. She's booked three nights in this excellent, funky place on High Bridge street, which is right in the middle of the action, but apparently has good double-glazing (plus, Sheila assured me she could sleep peacefully in the middle of a football match). I've checked it out on the booking site and it's amazingly cheap, considering how cool it is.

Unfortunately, the planned lazing-about-in-bed doesn't really go to plan, because even with earplugs in, you can't help but hear someone hoovering outside your bedroom and accidentally-on-purpose smacking the heavy nozzle on the door several times. Much as I love my mother, she's an absolute devil when she wants the rooms of her house vacated, and after half an hour of varying loud bangs, mutterings, singing of pop songs and slamming of the bathroom door, I secretly go back on the website and book myself three nights that I can't really afford in the same hotel as Sheila. If I stay here another night, I won't be responsible for the actions of my strangling-hands, and I'm sure it'll be more fun having good coffee from a machine at breakfast time, while talking about all things spooky, than sipping at instant coffee-water and being told off for attracting trouble to little mam's dreams.

When I pick up Milo, he looks different. Like he's standing taller and inhabiting his own frame more comfortably. Whoever this boyfriend is, he's done Milo the world of good, I can't deny it. His skin looks fresh and his eyes are twinkling. When he hugs me across the seats, he smells all clean and gorgeous and I ruffle his head like he's a baby starling.

'Hello, handsome!' I say.

He grins at the compliment and smooths his hair back down. 'Hello, witchy-poos. How you doing?'

'Not as good as you, obviously. You look scrumptious. Someone seems to have had a good time this week.'

Milo winks. He's not usually a winker, so it makes me laugh.

'I don't suppose I'm going to get any details about the new boyfriend and the other night's date?'

'We ate chow mein and he made me laugh. That's all anyone needs to know.'

'Fuck me, you're cagey.'

'Anyway I think it's much more interesting to find out what the hell is going on with you. Not back five minutes from a haunting in Lapland, and you're up here and Sheila's come to join you. Something's happening, so spill!'

'Let's just say that you calling me "witchy-poos" isn't that far off the mark. I feel weird as fuck, and my mam and I are dreaming the same stuff about witches being hanged and people being tortured, and all sorts. I've done some research about the Newcastle witch trials . . .'

'The what now?'

'Exactly, it's like the most tight-lipped historical event that ever happened in the North – cagier than you, about your fella. But it's probably better to get to the hotel and the three of us can discuss what's been happening.'

'Oooh, exciting!'

I park my glorified bean-tin in an overnight car park on the quayside, which costs a lot less than it would in London, and we walk up to High Bridge Street. The hotel is even funkier in real life, and I go to the desk with my case and check in, in two minutes flat. I told my little mam that it might help her dreams if I fucked off and stayed with Sheila, so she took it quite well. Dad just gave me a hug and a squeeze. He obviously 'gets' it. Mothers and daughters always seem to have complicated relationships. That or they're weirdly over-close, which always freaks me out.

Sheila exits from the lift, resplendent in a midnight-blue velvet top, and Milo emits a jokey wolf-whistle when he sees her. These two get on like a house on fire, and it's lovely to know my mates enjoy each other's company so much. We all order different cuppas and sit in the front window on cute teal armchairs, before a cool fire that has a screen with flames on it where the actual fire should be.

I spill about absolutely everything – some of which Sheila knows, some of which she doesn't – and Milo's face becomes a mask of joyous terror when I talk about the shadowy woman in my bedroom, then of Mag's little performance in the old graveyard.

'Tanz, that is fucking terrifying. How the hell did you sleep in your bedroom since then?'

'I left the lamp on all night the first night, but actually I didn't worry much last night and my dreams were definitely calmer. In fact I was feeling pretty much okay, until Mam started smashing the Hoover against my door, like a little Geordie jackhammer. I hope you don't mind, Sheila, but I'm staying here now too. The receptionist let me have the room next to yours. Another night with the parents and I'd either die of fright or murder my own mother in cold blood.'

'Oh, that's fab. I love that we've got rooms next to each other. We can research the witch trials, go to all the relevant places that might put the jigsaw together, then debrief at night in this cosy bar with good wine. Or in one of our rooms, with our notebooks out, like *Murder, She Wrote* but two Jessicas.'

'We can indeed.'

Milo looks positively jealous at this. 'Bloody typical – some paranormal shenanigans kick off and I've got to go to Manchester tomorrow for a brainstorming session with a TV company. It's a workshop and they're paying me, so I can't even pretend I've got the lurgy and pull out.'

Sheila pats his hand. 'Come for a debrief when you're back, Milo. I'm sure there'll be something juicy for you to join in with.'

Suddenly he looks less sure. 'As long as I don't get possessed again, because that was shit. I mean, I could just man the desk, if you like?'

I nod.

'Okay, Milo, we'll keep you in the loop with any excitement. I'm sure you won't miss anything much. You want to come on a little tour of relevant places now with Sheila, get her up to speed with everything I told you both?'

He shakes his head regretfully. 'I'll have to go soon – have to prepare my pitch.'

'Fucking hell, Milo, you didn't even do this much homework at school. Who are you?'

'I'm an important and terrifying figure in the writing world actually.'

I look at his gentle face and cheeky glint and roll my eyes. 'I know you are, pet. I hope you don't mind that I'm trying to write something as well, by the way? I promise I'm not trying to muscle in on your career.'

'Muscle away, witchy-poos; if it brings you back north to my loving arms on a more permanent basis, then all will be well.'

'I think your loving arms are pretty much booked up at the moment, buggerlugs.'

Sheila cocks her head. 'Woooh, is love in the air, sweetheart?'

Milo actually goes red. 'I'm not sure I'd go that far.'

'Sheila, he's got a fella. Just like you and your not-very-secret lover.'

She eyes me seriously. 'What about your not-very-secret Icelandic tour guide?'

Suddenly I'm the defensive one. 'He's not "mine", I told you. Thor lives abroad; my love life always ends up as a fucking bin-fire, and he's so beautiful that I hate thinking about him, so all in all it's probably best if I don't.'

'Bloody hell.' Milo stares at me. 'She's got it bad.'

'Okay, can you both leave it now and get back on with the matter at hand? Sheila, we definitely need to go to the Town Moor and stand where the hangings happened. The power of two might unlock more than I could do on my own.'

Milo jumps up. 'Well, before it all goes spooktastic, I'll love you and leave you. I've got some stationery to buy and I fancy a new pencil case as well.' I absolutely love how old-school he is. I hug Milo hard and he holds me a little longer than he normally would, then whispers in my ear, 'I've been worried about you. Please take care of yourself.'

'Stop being weird!'

He laughs, then hugs Sheila and trots off with quite the spring in his step. Yes, being busy and being loved-up suits him well.

'Okay, London magic woman. Let me show you around my town of birth. I'll just drop my case upstairs and we can get our big coats – that lovely velvet top of yours is no match for Newcastle at this time of year.'

# HUMAN SPARROW AND A SAD BLANKET

Sheila absolutely loves the Lit & Phil. I'd told her it was like the big library in *Ghostbusters*, but I don't think she fully believed me until she saw the place herself. I show her around as much as I'm allowed, and at one point outside one of the downstairs reading rooms she has a whispered conversation with 'no one', until she realizes that she's speaking out loud, and then she remains standing in the same spot, obviously listening but not speaking any more.

As I start to lead her outside, ready to show her the graveyard next, I spot Lydia sitting in the same corner of the library where I met her last time. She's in another shift dress, black this time, with her biker jacket, DMs and piled-on-her-head bleached hair. Her lipstick is more orangey this time and a little smudged, but it goes with the also-smudged black eyeliner. She spots us as we're walking by and, shooting a curious glance at Sheila, gives me a little wave, which I return.

'Wow, who was that? Big energy. Quite frenetic.'

'That's Lydia – she looks like a Valkyrie, doesn't she?'
'She does.'

Sheila and I head up the drizzly street, stopping in the hotel on the way so that Sheila can put another jumper on, then we head towards the graveyard. My transparent plastic umbrella shields both of us while we walk in companionable silence for a bit, until I can't resist it any more and ask the obvious question.

'Who the hell were you talking to in there, Sheila? I saw you whispering. Then you stopped, but they were still standing beside you. I could see the heat-haze.'

'Bloody hell, nothing gets past you. If you must know, it was an older lady. Well-spoken and the size of a human sparrow, with bright white hair. She was very cute.'

'Whoa. What did she want?'

'Well, you know how the spooks are attracted to people who can see them? We're like beacons of light to them, and she was interested in me as she could tell from the accent that I wasn't from around here. She said you'd been in there before and hadn't spoken to her. She said she wanted to tell me something about you. Apparently you have a humongous light around you – bigger than most people's – and it worries her. She wonders if maybe you shouldn't tone it down a little, as it won't just attract the good ones.'

'WHAT?'

'I know. She seemed a bit too in-the-know for some passing spirit tootling about the library. I wasn't sure what to make of it or what I should tell you, but you've asked now. And I told her that you protect yourself really well, so you'll be fine. But it did make me think: have you done any proper protection spells recently?'

'Well, no, but I always do the "surrounding myself with light" thing every morning.'

'Okay. So maybe later we'll do a proper "thing" in one of our rooms. Get you properly guarded. In my experience, *they* don't give these reminders for no reason. Seeing as you went up a notch spiritually *again* while you were in Reykjavik, it's probably a good idea to do a cleansing. I've never experienced a meeting of spiritual worlds like you did there, but I imagine it took quite a lot out of you.'

'Honestly speaking, I've not felt right since. And, look, here's the church.'

'Oh, how beautiful.'

And it is. Seeing it through an outsider's eyes makes it appear even more stunning than I already thought it was. We amble into the graveyard and Sheila stops suddenly and stands there, staring towards the wall where I saw Mag and the ghosts yesterday.

'What, Sheila? What do you see?'

'Nothing solid. It's a cloud, like a dark mist, and it has such sadness attached. Someone's guilt.'

'Guilt?'

'Yes, that mass death really stirred up some huge emotions, but this burial ground . . . Someone spent time here and, boy, did they feel guilty. It's still settled over the place like a sad blanket.'

'Sad blanket? I like that. Do you see anybody?'

'Nope. Just the fog. And something that's hidden. I

feel that strongly. And I do feel like I'm being watched – do you?'

'I've felt so off the past week I'm not totally sure what's going on half the time, but there's defo a feeling we're not alone here. Not that that should be a surprise in a graveyard!'

'Well, we certainly weren't alone in Cross Bones Graveyard.'

'Oh man, don't. Imagine if this place lit up with all the dead, like it did in Cross Bones. I think I'd have a nervous breakdown.'

'At least they'd all be Geordies like you.'

'I'm not sure that would be any kind of improvement.'

We both laugh and link arms as we head out of the graveyard on the next part of our quest.

# MY PARK'S BIGGER THAN YOURS

I take Sheila on the Metro. I love how shocked people are when they discover that Newcastle (and indeed Gateshead) has a Metro. It's not that far to the Town Moor, but Newcastle's a big place and where the gallows was erected is a very specific spot on the Nuns Moor. I read that they erected it not too far from the barracks at the time, as they were worried about the crowds getting out of control, so they wanted soldiers nearby, just in case. There were nine cattle-rustlers hanged that day as well as the 'witches'. It absolutely horrifies me that taking livestock could mean that you were killed. That's a crime in itself. But it certainly doesn't surprise me that the authorities worried about needing an army presence there, now that I know how much people didn't even believe in this witchcraft shit – they just had it thrust upon them. Anyway, a couple of Metro stops will make the whole trip quicker and less 'wet', as the cold drizzle has intensified.

Sheila is entranced by the Metro's lack of crowds and the soft seating.

'What, did you think it would be horse-drawn, have wooden seats and be full of inbreds carrying chickens and small goats?'

'No, I thought it would be rammed with cheeky sods as mouthy as you are.'

'Bet you didn't bank on us having a Metro like Paris, though?'

'No. It's nice.'

'Well, don't get comfortable, because the next stop is ours. How about a little jaunt on here tomorrow? Mystery tour.'

'Oooh, sounds great.'

'Excellent. Oops, come on – this is us.'

The Moor is huge. A thousand acres, bigger than Central Park in New York. We northerners are weirdly proud of this fact – no idea why; people seem to get very proud about bigness. The Freemen of the city, whoever they are, have cattle-grazing rights here to this day, and it's true that you'd not expect such an unspoiled swathe of land in such a built-up place. We walk the thin paths, huddled under my umbrella, and admire the landscape, which is actually pretty treeless. Sheila keeps looking around her in shock.

'This is weird. A massive tract of farmland in the middle of a city. I feel like this should be in Wales or something. And it has quite a lot of magic attached, you know.'

As a child visitor to the Hoppings, I was unaware of 'magic' in that sense, but now I can feel it all right. Hugely spiritual things, both negative and positive, attached to the ground here. Much death and much life. It ties in with the ancientness of the castle and Black Gate, and the fragments of original walls dotted around Newcastle.

As we approach the Nuns Moor, with Nuns Moor Park bordering it, I start to feel distinctly strange. Sheila grabs my hand hard as we get to pretty much where the 'action' took place. A cold breeze whips up suddenly, messing with the umbrella, and we both look up as the most unexpected yellow-grey clouds zip across the sky and there's a flash of lightning.

'Oh my God, Tanz, what's happening?'

'I don't fucking know.'

The thunder is mighty and we both instinctively pull up the hoods on our winter coats. 'Sheila, should we go?'

'I can't move my bloody legs.'

'Holy shit, neither can I.' My legs are absolutely rooted to the spot, and now I'm suddenly scared that we're going to be hit by lightning while we're trapped here, stuck in the grass like bloody golf flags.

Just as I'm thinking we're fucked, I see a heat-haze appear to my right and it 'hardens' into the shadow form of Mag. She points ahead of us both. Sheila doesn't notice her, which is unusual, but I can feel Mag's energy like a radiator.

*'Look upon't.'*

I squeeze Sheila's hand harder. And suddenly I'm at the front of a crowd with a large three-sided gallows before me. The weather is calm, but cold, and it's lighter than it was a minute ago. The smell is of animal shit, farmland, bonfires and some kind of incense, which may be linked to the fumigation stuff they burned when the plague returned a few years before the hangings in 1650 (I read about it last night on my phone, when I googled the seventeenth century in Newcastle). The crowd is charged with emotion: some worked-up drunken numpties, exactly like you get now, shouting shit about witches and evil, but also a lot of weeping and fervour, from what I feel to be devastated family members and friends. An older woman keeps shouting, *'No, no, no-no, noooo . . .'*

It's quite the lament. There are wooden forms the length of the gallows, with nooses above and a little ladder at the right of each, leading upwards. It's the same on each of the three sides, and the sheer number of nooses is fucking horrible. I 'know' that it's Mag standing next to me, though she has the hood of her woollen cloak pulled up over her head, so her face is invisible. Her scent is unmistakable and she's very quietly humming her usual song to herself, seemingly in an attempt at self-comfort.

I can't see Sheila; maybe I can only see those who were 'there' at the time. There's a wave of tension and . . . excitement, maybe, through the crowd, as three open-backed carts approach.

Mag leans towards my ear, hood still up, and whispers, *'Those two carts are filled with the poor innocents who were deemed to die by the witch finder; and that be the cart with nine moss-troopers.'*

As far as I can tell, the 'moss-troopers' are the nine cattle-rustlers that I read about and, as they are ordered off the cart, I just see men, scruffy-faced and ragged-clothed, their hands bound with ropes, who had simply been doing what they could in order to survive. I mean, fuck it, it was pretty much like executing people for shoplifting – what kind of world was this? I almost join in with the crying from the crowd, though, as I see the supposed witches being taken off the carts. The state of them. I knew they'd been held captive in Newgate gaol (and one of them in the castle keep) for a year, but I didn't properly envisage what they must have been put through.

Fourteen women and one man, with hollowed-out eyes and cheeks, multitudinous scabs and filthy rags for clothes. Their matted hair looks thinned-out and crusty, and I can imagine it's teeming with lice and all sorts of other little biters. The man is being held up by an old bloke in a cassock-type robe, as his feet are deformed and broken. What the fuck were they doing to them for that year? The women are so bent and defeated, it's hard to look at them. A man behind me begins to sob uncontrollably. He's older and well-dressed, compared to many others in the crowd. I wonder if this is the miller whose wife was accused of chicanery by a jealous cow who felt her inheritance had been scuppered? I steal a glance as the man wipes his nose on a large handkerchief, whispering to a younger woman, who I assume to be his daughter and who is also crying, *'She is no witch, my dove. I just wish I could have saved her.'*

As they are led to the gallows, there are ill-dressed uncomfortable-looking men on hand to help; they look like guards, but they also don't look all that happy about what they're having to do, as very few of these women are well enough to climb the ladder on their own, so they've obviously been mistreated. Even the cattle-rustlers seem horrified by the pitiful sight of these broken souls. The man with the knackered feet has to be all but carried. There are eight nooses on each side. Twenty-four in all. Twenty-four people to die today. What the hell must that have done to this part of the Moor, energetically? All of this innocent death. I want to hug all of them.

That's when I have an idea. I remember the whole thing with the successive ancestral line of Irish women who thought I was their family guardian angel – 'the Clíodhna'. I 'reached back' then, so could I do it again? The crowd surges behind me and I allow myself to be carried forward. A few military-looking men shout at us to get back, and some of the more lively members of the crowd are shoved away, but I stand calmly and lock eyes with an older woman standing on the bench, whose demeanour is more alert than that of the others. A noose is being put around her neck and she stares right back at me, a tear rolling down her mucky face. I think of all the healing energy I've been harnessing since I began experiencing spooky happenings, then in my head I call on Jemima, the 'healing angel', and ask for her help.

As I look up into those kindly but terrified eyes, I begin to weave a halo of light around the woman and all of those to be hanged at any minute, including the rustlers. I don't know anything about them – perhaps they did worse than nick cows – but right now I couldn't give a monkey's. Being put to death in this barbaric way for theft, when the rich and powerful were murdering people and stealing land all over the world at the time, with no punishment at all, doesn't sit well with my sense of fair play.

So I weave light and warmth for all of them as they are

made ready to be hanged. I pray for healing and love to take over their minds and hearts as the wooden forms are kicked from underneath them, and cries of excitement, anguish and fear go up in the crowd as they wriggle at the end of twenty-four ropes. I channel and channel and try not to let emotion in, as I reluctantly witness this mass of people struggling and gasping and turning a different colour. And as the life drains from them, I will as hard as I can that their spirits leave their bodies as quickly as possible and that they feel only the love that I'm beaming at them right now. Seeing them die like this – all of them quickly losing the struggle and going limp – with the love and compassion I channelled at them so that they died feeling kindness, not fear, without warning I suddenly also feel a rage like no other.

As I do so and my blood begins to boil, a man comes at me from the crowd. He was standing with the others in hoods and robes, and now as he pushes his hood back and stares right at me, as I finally lower my eyes from the spectacle of ugly death – there he is. The witch finder himself. I know it's him because I can feel the self-importance leaking out of him. And this pathetic inadequate with the psychopath's eyes is staring at me with cold fury, as if I should be intimidated. I can see that he looks like me, but he's not really like me at all, because he's weak. The weakness radiates off him and my rage is all-consuming. These men – always men – ruling the world by force and cruelty. Bringing women down because they fear them or want them, or both. My rage absolutely matches his, surpasses it in this moment, so I do something I've never done before in my whole life. I spit at him. I spit in that bastard's face because of what I witnessed, what he brought about. A display of power and ugliness that was murder for fun, and gain. Plus, a year of torture for those poor souls. How I despise him.

The witch finder doesn't flinch – there's an otherworldliness to this whole thing. Like I'm here, but not here, and so is he. I don't think I'm in a vision; this is some kind of halfway place. And his facial expression is one of absolute waxy unkindness, but it doesn't change, it stays fixed there, as he mechanically raises his arm. I see something metal in his hand, but I can't make it out properly before he raises it high and swings it straight towards my eye. I dodge my head quickly, but feel something pointed graze my cheek, just before I scream and the lights go out.

They come on again pretty sharpish when I hear Sheila's voice screeching blue murder. I squint one eye open and find I'm lying in the wet grass, with a sore face and mud all over my coat. I hear distant thunder, and the thrash of sleet suddenly subsides, leaving a fine drizzle. It's bloody weird. Sheila is next to me, getting her knees muddy, shaking my arm and looking like she's had a real fright. I smile up at her and she gives another little yelp.

'Thank *God*, Tanz. I thought you were bloody dead!'

'Why?' I sit up and put my hand to my cheek. It really smarts and, when I look at my fingers, there's blood. I'm bleeding! I take my little round mirror out of the front flap of my bag and, despite the burgeoning darkness, I can see a small cut quite clearly on my cheek.

Sheila sits in the wet sods beside me. 'You went down

like a sack of spuds, darlin'. I was seeing all sorts: an imprint of the hangings on the Moor, vivid like a really upsetting film. Those poor sods, so much death; but I couldn't see as well as I normally would, because that thunder and lightning hit with the sleet and made my vision hazy. I was about to drag you away, then this nasty-faced bloke approached and stood in front of you, and suddenly you didn't look solid; you were sort of . . . well, *hazy*, and he lifted his arm up and then you screamed and were solid again and on the ground, and I thought he'd stabbed you, the horrible man.'

'Nah, he missed my eye, which is what he was aiming for, the twat.'

'You saw him too?'

'I was there, Sheila, I was actually in that crowd.' I feel myself shiver. The cold is getting into my bones.

Sheila stands painfully, then holds out her hand to me. 'That strange storm disappeared as quickly as it started, but I think we need to get into dry clothes and discuss this with wine and some duvets around us. Early pyjama party.'

'Sounds good to me. Let's find a cab.'

# GATESHEAD GOD

It doesn't take long at all to get back to the hotel, put on some warm clothes and then reconvene on my bed, with a bowl of fries each and a bottle of Malbec delivered by room service. Sheila wraps a fleecy grey blanket around herself, brought from her room, and I make a nest of my duvet as I can't seem to get warm. I've already put a dab of Savlon on the cut on my cheek, which isn't that deep, to be fair, and have stuck a plaster over it, but it still tingles. My coat is on the radiator. I'm hoping it'll dry out enough to be able to rub off the soil stains.

'Sheila, what did you mean when you said I went "hazy"?'

She shakes her head and snaffles a chip. 'It was something I've not seen before. The imprint or mark of that awful day was playing out in front of my face. That's something I've experienced plenty – comes with the territory, and it intensifies if you watch it with another medium, like a live action film. But this time something else happened, something next-level strange. You became part of the imprint. You weren't fully "here" any more; you were in two places. And that's mad. And that's why I thought he'd killed you. You were "there", so whatever he stabbed at you with could have been lethal.'

'And that's how I got the cut face. The man actually managed to connect with my skin, the little dweeb.'

'Which is crazy, Tanz. And really very dangerous. If you think about it, though, it has been progressing this way for a while. First you got into folklore in three generations of Nelly's family. Then you went to Iceland and physically hung out with someone in *their* time in the 1970s, and didn't even know it. And now you've been injured by a nasty-faced witch hunter from the 1640s. If they can physically connect with you, then a bad one might seriously injure you. He very nearly did. Do you know who he is?'

'Sort of. He's the witch finder. Some Puritan bastards from the local council sent for him to weed out local witches, and I think I'm related to him. For some reason I've been drawn here now and I have no idea what *they* actually want from me. But me and my mam are dreaming the same stuff, and he's an absolute horror.'

'Well, I don't like this at all. If he can cut you, what else can he do?'

'I won't let him that close to me again, and I'll get Mag to protect me.'

'Do we know who Mag is?'

'Not a clue, but she's really not happy with that bastard. She wants me to sort him out, I think, but I don't know how to. How do you punish someone who's already dead? I mean I'll have to figure it out or I think she'll haunt me permanently. I'm pretty sure she's the one inflicting the matching dreams, and as for those freaky thunderstorms... that's two now. They come and go so fast. It's crackers.'

Sheila pours two globes of the wine. The glasses are really nice. This hotel may be budget, but you'd never know, as it's very cute and well equipped; the rooms have everything you could need and they feel cosy, plus the double-glazing really works – there's hardly any sound at all from outside. I take the proffered glass and, as soon as I take a sip, realize I don't want it.

'Fucking hell, Sheila, here's another weird one: I can't drink. I've not wanted alcohol at all since I landed from Iceland. And before you ask, I had a couple of early-indicator pregnancy tests in my drawer, from last time I had a scare, and so far they've said no. So it's not that, I'm sure it's not. Something's going on. I *never* don't want wine.'

Sheila looks at me thoughtfully, then gets up and closes the curtains. It's dark outside now anyway, but this seals the deal. She then takes a tea-light out of her bag, which makes me laugh.

'Always got a candle with me, love, just in case. Here, let me light it and you can turn that lamp off.'

Next thing I know, the room is bathed in shadow, except for this one point of light, sitting on the tiny desk space with the hairdryer and the mini coffee machine. Sheila sits in front of me and takes both of my hands. Instinctively I breathe deeply and slowly, and wait. I trust Sheila with all spooky shenanigans, so if she wants to form a circle of two, then she's about to do something magical, and I'm always here for the magic. She closes her eyes and begins to speak.

'Whoever is guiding Tanz right now, please let us know what's happening? She's been through a lot of intense experiences and now there's this mystery in Newcastle. Please tell us why everything has escalated, what is required of us and why the hell she suddenly can't stomach drink?'

I close my eyes and savour the silence and peace. Quickly someone 'joins' us on the bed. I feel the pressure on the left-hand side of my head, and Sheila gives the tiniest extra squeeze to my hand to acknowledge it. I feel I should keep my eyes shut, and while I don't hear anything new at all, I have a vague feeling of being wrapped in warmth.

Sheila begins to speak, her voice hushed. 'You're elevating, Tanz. That's what I'm being told. You've gone up more levels in a short time than most people do in years, and you're connecting with energies that other people would only aspire to. The reason alcohol isn't working for you is that it lowers your frequency, and that isn't a good idea right now. It's a shock to your system and will knock you out of balance. So, basically, you're experiencing a reset for a few days.'

'Okay. How come they can't tell me this personally?'

She's quiet for a moment while she's listening and the energy in the room gets heavier. Whoever Sheila's talking to is powerful.

'You're very open, you have strong guides, but so many from the other side are trying to speak to you at the moment, it's confusing. So your receptors are only allowing a small sliver of the "chat" while you work on this latest mission. They're calling it a mission, Tanz, so it must be one of your life's turning points. Karmically, you're about to solve something. Or not, if it's too much this time. That's what they're saying. Making it clear that even *they* don't know the outcome of every situation – no one from the spirit realm does, because humans have free will and sometimes get overwhelmed. In this case, you just have to go with things and see how much is doable. They're saying that if it's too much, they'll step in, but they can only help so much. You may get overwhelmed, and that's allowed. This person is new to the ranks and is watching over you, night and day.'

'What does "new to the ranks" mean, Sheils?'

'Who knows. New to helping you? New to that realm? New to this kind of soul work – may have been helping elsewhere.'

'Where's Frank at?'

Sheila goes silent again, then chuckles. 'In this case, he's on "other duties" – too close to the case! Of course he's always with you, but this is something else. Just because he's in spirit doesn't mean he doesn't get feisty, though. From what I'm being told, given the choice, he'd be on Tanz duty twenty-four-seven. Whoever is speaking to me has a good sense of humour, Tanz. They're definitely your people. But – and I don't want to scare you – *but* they're telling you to tread carefully and to listen hard to your intuition at the moment. It's not always easy to know what's *them* and what's a sacred voice inside you, and there's definitely danger around.'

'Of course there's fucking danger. There's always danger. Someone's always trying to finish me off when this stuff happens.'

'Well, you're protected, as always. They're giving you extra protection in fact, so we don't need to add to it. That's what they're saying. But keep your eyes peeled, because not-so-nice energies are pressing in.'

'Well, that's bloody comforting, isn't it? "Not-so-nice energies." *Again.*'

As Sheila listens to whatever she's being told, I hear a small whisper in my head, from a familiar Geordie voice. *'I've gone nowhere. I'm omnipresent, I told you. Like a Gateshead GOD. Hang tight.'* This almost makes me laugh out loud. Frank is still funny, even as a ghost.

Then Sheila speaks again and breaks the giggle off at the root.

'They've said to tell you what I saw at the Moor. I wasn't sure if I should repeat it, but I've been told it's a good idea. Just so you know: before that man took a swing at you, I could only see the gallows. It was suddenly in close-up, and when I found myself zooming in on all those poor sods about to die, one of them had your face, Tanz. You had a noose around your neck. Then suddenly you were in front of me again, being attacked by that nasty swine. That's why I got such a fright. It felt very real and I was terrified for you.'

I let go of her hands and open my eyes.

'*Fucking hell*, Sheila, you weren't going to tell me?'

'How was I going to explain that, without scaring the hell out of you?'

As she says it, the tea-light suddenly goes out. I give a tiny scream, then the room fills with a song that starts with words and turns to a hum.

*'Sleepe, sleepe, though greife torment . . . Hmmm-mmm . . .'*

Weirdly, it calms me, I don't freak out; instead I go stock-still as Mag's energy descends over us on the bed. Her smell is so familiar to me now, and I even quietly hum along like it's my song too. After about twenty seconds it fades and the heaviness lifts, until it's just Sheila, me and two half-eaten bowls of chips that I'm suddenly ravenous for.

Sheila switches on the lamp and stares at me.

'Who the actual fuck was that?' She rarely swears like I do. I'm the potty mouth in this relationship.

'Sheila, meet Mag.'

'That was *her*? Bleedin' hell, Mag is one strong spirit. But she's been in torment – I can feel it. What the hell have you attracted, Tanz? This is big-league.'

'In what way?' I grab my chips, while Sheila takes a huge swig of wine.

'There's something about her – Mag can move mountains. She's an old-school witch. She healed and helped people in the most dangerous of times and was never caught. She was careful, but she was also genuine. "Pure" witches are rare. Her bloodline stretches back, exactly as both of ours do. I now feel like someone kicked me in the forehead. I'll tell you what: it's certainly never boring with you around.'

'You almost didn't tell me that you saw me being hanged!'

'I didn't. I saw your face on someone with a rope around her neck.'

'What's the *difference*?' I ask.

I grab the wine that Sheila poured for me. Take a gulp. It's like drinking sour acid. Fucksake. I put it back down and shake my head.

'You know what: I bloody refuse to get freaked out by this. If I'm going to continue to have these spiritual "adventures", then – as they told me at drama school – I'll have to "trust the process". But if I end up in peril again for the umpteenth time, I'm going on fucking strike. It's all very well, them lot sitting on high, setting me missions; it's quite another thing being me, walking around on this Earth, tired and lonely and sick of acting, and not knowing who I even am any more, and then being expected to suck it up when everyone's either dying on me or trying to bloody murder me. I'm actually getting a teensy bit pissed off with these constant shenanigans. I'm not even *paid* to do this. Also, if there's so much danger around, I don't want you involved in it, Sheila. I already nearly got you killed in St Albans. Plus, you only recently recovered from that horrible chest infection. You can't be rolling around in sleety mud, trying to wake me up from ghost attacks. It's not on.'

Sheila begins to laugh. Proper throaty giggles.

'You do know that I live for this stuff, don't you? This is my life, and is actually a job that I *do* get paid for. Plus, I find it fun. Even the scary bits. And I'm older than you, so pack it in. What happens to me is not your concern or responsibility. Now let's watch a rom-com and shake off all that drama.'

I wrap the duvet warmly around me and snuggle back against the headboard. A rom-com could be just the ticket.

# WHAT'S IT LIKE BEING DEAD?

Watching a romantic piece-of-fluff of a film with a sore cheek after a ghost attack turns out to be a really good idea. We watch one of the shittest movies I've ever seen and we both enjoy the simple silliness of it. Sheila carries on with her wine and I sip on a peppermint tea and by nine o'clock we're both completely pooped. Obviously channelling a horrible hanging event from 1650 has taken it out of us both. I tell her to set her alarm for 6.30 a.m. as I suddenly have a plan. She smiles fuzzily and sets her phone alarm there and then, then heads off next door to her own cute room.

I clean my teeth, then bed down. I still don't feel like 'me'. The sense of not quite being inside my own body continues, though now it's accompanied by the conviction that something big and uncontrollable is about to happen. Not right away, but soon. On that comforting bombshell, and with earplugs in so that no hotel noise rouses me, I nod off quickly, comforted by the thick luxury of the pillows and the high-tog duvet.

To absolutely nobody's surprise, my eyes open again and I'm not in the hotel room any longer. I'm on top of a mountain. Of course I bloody am – I can't just be asleep and stay asleep, can I? It's not cold and rugged here, like on Esja, the dormant volcano overlooking Reykjavik bay. No, this is a high rocky place, but with grass, trees and a myriad of different-coloured wildflowers. The view is of hills and dales below, and the air is fresh and warm enough to feel comfortable in a thin shirt, which seems to be what I'm wearing – a linen-looking item that I don't own in real life, but feels gorgeous against my skin. I'm sitting on a sheepskin rug and I'm the most warmly relaxed I've felt in years. No worries or intrusive thoughts; simply chilling here, breathing life in.

A rustle to my right makes me turn and, out of the blue, there's another sheepskin rug and a woman sitting there in the same kind of light linen as I'm wearing, shirt and loose trousers, legs crossed and smiling widely. For a second I don't recognize her, but I know I should. Then it hits me: Caroline. Caroline May, the horrible lead woman from *Penshaw Investigates*, who stole my heart as a friend when we worked together on that miserable TV show, then died unexpectedly just as she was finding happiness. I stare at her in disbelief, then dive on her. She laughs her head off when I wrap myself around her and kiss her repeatedly on the cheek and ruffle her hair, which is now not a manicured hard-hat, but tousled and longer, with grey in it.

'Caroline, Caroline. Oh my God, Caroline, it's lovely to see you.'

She grabs my face on both sides and leans back to look

at me. Her eyes are deep pools of warmth, and the wariness and sadness are gone.

*'Hello, Tanz, my lovely girl.'*

'Lovely girl' – that's not something that would have come out of her mouth when we worked together. She smells of fresh air and something powdery and soft.

'What's going on, Caroline? I've not seen or heard from you once since . . .?'

*'I was adjusting, darling. I didn't really enjoy being Caroline May. I was the loneliest woman in the world.'*

'And the snobbiest.'

She laughs an easy laugh and grins in my face. *'Yes, I was a bit of a snob, wasn't I? I've been in the energetic equivalent of a lovely care home since then. Enjoying the calm and adjusting to other vibrations. How are you?'*

'Me?' I have to think about this. 'Lost, mental, emotional, happy sometimes, sad sometimes, fairly tired of people and ghosts trying to kill me. You know – the usual.'

I plonk down next to her on her rug, and she puts her arm around me as we both sit there and take in the view. My heart is so full, being next to Caroline again. She is vibrating with health and warmth. So different from the broken butterfly I knew. We don't speak for a while, then she takes a deep breath.

*'I need to give you some information and I haven't got that long.'*

'Ha, you sound like a Russian spy.'

*'Hey, concentrate! Now, to precis it: I think it's safe to say it's not easy living in the world right now, Tanz. Not for anyone. You're doing great.'*

I take this in, as I wasn't expecting a pep talk from a woman who spent most of the time I knew her wishing she could leave the world at the earliest possible convenience.

'It doesn't bloody feel like it. You say you were the loneliest woman in the world. Well, I'm not far behind you. I feel like an alien.'

*'You'd be surprised how many people feel the same. I didn't realize until I "crossed" and felt the collective howl of isolation coming from a lot of humanity right now.'*

'Flippin' heck, woman. Deep!' A warm breeze makes all of the blooms move and the grass sway. I think I can smell passionflowers from somewhere. I study the profile of this woman, who was such a sad soul before, and tears well up – not from being upset, but from the joy of knowing that she's happy now.

'What's it like, Caroline?'

*'Being dead...? As if I can tell you any details! Let's just say that people put far too much emphasis on death. Like it's this final horrible thing that looms night and day through life and scares everyone with its finality. The truth is: everything is merely a flow. Including death as a wonderful part of the process would be so much healthier than what "we" do. Other cultures handle it much better than Western cultures, but even then most people are scared of death. Instead they should enjoy all the things you can enjoy when you have a physical body, but also cherish the thought of being weightless and carefree.'*

'Is that what you are now?'

*'It's slightly complicated for me to answer that, because in real terms there is no "me", as you knew me. This is how*

*I present myself to you, because that's how you recognize "me", but in essence: yes, the weight of the world is off my shoulders and I feel only gratitude and love.'*

'That sounds fab.'

She turns and looks me in the eye. *'That doesn't mean you should get any ideas about bailing out before your time, though. I know what you're like – you're a Geordie tornado of emotions, with a still place in the centre. A sad, silent place that longs for "home". You'll be home soon enough – in the blink of an eye in fact – believe me. But for now I need you to know that we're all watching you and rooting for you, and trying to protect you from the worst excesses of low-vibrational beings.'*

'What, like devils?'

*'That's one word for them, I suppose. You've got a bit of a task to complete at the moment; it'll help your whole family line, and the lines of others. But it's not without danger.'*

'Here we go. Danger again. Are you the one who was talking to me through Sheila earlier?'

*'No. That's someone else. I just wanted to give you a hug. I thought you might need it.'*

'You have no idea. And now you've got me trying not to cry. I always used to cry when I saw Frank in visions, and all that. Then when he popped up in Southwark and saved me from a knife-wielding dickhead, he told me that I needed to man up; but here I am again, nearly crying because I thought I'd lost my mate for ever and I haven't, because you're sitting next to me.'

Caroline wraps both arms around me from the side and

kisses my hair. The Caroline May I knew would be as likely to skydive without a parachute as to get all cuddly like this, but it's absolutely lovely.

*'Tanz. You could never lose me. While you're alive, I'm alive. You showed me more love in a short time than I'd experienced – or allowed myself to experience – in years. Believe me, I'm your friend for ever.'*

We sit there, arms around each other, and breathe. It's divine. After a while Caroline moves again, leans away gently and looks in my eyes once more.

*'I have to go. But before you wake up over there, I need to tell you one more thing. You'll get a choice soon: a big one. Just remember us eating chips and looking out to sea, while you think about it. Don't make any rash decisions, my darling one. We're all with you. Always. You are very loved, you know.'*

There isn't even a transition. She says this and all at once my phone alarm is going off and I'm not 'there' any more. I'm in a warm bed in the darkness, fumbling for my phone and thanking the universe again and again for allowing me to see Caroline.

And yes, there may be one or two tears on my pillow, but they're tears of gratitude. Which makes a nice change.

# YOU'RE NEXT

Sheila is beside herself on the Metro. (Well, technically she's beside *me*, but you know what I mean.) It's 7 a.m. and we took coffees away with us from the hotel, along with a fat croissant each, and we are nibbling while sitting in the 'prime spot', which is the seat right at the front of the train where you can watch out of the big front window to the right of the driver's 'box', like you're actually driving the train. Most of the journey is outdoors and it may be cold, but today the sky is bright, which makes the whole trip feel cheerful.

'Where are we going, Tanz?'

Sheila has croissant crumbs down her coat and a big smile on her face. The early rise hasn't phased her at all. 'I'm taking you to the sea.'

'Wow, I feel even more like I'm on holiday now.'

I haven't told her about my Caroline May dream yet. I'm keeping it to myself for the time being. It's like I can feel the glow of my friend's new-found serenity sitting in my soul. Also, the cut on my cheek was easy enough to cover with concealer after my shower before I left the hotel room, so I can almost pretend that weird thing on the Moor didn't happen yesterday. I don't feel totally grounded yet, and I still haven't shaken the totality of my rage at the cruelty of humans towards other humans, but at least I'm cheerful right now, hanging out with my friend at stupidly early o'clock. Watching the track ahead, with trees and greenery and a big sky, is almost like being abroad. I mean who needs the Paris Métro when you've got West Monkseaton station up ahead and a going-cold white Americano slopping onto your hand every time you try to drink it?

The walk from Metro to seafront is really short, and Sheila's eyes are wide and amazed when she first spots the ruined priory that dominates the landscape and overlooks the grey-blue slightly choppy sea. I tell her that they have beautiful open-air gigs there sometimes, and she decides that she wants to come back one day to watch a band in the ruins. To the left of it is my favourite stretch of beach, which has a fish-shack at the back that serves great food and drinks. It's famous in the area, and if it was later in the day I'd have booked us a little table on the sand to have fish and chips. As we walk to the railing overlooking the sea below, I spot the bench where I sat with Caroline that time I 'kidnapped' her from hospital, and remember vividly how she tried to hide the rekindled light in her eyes as the sun went down so beautifully on the horizon.

'Fancy a paddle, Sheila?'

She looks at me, then laughs. 'It'll be a bit nippy for me, but I'll watch, if you fancy it . . .'

We descend the stone steps, of which there are many,

and I stick by Sheila, going at her pace, as I don't want to be the reason for her falling, because of me running ahead – I've caused her enough trouble already. The beach has a few dog walkers on it; and a bunch of people, mostly women, near the water's edge, taking off clothes.

'What are they doing, Tanz?'

'They're going in for a swim. It's a thing here: cold water apparently brings you right back into yourself. Wakes up your mind.'

'It's freezing – they're insane!'

I produce a towel from my bag, which I fold in half and put down far enough away from the water to stop the tide getting to it.

'Sit here.' I take off my coat.

Sheila looks confused. 'What are you doing?'

I take off my jumper and vest. I'm wearing my crappy but still serviceable swimming costume underneath. 'I'm going in, pet.'

'You're bloody *what*?'

I laugh and drag off my ankle-boots and black jeans. 'My mind's basically soup at the minute. I need waking up. I'm fucking terrified of seaweed. And jellyfish. And waves. But I packed a costume, and why would I do that unless this was subconsciously on the cards?'

'Well, this I've got to see.'

'You don't mind watching my stuff?'

'Of course not.'

It's absolutely Baltic, standing here semi-naked in the brittle winter sunshine, but I look at the sea and the people already in there, brace myself, then walk towards the water's edge. As soon as my feet feel the first laps of seawater I regret my decision, but I'm always regretting my decisions, so this is simply another one. I wade in further, but get so cold and scared at knee-depth that I stop dead and realize that I can't go any further. I turn and wave at Sheila, and she waves back. Then I just stand there, watching others whoop and jump in the brine. That's when I feel a presence beside me and look down to see a little girl, who can't be older than six. She has salt-matted long hair and is in a tiny orange swimming costume and those neoprene bootie things that stop your feet from freezing in cold water.

'I'm Katie. Are you a bit scared?' She has the cutest Geordie accent.

I nod. 'I am a bit, actually.'

'Well, I promise you, it's okay once you go further in. Come on.' She puts her wet little hand in mine and I'm so disarmed that I don't even think about it, I just move forward with her.

The sea knocks the wind out of me as it reaches the height of my lungs, but Katie doesn't falter and has already started to swim. A lady who's further out smiles and the little girl says, 'That's my mam' and splashes towards her. As she reaches her, Katie turns and waves at me and shouts, 'You did it!'

And I have done it. I'm up to my shoulders in freezing water, and suddenly it doesn't feel so cold and I let go and allow myself to float. The little girl gave me courage that I wouldn't have had otherwise. I wave back at her and her mum and call out, 'Katie is a legend!'

Her mum shouts back 'I know!', then they have a little swim together before heading back in.

I remain in the water and look at women of all ages going further out, dancing through the choppy waves like shiny seals, some with swimming hats, others ducking under, with hair free and soaked. A gang of three women who look to be my age, and who are emitting little squeals as the water gathers momentum and splashes over them, grin in my direction, and one of them wades closer to speak to me.

'This your first time?'

'It is. I had no idea how amazing it would be.'

'It's addictive. You come once and then you just crave the high. Who needs sex, when you've got the sea?'

All three women start to cackle and I join in. They then go into deeper water and I realize I probably have to get out soon, as my body isn't used to it and, from what I've read, it's very easy to get hypothermia. But still, in the five or so exhilarating, freezing minutes I've been submerged, with the sea splashing my face and hair and the breeze freezing my nose, I get a feeling of being in my own body and alive that I've not had for a while. Then I feel some seaweed brushing my leg, which breaks the spell and makes me think that something terrifying might eat me, and I exit as quickly as possible, my skin a livid red and tingling from the cold.

Sheila is waiting, having shaken the sand out of the towel, and helps me wrap it round myself, as my hands are currently blocks of ice. My teeth are chattering, but I feel incredible. It occurs to me at this point that maybe driving here would have been the warmer option for getting home, as we now have to get on a rackety train for half an hour, but I wanted Sheila to have the Metro experience, so that's that.

She helps shield me as I dry off as best I can and get my clothes back on. Luckily I discover I still have my orange beanie stored in the side-pocket of my rucksack, because my hair is damp and full of salt, despite me piling it up in a clip before I got in the sea. I pop it on, then put on some bright lipstick in an attempt to make it look like a fashion statement, and we head back up to the coffee place on the coast road, where I get us both a truly delicious hot chocolate, allowing the central heating in there to thaw me out.

'Want to tell me why you suddenly fancied a dunking in the North Sea in winter? You've never expressed a love of freezing yourself half to death before. That's something you try in summer first!'

Sheila looks amused, but also baffled. And she's right – it's not something I've ever expressed a wish to do before, and I'm not exactly a lover of the cold. But last night as we sat on the bed, glazing over in front of that daft film, the thought of all the love I'd sent to those poor sods who were being hanged grew more and more important in my head. The healing I'd felt and channelled into them seemed to be pinging back at me, and this warmth crystallized into the absolute conviction that I should get in the sea and 'reset' myself as soon as possible. I don't know much about sea swimming, but the cold water definitely did something for me and I'm tingling right now. I haven't told Sheila about this channelling. Nor have I spoken about the dream last night. I don't know why I'm being so secretive.

'I'm not sure why. I saw a documentary about it ages ago and got a gut feeling last night that I needed it. I'm probably just getting more mental than ever. What do you think of Tynemouth?'

'I think it's beautiful. I think your heart's here.'

'What do you mean?'

Sheila raises an eyebrow at me. 'I think London's lost its appeal. I think you know a lot of people here, and your family's here, and you've felt lonely for quite a while.'

'Fucking hell, mate, you'll have me in tears in a minute.' Right then my phone rings and, to my surprise, it's my mother. My little mam doesn't call on the mobile, ever. Not unless nuclear war's kicked off or the family home has burned down. She unreasonably believes that calling me on the mobile will cost thousands of pounds and will ultimately bankrupt her and dad and have them in the debtors' prison.

'Mam?'

The squawking down the phone is immense. Even Sheila can hear it and her eyebrows shoot up high.

'Mam, Mam, calm down, speak slowly. What's going on?'

I listen to a garbled and still over-fast story, which goes on quite a while and ends with 'This'll be the bloody death of me, Tanz.'

'Mam, I'm in Tynemouth. I'll get back to Newcastle, grab the car and come straight over, okay?'

Mollified, she kills the call at her end, and Sheila looks at me with genuine concern.

'What the hell's happened, Tanz? Are you okay?'

'I'm fine, but I think my mam's half a millimetre away from levitating onto the roof with anxiety. Seemingly she got up half an hour ago, washed her face, then came down and made her usual pot of tea and some toast – yes she really did go into this much detail – and said it wasn't 'til she'd taken my dad a cuppa and come back downstairs that she looked out of the front window and saw something in the rockery in the front garden, then went outside to check what the hell it was. Turned out to be a dead hare. Neck wrung and head the wrong way round. There was a note tied around the neck with string. It said, '*You're next.*' I mean, what the fuck?'

'Jesus! Let's go. Even I would be losing it, if that happened. And a hare at that. Quite specific, isn't it?'

I feel my stomach sinking deeper than it already did while my mam was freaking out on the phone.

'She thought it was a rabbit, but Dad knows his animals and said no, it's a hare. I mean, it *is* specific, isn't it? Hares are associated with magic, and witches were rumoured to be able to take the shape of hares. I read that recently, it's one of the stupid things that people accused women of in the olden times – got them hanged for it. Why has one been lobbed into their garden, though? My parents are just normal people who live a perfectly ordinary life.'

'No idea. The Celts saw hares as a symbol of prosperity and abundance, you know. Wouldn't eat them. Let's go and see your mum, and check out the unfortunate hare; there might be some clue she's missed.'

Oh God, I forgot Sheila loves this kind of thing. Her cogs are obviously whirring.

'Come on then, Miss Marple. Come and meet my parents. My mam's much scarier than a strangled hare, that's for sure.'

'Not scarier than you suddenly ripping your clothes off on a sub-zero beach, though.'

'Shut up.'

# YOU DON'T GET THUNDERSTORMS IN WINTER

When we get to the house, my mam is talking fifty to the dozen. My dad greets Sheila and me with a warm smile and a nod, then excuses himself to the shed to 'do some work'. Mam smooths down her salmon-coloured ensemble of jogging trousers and matching jersey top and smiles as best she can when we walk in. She's wearing brown tartan slippers and has put some pearlized lippy on, probably in Sheila's honour, but her short lacquered bob is not as neat as usual and her eyes are haunted.

'Would you like a cup of tea, Sheila?'

'That would be lovely.'

We follow her into the kitchen and there, laid out on yesterday's newspaper, is the dead creature with the note tied around its neck. The hare is a beautiful specimen, quite big and healthy-looking, with thick brown fur and those huge ears. I've decided it's a he because he's so large, but I might be wrong. I can't resist stroking his fur and Sheila does the same. My mother stands back and shakes her head as the kettle boils.

'Be careful. God knows what diseases those things carry.'

'I think we'll be all right, Mam. That's what soap and water are for. What are you thinking, Sheila?'

Sheila strokes the hare's pelt again and looks at the neck more closely, then inspects the note, which is actually one of those brown cardboard labels on a string, like you'd tie around the neck of a jar to identify the contents or would attach to a gift. '*YOU'RE NEXT*' is written in black Sharpie in strong capitals. It's ridiculous, but also scary.

'It's clean, but I can feel some buckshot under the skin in the neck,' Sheila says. 'My grandad used to hunt, and my nan would skin rabbits and make them into pies. She'd let me stroke their fur before she skinned them, so I know what I'm talking about. You can buy shot game from specialized butchers, this doesn't mean someone with a gun actually shot and left this – they probably just bought it.'

I look at her with the usual admiration. This woman is a constant source of surprise to me.

'Where exactly was it, Mam?'

Mam leads us through the living room. The view from the bay window is straight onto the front garden, which in summer is a riot of bedding plants, studded with rocky bits. At the moment most of the plants have died back. She points to the middle of the garden.

'It was there: half on the rockery, half off. Like someone had thrown it, and it had landed funny.'

Sheila nods. 'Do you think someone could have walked

past early on, or in the night, and quickly lobbed it over the wall?'

The wall to the street is low, about four feet tall, so anyone over two years old who fancies throwing anything into the garden can. My mother heads back to the kettle, which has now boiled and is filling the room with steam.

'Yes. I think it would be too risky to come down the path, as Zorro would start barking, so that's probably the best explanation.'

We go back to the table and inspect the hare. It's not stiff and it doesn't smell. Sheila cocks her head, remembering something as she gives her hands a quick wash at the sink. I do the same. The soap in the little dispenser reminds me of being five years old. My mam doesn't change her habits easily.

'When my last cat died – Sula she was called – I was so heartbroken that I gave up ever having a pet again,' Sheila tells us. 'And the vet told me then that once rigor mortis sets in on an animal, within four hours of it dying, it takes about twelve hours to wear off. That hare isn't stiff and, seeing as it's been here a while, if it was freshly killed it would have rigor mortis by now. It's not warm, it's actually freezing cold, and it doesn't smell, which it would after a few days, so I think this either died pretty recently or it's been kept frozen and thawed out.'

I grin at my friend in wonder. 'Sheila, that's amazing. You see Sherlock Holmes on the telly coming up with stuff like that. I'm not sure about me being Dr Watson, but still, well done!'

She gives a little bow. 'Elementary, my dear Geordie.'

My mam pours us each a mug of tea, looking like she's sucked a lemon. She really hates anything to do with death.

'Mam, did you hear anything at all?'

She hands a mug to Sheila and they both sit down, while I pace about, because there are only two seats at the table and because I'm restless.

'No, nothing. Usually if the postman comes, or anything like that, I wake up, but I've been so tired this week I think it's caught up with me. At first I couldn't get to sleep last night; I kept seeing in my mind's eye that horrible man's face. Looked like thunder he did, mad eyes—'

I hide my shock and shoot the tiniest of knowing glances at Sheila.

Mam looks accusingly at me over her cuppa . . .

'Why are you looking at me like that, Mam? I'm as surprised by all of this as you are. Once I got back from Iceland I wanted time to recuperate. I didn't want another load of strange business to sort out.'

'Well, in any event, I eventually managed to clear all of that out of my mind, but it took an hour or two, so I think I slept really heavily after that. Your dad said I snored, but he can bloody talk – he tosses and turns half the night sometimes, it's like sleeping next to a whirligig.'

'So, Tanz tells me you've been sharing dreams? That's an amazing link to have.' Sheila seems to have learned in five minutes what I finally worked out later on in my childhood. Distraction: that's the only way to stop my mam going off on one of her rants.

Mam gives a thin smile. 'Eeeh, well, I suppose you could say it's a link. I'd call it more of a curse.'

'Do you think so? I'd love to be that connected to someone. And I have to say, I couldn't tell you before now, but some of the things you've picked up on when Tanz has been solving her mysteries have been absolutely outstanding. The mother–daughter connection is on another level.'

Mam sniffs and reaches into the biscuit barrel, which she seems to have no problem leaving open three inches away from a supposedly disease-riddled animal corpse.

'Would you like a custard cream, Sheila, or maybe a malted milk?'

Sheila smiles her thanks, takes a custard cream and dips it in her cuppa.

'The truth is, Sheila, my grandma was a psychic medium. Everyone knew who she was in Springwell, and beyond. She was dripping in other people's jewellery, which they'd pay her with because they were all poor, and her house was apparently *teeming* with ghosts. Couldn't move for the undead, or whatever you call them. She did seances and readings and all that. My mother hated it. Grandma died when I was little, so I don't really remember her, apart from all the rings, but my mam banned any kind of spooky stuff from our house. Hated all of it. And when my lovely friend went on one of them awful Ouija boards, I asked her not to and then I stormed off home, leaving her and the lasses to do it on their own. Afterwards I found out that the horrible board said she would die young, and she did, two years later. I'm sorry, but I can't be doing with it; it never brings anything good.'

'The thing is, though, if you have those sensibilities, plus you dream things that actually come true, isn't it better for you to protect yourself and let it happen, instead of fighting it so hard?' Sheila replies. 'Tanz hasn't done this on purpose to annoy you; her gift is so strong she just has to take notice. Things go terribly wrong when she doesn't.'

Mam chews her biscuit and looks uncomfortable. She doesn't enjoy being questioned or having her life decisions poked at – she's very stubborn like that.

'Mam, Sheila's right, you know. Some of the stuff you come up with is so amazing, I wish you could see it as a bonus and not a bad thing. Sheila can put a light around you, if you like, and show you how to stay protected. I know you won't take it from me, but she's been involved in that side of things for years and she's an expert – maybe you'll let her do that at least.'

'I'll think about it.'

Sheila winks at her, then looks back at the hare. 'Do you want to call the police about this, do you think?'

'Eeeh, I don't know. What if it's a prank gone wrong or it even wasn't meant for me?' Mam stares at me meaningfully.

'I know why you're looking at me like that, Mam – I was thinking it might be for me too, although who the hell but the neighbours knows I'm here? I live in London, so someone would have had to see me coming in or notice my car pulling up and recognize it. But the hare thing: that's about witches, and that's what I'm researching. If this is a prank, it's a shitty one, but it makes sense that it might be for me and not you. Do you want me to stay here again tonight?'

To my relief, she shakes her head vehemently.

'NO! God knows what you'll attract into the back

bedroom, with all this going on. I don't want stray ghosts clogging up my hallway. If anything else happens, then maybe we should call the police, but for now I want to know what to do with that overgrown rabbit.'

I shrug. 'Has Dad still got the little chest freezer in his shed?'

'He has. It's not plugged in at the moment, but it works.'

'Well, get him to plug it in, put the hare in a carrier bag and shove it in there, in case it's needed later as evidence.'

Mam takes a glug of her tea and nearly chokes on it. 'Evidence? Eeeh, whatever next? How do you cope with all this palaver, Sheila? Trouble follows this one around.'

'Well, actually I'm in awe of her. She learns new things all the time. And she's one of the bravest women I've ever met.'

I wasn't expecting that, and it makes my heart swell.

'We've always known she was different. And don't get me wrong: we're very proud of her.' Mam almost chokes on her words. Compliments don't come easily to her; they were in short supply when she was growing up and she never got in the habit of dishing them out.

I jump in before this gets worse and I end up completely and utterly mortified. 'Mam, if it helps you to know this, what we're doing right now is trying to help right a wrong against a bunch of innocent people – almost all women – who died because certain people – *mostly men* – have always been, and continue to be, cruel, power-hungry loons. And a dead hare isn't going to stop me. But I understand how scary it was finding it, and I'm sorry.'

Just then Zorro wanders in from the garden, sniffs at

Sheila, who gives him a pat, then lumps down at my mam's feet and heaves a tragic dog-sigh.

Mam straightens her back and seems to resolve herself to saying something.

'Ah, bugger it, pet. If whoever it was comes back, I'll set Zorro on them, then they'll know about it.'

I look at Zorro, all sorrowful eyes and fat belly, and really wonder whether he would be much of a deterrent. I suppose he could lean heavily on them and make them fall over, but that's about it. Still, if it makes Mam feel better, then who am I to bring down the vibe? My eyes then stray back to the hare and the note. I mean, it really is a weird thing.

'Right, Mam, I think you should finish your cuppa and let Sheila put a protection around you. Then we'll put one around the house. If I'm not staying here tonight, I at least want to feel like whoever did this will feel very uncomfortable if they try to come back.'

Mam nods. 'Do whatever you feel like, if you think it'll help. Just don't leave any ghosts trailing around the place.'

'We won't. And hopefully no more weird thunderstorms will kick off while we're doing it, either.'

'No more what?'

'Like the other night, Mam, when it suddenly thundered and there was sleet.'

'Thunder? It's winter, pet, you don't get thunderstorms in winter.'

'You didn't see that violent thunder and lightning the other night? And the storm yesterday afternoon?'

Little Mam starts to laugh. 'No. A bit of sleet fell, but it stopped pretty sharpish. Either I'm going deaf or you heard a lorry going past and thought it was thunder. They're a bloody nuisance round here. Banging and clattering and making the house shake.'

I don't say anything else. It's just too odd, but I catch another glance from Sheila, whose brow has furrowed. Curiouser and curiouser.

# WINDOW PRICKER

Sheila and I are in a cafe on the quayside, sitting in two baggy leather armchairs, with still more coffee and a slice of Victoria sponge each. I seem to have a bottomless capacity for caffeine right now, especially as the early start has started to kick in, making my eyeballs itch. The river is a lovely sight, as is the Sage building opposite, like a beautiful, gigantic iridescent snail shell.

'So let's get this straight, Tanz. Someone lobbed a bloody great hare into your parents' garden at some point overnight. You're sharing dreams that aren't dreams – they're more like visions of the past as if it's happening now – with your mum. You got cut on the face by a malevolent witchfinder bloke that you're pretty sure you're descended from. Plus, you've got a ghost mate called Mag who's full of magic, brings thunderstorms when she's about that only we can hear, and keeps slamming you into the last moments of accused witches who are about to be hanged.'

I get out my notebook. My handwriting is a nightmare mess of jangled letters, but I can decipher it, which is lucky, because I took a lot of notes and want to remember the details properly.

'Yes, though I also had a vision about the same nasty witch finder at a burning, which doesn't surprise me, because when I was reading about the witch trials I found out the "witches" were burned in Scotland. In the vision that I saw, Mag told me that they were strangled first and then burned, to cast the demon energy out of the dead bodies. And the man that the Puritan blokes sent for, to be the witch finder in Newcastle, came from Scotland, so it looks like he didn't just get innocent people killed here – he did it in his home country as well.'

'Do we know who he was?'

I take a bite of surprisingly moist cake and shake my head. 'He was never identified, which is a disgrace. But from what I can tell, he took his methods straight from the playbook of Matthew Hopkins, the self-proclaimed Witch-finder General.'

'Oh, *him*. One of the worst people who ever lived.'

'Yup. Him and General Custer make up my top-five worst men who ever lived. Some people dry up my eyeballs with rage. Hopkins was earning money for every accused woman he "proved" to be guilty and, believe me, accused men were a rarity, so he put a lot of vulnerable and ageing ladies to death by lying through his back teeth. He really was a cunt. A lawyer as well, so a double cunt. Interestingly, though, he disappeared completely from the records in 1647. No trace of him after that apart from rumours of a death from tuberculosis that were pretty much disproved later. I just hope he didn't live a prosperous life – the absolute shit-house.'

I feel that force again, the welling of a fury that seems to simmer within me all the time at the moment. I don't know where it's coming from, but I never used to be quite this furious. In its own way, I suppose it's a good spur. The power of anger is as useful as any other power when you need strength, I reckon; just look at *The Incredible Hulk*. Sheila nibbles at her cake, probably too full of custard creams to really appreciate the full hit of jam, cream and sponge. I'm used to cake-slices in coffee shops being a bit stale, but this piece is not that and I lick luxuriously at the filling.

'I didn't know he disappeared, Tanz. That's interesting.'

'It is. And even more interesting is that Mr Anonymous, who came to Newcastle in 1649, also disappeared soon after the hangings in 1650, when he tried his shit somewhere else and they didn't believe him. There's not enough documentation to find out how he was discovered and discredited, but it was rumoured that he'd been put to death for causing so much murder and mayhem. How mad is that? History is such a strange thing. We hear about what these bastards did and about all the women they hurt, but we don't hear about what karma did afterwards and whether they suffered in life for what they did or whether they had to wait for death to get their just deserts. We also don't hear how intelligent people knew this witch stuff was horseshit – demonic panic brought about by Charles I being a paranoid numpty – and that it was only perpetuated by the usual superstitious sheep, who are still around these days and who, instead of burning witches, vote for absolute bastards and thieves who make everyone but rich people's lives even worse.'

'Jesus, you're a Geordie tempest today. Thank God you got into the sea this morning to cool your brain down or you'd probably be swinging a sword around your head by now.'

I don't disagree with any of this. Right then I look down at my notes again and notice something I'd forgotten.

'I think it's very interesting that when women were accused, some were immediately let off because they were "too pretty and young" to be a witch. I mean, this was misogyny in its purest form. The only women worth saving, according to the men, were the fuckable ones. The rest of us were expendable.'

There is a little old lady who until a minute ago was sitting in an armchair a few feet away from us – the cafe's only other customer in fact – who's now gathering her bag and belongings together, after putting on her green woollen coat. I assumed that she was too deaf to hear me, as I'm trying to keep my voice down, but she turns as I finish speaking and holds a fist up.

'Go on there, sister. Absolute bastards, the lot of them.'

She stalks towards the door and exits, then waves through the window before wandering off up the street.

I raise a defiant fist in return and smile as she disappears.

'Look at you, whipping up the masses!'

'Sheila, I don't know what's going on, but reading about this stuff makes me livid. Nothing changes – they just can't burn us now.'

'Oh, I want that on a T-shirt! *"They can't burn us now."*'

'You don't seem to get as furious as I do.'

'Yes, I bloody do. I've just been on the planet longer than you and I'm more world-weary. Until recently I didn't even bother having anything to do with men any more.'

'Actually you've told me several times to be careful of men. Gladys is the same. Speaking of which, I'm going to message her later, as she's missing out on all the fun. She knows a lot about witchy stuff. But I don't want to intrude on her trip, when it's about her son, or try and entice her home before she's ready.'

'Yes, best to let Gladys come back when she's done what she needs to do, but I'm sure a message telling her what's going on won't hurt.' Sheila takes a contemplative sip of her coffee and momentarily her eyes drift away. I've always known that Sheila has a secret and it always seems to hover closer to the surface when I speak about Gladys's lost son. She rallies quickly, though, and changes the subject. 'What do you think about that hare anyway? Who the hell would do that?'

'I really don't know, Sheils. It's bugging me, because I don't know anyone in the area who is aware of the side of me that developed in London – or anyone who would do something so dark. I mean, Milo knows, but he's away now, and I doubt he'd touch a dead hare with someone else's barge pole, let alone scare my mam with it. Then there are the people I met on the ghost walk, back when I was ghost-busting that evil man from the Black Gate, but none of them would have my home address. My only other thought is that it's a coincidence, and either it was meant for someone else completely and they got the address wrong – unlikely, I know, but not impossible – *or* that hare was meant for my parents because one of them has annoyed someone. But that seems so ridiculous when you consider that the pair of them don't see many other people or even go out. Apart from my dad walking the dog and my mam getting the groceries in, they mostly potter in the garden and watch TV. Also, wouldn't a hare be expensive? Who can afford to be chucking expensive game animals about the place? People in that part of Gateshead would be more likely to chuck a squirrel that they shot in their garden with an air-rifle.'

Sheila begins to laugh at this and I get a sudden burst of gratitude that she's here with me, one of the only people in the world who knows the extent of how mad my 'secret' spooky life is, and who actually likes it. She's sitting here in a cafe with me, watching the river of my home town flowing slowly by and nonchalantly discussing a dead hare with its head facing the wrong way that landed in my parents' garden.

I see her eyes drift again and I can't help asking, 'Are you missing him, Sheila?'

'Who?'

'Who? Oh, come on now – you know exactly who I mean. Pan, the beautiful fella that you actually care for, the one who proves you don't hate all men across the board. You two have a bond; it's really obvious, so please don't say that you don't.'

'I didn't say I *hated* men and, when it comes to Pan in particular, I'm not saying anything at all.'

'Why not?'

'Because what we have is lovely, but he will eventually need someone who isn't a million years older than him, and I'll have to let him go. I'm working very hard on not acknowledging that I miss him at the moment, so please let's stop talking about it.'

'Well, I miss Thor, and I've hardly known him any time at all, so it stands to reason that you miss your lad. Some men are like us: that's the truth of it. There's a horrible aura that comes from people – both women and men – who only have the worst of masculine energy in the world. We, you and I, have a good mix of female and male energy, and so do some men. They're the good ones. You've met one of them, and so did I for a few days.'

'You really like this one, don't you?'

I nod. 'I do, but Thor's so far away. It probably won't work if we meet on less dramatic terms, because real life has a habit of scuppering even the most pure of romances. But I don't just like him – I love him, and that's very annoying.'

'You definitely think it's not just because you had such an intense time with him?'

'Definitely. Sometimes you just know.'

Sheila lets out a high whistle. 'What's meant for you doesn't pass you by.'

'Yeah, well . . .' I don't get any further because, as we've been talking, some yellowy-grey clouds have gathered over the river. Suddenly there's no one to be seen on the quayside and all the cars have gone. This can't be true obviously, but I jump up and stand at the window glass. Sheila joins me.

As the low-key music of the coffee place disappears, suddenly there's the sound of a ringing hand-bell from outside and a man's voice crying down the street, 'All people who would bring in any complaint against any woman for a witch!' The inevitable flash of lightning cuts the sky agape and there's distant thunder, but no rain falls this time.

'Are you getting this, Sheila?'

She whispers back, 'The town crier and the storm?'

I nod. Then a shadow comes that falls over both of us, as I smell Mag and feel her presence around us. Her voice, when it comes, is a millimetre from my ear. *'The Guildhall. They didn't stand a chance . . .'*

Right then he appears: the witch finder. Weak-chinned and with his mad eyes, outside the window, staring straight in, looking me right in the face with a jubilant smirk on his wet mouth that gives me goosebumps. I don't know what he's so pleased about, but I hear Sheila give a little gasp as he raises his hand while lightning flashes above him, then strikes at the window with the object in his hand. There's a cracking noise on the glass and then I hear Mag again. Close to my ear, urgent in tone.

*'Find it. Find it and burn it. The witch pricker be close by. You're the one. Burn it, Chosen One.'*

Just hearing the word 'Chosen' makes me flinch in shock. The name Alfvin gave me – the word that made me feel safe and loved – has now taken on a different meaning.

Sheila grabs my arm as the vision fades, like she knows my knees are about to buckle. Luckily I gather myself enough not to fall over and I grab Sheila in return, to keep me upright. The sky is now suddenly how it was before, and there are people and cars and life is carrying on. There's also a crack in the glass in front of my face. The girl behind the counter obviously didn't hear anything, because she doesn't even raise her head from whatever she's doing on her phone as we sit back down, then she gets distracted by a family with three boisterous, chilly little kids coming through the door.

I need a moment to get myself calm again. Sheila looks up at the hairline crack in the window in disbelief.

'What the bloody hell is going on here?'

'Don't know, Sheila, but it looks like she wants us to walk back via the Guildhall around the corner.'

'Well, I, for one, am not arguing with Mag. This is *wild*.'

I'm not sure Sheila should be looking this excited. She's got one thing right, though. This is *wild*. And it is actually starting to feel dangerous. That mad fucker seems determined to slash me with that pricker of his, and it looks like he can show up wherever he bloody likes. Not only in dreams and at the Moor, but on the quayside when I'm trying to finish my cake. The bald truth is: if he can damage a window like that, he's probably getting stronger, and that means he's more likely to damage me.

It's definitely time to sort this out.

We're outside the Guildhall and it seems to be a bit of a dud tip, because it's a mixed bag of architecture and remodelling and wasn't built until 1655, a full five years after the witch trials. I've looked it up and am actually reading about it right now. Seemingly it's on the same site as the previous Guildhall that burned down in 1639, so I'm not sure what the hell was standing when they tried the accused. Anyway, it's the right site and it looks clean and pretty in the fading afternoon light. Not open to the public, though, from what I'm reading; it's guided tours only, and they don't happen very often.

We stand outside on the street while Sheila sucks on her fruity vape that smells of grapes, and I just breathe, wondering if we'll get another 'visitation'. And in a way we do, because suddenly walking towards us is Lydia, the Glamazon from the library. Today she's in a dark padded long coat with a hood and black DMs, smoking a fag. Her bleached hair is piled up, as usual, and the smudged lipstick is purple, which makes her black-rimmed turquoise eyes pop. I didn't notice in the library how intensely bright her eyes were.

At first Lydia seems lost in thought, but as she draws level I say 'Hi' to her and suddenly she focuses on us and smiles. Her teeth are big and square and slightly discoloured in natural light; she's also even taller than I thought and sturdily built, and once again I'm impressed at the gravitas that her size brings. She's a force of nature and no mistake – she truly does loom at you.

'Hello, Tanz, how's the research going?'

'Okay, thanks. Just showing my friend Sheila around town at the moment.'

'That's nice. Staying somewhere swanky while you're here?'

Sheila smiles. 'No, we went boutique instead, didn't we, Tanz?'

'We did indeed. I like it better – the lobby with the pink neon is a total winner, for a start.'

'Yeah, and there's a bloody good Merlot at the bar.'

Lydia smiles at Sheila, then looks at me shyly, opens up her bag and takes out a little notepad.

'Listen, I know this is a bit premature of me, seeing as we don't even know each other, but if you do want to know anything else about the witch trials, or the history before and after the hangings, get in touch. It's a pet subject of mine, and I love meeting other people who are interested in it. I really don't get to explore it as much as I'd like to. It was actually great to meet someone else at the Lit & Phil who wanted to look through my favourite books. The thing is, though, I've found out some extra little nuggets since I started digging, which you don't find in the usual places, and it really is fascinating.'

She hands me a slip of paper and I put it in my bag.

'Thank you so much. If I need to find out anything else, I'll give you a shout. It's certainly an interesting one, but it's more curiosity than anything else and we're off back to London soon.'

I don't know why I'm keeping so much to myself, after Lydia was so open with me at the library. It was her who told me about the town crier and we just heard him; plus, other stuff she said is all turning out to be absolutely true. But still, talking about ghosts and paranormal stuff with people I don't know doesn't always go down well. Thor loved it from the get-go, but he's a wizard. This woman is quite the eccentric, but I don't know her and she might be mental, or she might suddenly recognize me from the TV, then start telling everyone that the actress playing the generic slut from *Penshaw Investigates* (which is airing at the moment, in fact) is a loon who speaks to dead people. I don't want to risk it.

'Okay. Enjoy your stay, Sheila, and I hope you both have a lovely night. I've got to get back to work now.'

'Bye, Lydia, nice to see you again.'

Sheila smiles and waves, then turns to me as Lydia disappears around the corner. 'Tanz, that's the most unreadable woman I've ever encountered. Do you think she's connected to your Mag? Mag sent us to the Guildhall and then there Lydia was, walking down the street.'

'I know, and I'm not a great believer in coincidences. But what I can't tell is if Lydia's a good 'un or not. Her energy is impressive but, as you say, unreadable. What does that mean?'

'Right now, who can say?'

'Well, what I can tell you is this: one thing I heard loud and clear, when the storm came in over the Tyne just then, was "*Find it and burn it.*" Mag seemed to be talking about the witch pricker and I'm hoping it's the artefact she meant – that is, the sharp object the fucker keeps brandishing – because after all these years I can't see how we can burn *him*, even though I know he was also referred to as the "witch pricker". And if she is talking about an artefact or relic that needs to be burned, then does Lydia know something that can take us to it? I mean she handed me her number and told me she knows snippets that other people don't know. Perhaps there's an artefact that not many people know about, and Lydia has the lowdown on it.'

'That's a lot of supposition, but going by your latest exploits, I wouldn't dare argue, because your instincts have been bang-on. Anyway, it's getting a bit too chilly for standing still and chatting on the street – should we move on?'

# PHANTOM FLU

Famous last words from Sheila, as she's struck down like a bolt from the blue by a head cold within twenty minutes of us heading back to the hotel. It's extraordinary: one minute she's a bit chilly and needs a sit-down, and the next minute she's curled up on a big sofa near the bar while they make her an extra-potent hot toddy. I've literally never seen an illness hit so fast, but then I don't know why I'm surprised by anything these days.

Sheila's neck is mottled and her nose is running and she keeps clearing her throat, while I order the nice barman – who's called Trevor, and has the look of a fresh student who hasn't had life kicked out via his earholes yet – to put an extra shot of their best whisky in there. I'm pretty sure that taking Sheila to the Nuns Moor and getting her caught in a spectral thunderstorm has brought this on, so it's the least I can do to get her the best 'medicine'.

'Tanz, I'm so sorry, love – I don't know what's going on. I'm taking my vitamins, I'm getting enough sleep and I'm wearing plenty of layers, I didn't expect this at all.'

'It's probably the temperature change this week, then being on your knees in sleety mud because of me. I even took you to a chilly beach at fuck-off o'clock in the morning. I'm so sorry.'

'Don't say that. I always get a winter cold anyway, it's just a bit later than usual, so I thought I'd swerved it, with all of my precautions. Shows you can't be complacent.'

I take the steaming drink from Trevor, making sure I tip him, because this smells exactly the ticket.

'Come on, lass, let's get you comfy. At least the room's nice and you can watch a movie in the warm.'

We get into the lift and I can actually see Sheila's eyelids drooping.

'You look knackered, pet. And your neck's gone blotchy. Tell me you haven't got meningitis.'

'Stop it, you loon. This always happens when I'm getting a snotty cold. I can't believe how quickly it kicked in. And you're right, I'm suddenly exhausted. I reckon I'll be no good to anyone after this knockout potion.'

In no time Sheila's tucked up, with pillows fluffed, cardigan buttoned and hot toddy being sipped. I put the TV on for her – some programme about finding a holiday home – but I doubt she'll take it in. I take her room keycard and promise to return with a sack of cold remedies and decongestants. Poor lass. At least she looks cosy.

'Tanz, don't be worrying about me. It's nothing serious. I might even sleep the worst of it off tonight, seeing as we caught it so quickly.'

'Well, I'm not taking any chances, so prepare to be nursed to within an inch of your life.'

She gives me a regal wave as I exit, and I go and grab another layer to insulate me against the late-afternoon temperature drop.

Up near Monument Metro station there are plenty of people milling about and I can't resist a cheeky shopping splurge around the centre. I start at Boots, obviously, and buy Sheila so much stuff that she couldn't take it all in a month. Then I walk in an arc, going into any shop that takes my fancy. It's so nice wandering about, buying little treats, that I almost forget my 'mission' and simply enjoy being in my home town, listening to the accents and feeling no pressure.

By the time I head back towards the hotel I've bought her a hot-water bottle with a fluffy cover, plus a warm fleecy hat in bright colours with sparkly bits in the weave, so that it looks glam enough for her to wear outside. Sheila always looks glam, so you have to be careful what you buy for her. I've also bought her a vapour-rub for her chest, the best cold-and-flu pills on the market, a little bottle of freshly squeezed orange juice, a half-bottle of good whisky to pour in her herbal tea later, some hardcore vitamin C fizzy tablets, a box of nice tissues with balm in them so that her nose won't be red-raw from blowing and – last but not least – some truffles from the posh chocolate place, to keep her sugar levels up. I don't care how much I've spent, as this is an *emergency* and they're for my friend.

As I'm trotting back, I see quite a few lasses in little dresses and high heels with no coats on. It's just after 6 p.m. now and it hits me that any time after 31 October is basically 'lead-up to Christmas party-time' in Newcastle, so these women – well, girls, a lot of them – are out for a good time tonight. I almost feel bad for them, until I remember a drunk young lass at the bar years ago, on one of the rare nights I went to the infamous Bigg Market, telling me that I didn't have to worry about half-naked lasses in freezing temperatures, because they mostly 'necked a few vodkas' or a bottle of wine before they even left the house, to insulate them against the cold. This would explain why so many girls heading to the bars already look half-cut at teatime.

I nip down a little side-street to avoid the party-kids and see a vintage sign with neon above it, heralding a place I've never seen before, a basement cocktail place called 'Bougie Bar'. I peer down the iron stairs and see warm, dimmed light coming out of a window that is rather deliciously frosted, so that I can't see in. I like the intrigue of this, and make a note of where it is before carrying on until I reach our place, Hotel Number 1.

# BOUGIE NIGHT

There's no answer when I knock lightly on Sheila's door and when I enter, as quietly as I can, I find her dozing in her pillow nest. As I click the door closed, I hear her stir, then turn in time to see her groggily grabbing a wad of tissue and blowing her nose like a trumpet.

'Oh, Sheils, you poor sod. Not much of a holiday in Newcastle if you're ill.'

'Oh, I'll be okay, darlin', I just need to sleep it off. I'll be much better tomorrow.'

'Well, I got you a bunch of stuff – look at this lot!'

Over the next half-hour I fill Sheila's hot-water bottle for her, dose her up to the eyeballs with flu medicine, make her drink some fresh orange juice and leave the rest by her bed, present her with the chocolates, then leave all the other medications within her reach and even make sure her pillows are re-fluffed.

'Tanz, you're a natural nurse.'

'For a short time I am, but I couldn't do it for a living. I'd start getting very impatient with people.'

'You've definitely made me feel as comfortable as possible, and these tissues are brilliant. So soft! Thank you.'

'You're welcome. Do you want me to sit in here with you and keep you company?'

'What, and pass this on to you? No, sweetheart, run for your life. I've got everything I need. I'll message you or call if I want anything else, but I doubt it'll happen. I think I'll probably keep dozing for now and if I wake up too much later, I'll watch a film.'

'What about food? I have a couple of veggie flatbreads that I got from the deli up the road, if you want one.'

She wrinkles her nose. 'I'm not hungry, but I can call room service and get something if I feel peckish.'

'Right. Well, I might go to my room and make some phone calls then.'

'You do that. Night-night, love.'

'Night-night.'

Making phone calls doesn't take long. Because there's only one call to make, and my little mam has nothing new to report. She says that my dad reckons the hare was 'just kids messing about' and now she's inclined to agree with him. She always ends up agreeing with him, and I don't bother asking any basic questions like 'How did kids afford to buy a bloody great hare, and why would they chuck it in your garden with a threatening tag around its neck?' Mam sounds too relieved for me to rock the boat. I wish her a good sleep and eat a flatbread for something to do, then sit there twiddling my thumbs, wondering if I should put on the TV or go down to the hotel bar with the book that I packed but wasn't sure I'd read.

Neither option appeals that much, and my mind goes back to that interesting little place called 'Bougie Bar'. I mean, I'm sure they must do virgin cocktails, and it might be nice to venture out on a tiny half-hour adventure. I look in my case and take out my not-posh-but-tight-fitting-and-also-warm jersey dress, plus my best ankle-boots and some woolly tights. With a slick of red lipstick and my hair combed, this should look okay. I'm not on the pull, but I also don't want to look like a dump-truck in a bar full of hotties, so the dress is a good compromise because of its figure-hugging but practical properties. I get changed, then put in my favourite hoop earrings – classic hoops are my go-to – and top it all off with a slick of gloss over the red lipstick and a squirt of sassy scent.

For a moment I hesitate, as it feels like I'm abandoning my mate, but my restlessness wins this battle and, scooping my coat over my arm, I head out.

# EDNA AND HER HADDOCK

'Bougie Bar' is down a narrow, clattery metal staircase and I'm very careful as I descend, as this is not how I want to die. At the bottom is the dimly lit frosted window and a glossy black door. I open up and almost gasp, as I enter the kind of place I would never expect to find around the corner from the Bigg Market. When I first became an actress and was actually successful on telly, before it all went to hell in a handcart, I travelled a lot, for work and for pleasure. And if I'd found this beautiful gem in any other country, especially France or Italy, I would have been enchanted, but not surprised. Here, well, I'm gobsmacked.

It's one of the coolest speakeasies I've ever seen. It's small, with plaster walls, and the one behind the bar is cream, roughly painted and looks like it's peeling a bit with damp. I wonder if that's an effect rather than a knackered plaster-job. I suspect it is. The side-walls are a glorious deep blue. There are gilt-framed mirrors and small black-framed erotic paintings dotted about the place. The bar is gold and blue and has bar stools that are made of rough wood, with wine-red velvet seat pads. The smell is exotic and is coming from incense sticks. It's very compact down here, with a few small tables and a bunch of mini velvet armchairs to sit in. Currently it's not rammed, but I bet this place fills up fast. It's so cool, it has 'late licence' written all over it. The barman is tall and as thin as a reed, with greased-back hair, an embroidered waistcoat and a pencil moustache. I love his style.

I take a stool at the bar and he smiles.

'What would you like?' He looks to be in his forties, has a naughty twinkle and his accent is not Geordie – in fact he sounds Mediterranean. I reach for the cocktail list, fully intending to get something alcohol-free.

'Let me just have a look at this.' As I pick it up, a woman emerges from a back room and also stands behind the bar. She's got pin-curls in her black hair, perfect crimson lips and is wearing a mustard-yellow satin wiggle-dress from Planet Sexy-as-all-hell. She's also older than I am and about seventy times more beautiful.

'Hiya!' she says, and I fully expect a smoky-toned version of his accent. What I get is a high-pitched Geordie voice with a built-in giggle.

'Hello! I *love* that dress. My goodness, you are style perfection. You both are – I feel like I should leave before I vomit with envy.'

She snorts when she laughs, which sets me off. 'You're funny. I'm Raquel.'

'Hello, Raquel, I'm Tanz, and next time I come here, I'll dress for the occasion. I've also been off the booze for a week or so, but you know what, I suddenly want a Porn Star martini.' Okay, so I've been warned about drinking, but I've been under a lot of pressure the past day or two and maybe I can break this damned curse with a sugary cocktail.

'Oh, great choice. Paulo is the master of Porn Star martinis, aren't you, darlin'?'

He nods indulgently and squeezes her waist. 'She is a very supportive wife – I make a satisfactory Porn Star martini. Though I have to say, the freshly cut and pressed passionfruit with the specially imported small-batch vanilla vodka does make them rather moreish.'

'Well, let's start with one and see if I get through it without collapsing. Then we can examine the "moreish" claim.'

Raquel smiles, kisses Paulo on the cheek, then joins me on my side of the bar, taking the stool next to me. 'Make that two, sweetheart.'

He nods smartly, then gets to work. I look around at the two other customers, older ladies in smart office attire, sitting in armchairs in the corner, drinking what look like Cosmopolitans, then grin at Raquel, cheered up even by the thought of making my mind a bit fuzzy with vodka.

'Raquel, this is one of the most gorgeous bars I've ever seen. How long have you been here?'

'Oh, just a few months. We modelled it on a place in Valencia that we found on our honeymoon. When I got divorced from my first husband and we sold the house, we split the profit. We were a disaster as a couple but, to be fair, he was a DIY genius and the house did well because of the extension and the modifications. I pooled that with Paolo's nest egg, and here we are.'

'Wow, second marriage. I've not even been married once.'

'Marriage isn't for everyone. I never expected to go again, but you never know what's coming, and I felt within three days of meeting Paulo that we were going to be together for a long time. I tried to ignore it, but fighting the feeling only made me feel ill. Then he got out a ring when I least expected it, on a little getaway to the forest with a jacuzzi and a fire, and he reflected right back at me exactly how I felt. I knew he meant what he said, because he was so nervous. Paulo never usually loses his cool. He also said he'd wait for as long as I liked to actually marry me; he simply wanted to let me know how committed he felt. Lunatics want everything to happen fast, but he just wanted me to know how strongly he cared. How could I resist that?'

As Raquel finishes her sentence, two fabulously juicy-looking martinis are placed in front of us alongside a shot glass, each filled with bubbling prosecco.

We both pour our shots into the drinks and I lift my glass in salute.

'Here's to you and Paulo. Your story gives me hope and, believe me, I need some hope – and some help – when it comes to blokes.' I take a gloriously big slurp and it feels good.

Raquel lifts her glass, has a sip, gives her husband an approving nod, then places it carefully down again and appraises me, head cocked. 'Do you mind if I look at your left palm?'

You're kidding me – another fellow spooky woman? Here, in a hidden speakeasy that I didn't know existed?

I hold out my hand, relaxing my fingers so that she can see the palm properly. 'Go for it.'

She holds it under the low-hanging dimmed glass orb that hangs over the bar, then looks from it to me and back again, while I take in another mouthful of fruity tongue-gasm.

'Well, I wasn't expecting that.'

'What?'

'You. I meet a lot of people who come from a family line of psychics and clairvoyants, but you are *something else*. I doubt I'm the first to tell you that you're a powerful wise woman? I grabbed your hand to see what it said about men. I didn't know I had witch royalty coming here tonight.'

This tickles me. Another occurrence that can, in no way, shape or form, be described as a coincidence, when your life is so rammed with synchronicity. I look at my glass and note that I've already drunk more than half of my cocktail. I drain some more.

'To be fair, I didn't know I was going to meet a fellow spooky woman when I left my other fellow spooky woman alone in the hotel half an hour ago to sleep off a cold. I'm only here from London for a short time; it's random luck that I'm here at all.'

'So you didn't plan on coming here tonight?'

'No, I had a sudden free evening because my friend got

ill, and I had this feeling I should come in here. I noticed the sign as I was going back to give her some medicine.'

'Oooh, I love it when the stars align, don't you? Is she okay?'

'Yes, she just needs rest and vitamins, I reckon. We went out on the Town Moor and got very wet – I think she caught it then.'

'Paulo, we need another Porn Star martini here for Tanz. Her first one's evaporated.' Raquel looks back at my palm and nods appreciatively. 'This has happened to you before. Abroad. Someone read your palm. It all kicked off after that. You'd been hiding from your gift for years.'

'Holy shit, you're right. A make-up artist in Spain. Scared the hell out of me, to be fair.'

'Yes, there are all these crosses on your psychic line where you shied away from what you were. Got frightened of the spiritual realm. But looking here, those crosses are done now. There are some very faint ones, which will be you questioning your power in the future, but no more running away from your fate.'

'I can't bloody believe you can see all this.'

'Same as you: family line. My grandma taught me to read palms. I also "know" things about people as soon as I meet them. But you – I wouldn't be able to handle what you have . . . You're like a flashing beacon for spirits. Do you talk to them?'

'Talk to them? They never shut up. Unless I really need an answer to something, then they go as silent as the night. They don't do what they're told, speak in riddles, take the piss out of me; and Frank, my friend who died, well, he does a special line in trying to get me killed.'

Raquel's face is a picture of delight. 'I love meeting people like you! It sounds like your guides reflect your personality perfectly. It's your own fault – you should be more boring.'

Wow, I've never thought of it like that. We get the guides that match us. I'm erratic and crackers, no wonder my 'voices' are the same. I finish my first martini with a flourish, and Paulo replaces it immediately with the fresh one he made, before serving a young couple who just came in. Raquel looks even closer at my palm before giving a squeak. Right now everything is getting nicely woozy around the edges and I'm not feeling sick at all from the drink. In fact it has hit the spot *wonderfully*.

'So, Tanz, you know there are different kinds of "workers" for that realm, right? Me, for instance: I'm a facilitator. I tend to bring people together who complement each other's strengths. Others have dreams, others heal those who are depleted. There are many kinds of light workers and power sources. And from what I can see, you are all of them. Do you hear me? *All*. And on top of that, there's something else. The drink only magnified your power.'

'Sorry?'

'Your energy, I can feel it. The drink connected you even more; you're like an open channel suddenly.'

'Yes, that's it! I was actually warned recently that I have a lot of spirits trying to reach me at the moment. More than usual, though I have no idea why. My guides made it harder for me to drink recently, so that I didn't get a case of "overload". I mean, they've scuppered my wine intake. But these martinis are going down fine.'

As I say this, I see a haze in the corner of the bar, a few feet from Paulo, who is mixing a Negroni. I know it's a Negroni because I heard the bloke who came in order it like he was announcing running for prime minister. He hasn't exactly got a quiet voice and is currently manspreading in what I guess he thinks is a sharp suit, looking every inch the cocky estate agent (I have no idea what he does, that's merely what he looks like). I also heard him ordering a Cosmopolitan for his girlfriend, despite her saying that she liked the look of what I was drinking. She has the look of a young woman who doesn't argue when she's bossed about. She has a soft demeanour and her body language is extremely self-effacing. It's amazing that even while I'm sitting chatting, I always seem to soak up everything else that's going on around me, and in this case, from the energy I'm picking up, that bloke's an arrogant twerp.

The 'haze' in the corner starts to solidify – something I never used to encourage in the spooks, as I was scared to death of ghosts. These days I'm so accustomed to deceased people showing up in all different states of transparency and solidity that it's just another 'thing' in my life. Now I can see it's an older woman, buxom and round-faced, with a mop cap and a pinafore, the cap protecting what looks to be greying dark hair, tied up untidily. She's smiling, her cheeks are red and she's showing me what looks to be a gutted fish. She was either a cook or simply loved cooking when she was alive. Her apparent glee at being able to show me her fish makes me titter and Raquel glances to where I'm looking, then raises an eyebrow.

'What are you laughing at?'

'I don't want to scare you, but there's a woman in the corner behind the bar holding a big fish. She looks extremely pleased with herself. Her two front teeth are missing, but she's smiling away.'

Raquel's jaw drops. 'Oh my God. You can see her! We sometimes come in and smell stuff. Cooking smells that don't correspond with the offices upstairs. I could feel there was someone here from the minute we started decorating, and Paulo said one night when he was locking up that he felt someone breathe on his neck. We didn't do anything about it because it felt friendly enough. Then my mam visited and said it was a woman from about a hundred years ago, but that was all she got. Can you find out who she is?'

'Hang on a tick.'

I zone into the lady and smile at her, deciding it's probably better to speak to her with my mind, rather than out loud.

'Hello there, I'm Tanz, who are you?'

*'I'm Edna, pleased to make your acquaintance.'*

Her voice is earthy and warm. She reminds me of some of my mam's aunties who used to visit when I was little: salt-of-the-earth, no-nonsense women with hearty cackles.

'What you doing with that fish, Edna?'

*'Our Walter caught 'im. He's a beauty. Don't get to eat a lot of these. It's mostly kippers if we're having fish. I think I'll make a pie.'*

'Sounds delicious. I love fish pie.' (I do love fish pie, I'm not lying.)

Edna's smile gets even wider.

*'I'm stewing some rhubarb as well. The custard'll be ready in a bit.'*

'Do you live here, Edna?'

*'Aye, of course. We run the pub upstairs, I cook down here. Anyway I need to stir that custard.'*

'Okay, can't wait to try that pie.'

She grins and bustles off into the little back room off the bar. I look back at Raquel.

'She's called Edna. She's a nice woman. Seems like upstairs was a bar; she said "we" ran it, so I'm assuming it was a family thing. Anyway she loves cooking. She's off stirring the custard now and she's going to make a fish pie.'

'Ha-ha. That's incredible.'

More people are coming through the door now; there's a small queue at the bar and the seats are filling up.

'Oops, I'd better help Paulo. I can still talk to you from behind the bar once we've served this lot.'

I sip on my new martini, the second drink they've not yet taken payment for, and remember to put a protection around myself, because tuning in like that leaves you incredibly 'open'. I love how Edna's just getting on with her life. She obviously didn't die in torment. My guess is that she absolutely loved living here, and cooking, so she's left the human part of herself behind to carry on enjoying those experiences. If she seemed unhappy, I'd offer to 'clear' her, but she's probably a protective spirit in the bar;

and the way she's smiling, she must be perfectly happy with Raquel and Paulo running it.

As I listen to the northern accents of people getting served, I notice that the lad in the suit is now talking to his girlfriend about clothes. As I tune in more closely, he seems to be discussing a woman at work who knows how to dress, compared to the lass drinking the Cosmopolitan that she didn't ask for, who the man says needs to look less dowdy. I surreptitiously take in her appearance, being careful not to stare too long. She has long hair, which is shiny and straight, and not a lot of make-up, which she doesn't need because she has lovely skin. Her dress is understated and suits her, but she has the kind of figure that would also be completely *kapow!* in a low-cut number.

I look at the lad, with his smug face and his overconfident demeanour, and I see a control-freak little boy in an over-buffed, over-tanned man's body. He couldn't handle the attention she'd get, if she dressed up. He'd just find another way to knock her down. Despite the lovely glow from the cocktails, I feel that rage rising again, as I see his girlfriend's face drop and her eyes move to a spot on the floor. If I could get away with it, I'd kick him off that fucking chair, the absolute knobber.

As I'm thinking this, a shadow materializes beside him and, to my surprise, it solidifies into a very animated Mag, with a face as furious as the sudden storms she creates. She hooks her foot around one of the legs of his seat and gives a sharp yank. Suddenly he's on his arse on the floor, with his precious Negroni poured all over his pale-grey suit. He shouts out in impotent rage and looks around. There's no one near enough to have done anything. I cannot believe Mag did exactly what I wished for. She fades to nothing again, but not before I see her doubled up with laughter, floating over his head. I also get the quickest flash of Edna, giggling toothlessly as she whacks him over the head with a spectral haddock. His girlfriend has her hands over her mouth, completely confused by this sudden development.

Paulo jumps from behind the bar with a cloth and tries to help the man up. 'Are you all right, sir?'

I am trying my absolute best not to dissolve into giggles. Partly from shock, partly from booze and partly because I love when people get their just deserts. The lad doesn't take Paulo's hand, but leaps up on his own and glares straight at me. 'YOU FUCKING DID THIS.'

Everyone's already looking at him but now the room goes silent apart from the quiet piano music seeping delicately from hidden speakers.

I stare him in the eye. 'No, I didn't. I was sitting here sipping my drink, minding my own business.'

'Bollocks, you've been checking me out since we came in here, you desperate old bitch.'

That's when I stop holding it back and burst out laughing. 'Checking you out, you little orange windbag? I wasn't checking you out, I was wondering why your voice is fucking louder than an air-raid siren and what the hell that beautiful girl is doing with a man with *absolutely no chin.*'

One of the ladies in office clothes, who must be on drink number four at least by now, pipes up, 'I was wondering that 'n' all,' while her friend wheezes with surprised laughter.

So I wasn't the only one who noticed his bullshit then. The man lunges straight for me, but Paulo's ready for him. He grabs him by the back of the suit jacket, which rips down the seam like stitched toilet paper. It stops him long enough for Paulo to get in between us and stare down into the idiot's face. His voice when he speaks is icy-calm.

'If you think you're going to attack a woman in my bar, think again. I'm sorry you fell off your seat – maybe hard liquor doesn't work for you. I'd suggest you leave now and change out of that wet suit.'

The lad looks like he may have a pop at Paulo, but he's a foot shorter than him and his girlfriend is now on her feet, looking mortified.

'Come on, Darren, it's not worth it. That woman didn't move from her seat, I promise you.'

'I'm telling you, she did it.' He sounds deflated now. He shoots me daggers, then glares at Paulo again. 'You're a prick, mate.'

Paulo gives one of his formal bows. 'Good night, sir. And please treat your girlfriend with respect.'

Okay, so us liberated women are not supposed to be impressed by macho displays of strength, but come on: Paulo just showed everyone how it's done. As soon as 'Darren' storms out with his put-upon girlfriend, the place bursts into spontaneous applause. It doesn't escape my notice that all of the clientele in here right now are female. And the woman who piped up is grinning from ear to ear. She looks over at me.

'What the hell happened, do you know? Did he fall off?'

I shrug. 'I honestly don't know. One minute he was

telling his girlfriend she didn't dress well, the next minute he was on his arse.'

'Well, however it happened, it was beautiful. Hopefully she'll realize soon that he's a knob.' She holds up her glass to me, and I toast with her.

People go back to their drinks now, chatting animatedly, energized by this strange occurrence. Paulo straightens his waistcoat and then returns behind the bar, like this happens all the time. I thank him and he inclines his head, like it was nothing. Raquel kisses his cheek, then comes out from behind the bar and takes the stool next to me again.

'That was bloody magnificent, Tanz. Paulo's now making you another drink for the shock, and I want you to tell me everything, please.'

'What do you mean?'

She leans in and whispers, 'I saw a shadow moving by that knob's chair, and I "felt" something too. You must be magnifying my "gift" just by being close by. Tell me what's going on – why you're in Newcastle right now. I'm thoroughly fascinated.'

So, lubricated by tasty cocktails and good company, I tell her more than I tell most, including being haunted by the witch trials, my Icelandic adventure and the small-but-mighty Thor, who I really wish I could stop thinking about.

I have no idea what time I leave.

# BEER FEAR

Oh Christ, there's a brass band playing in my room.

When I wake up, I don't so much open my eyes as peel my eyelids back like unripe banana skins that aren't ready. The hotel phone is ringing and, after taking a deep breath, I pick up. It's Sheila, sounding groggy as all hell.

'Hi, lovely. I've just slept round the clock and still feel like a rhino stamped on me.' She sneezes and I hear her blowing her nose.

'Oh, Sheils, I'm sorry, pet.'

'Wow, you sound worse than me – have you got the same thing?'

'Not quite. Are you hungry?'

'Not much, but I think I should have something.'

'Why don't I call down to the breakfast bar and ask them to save us some pastries and make us two big coffees? I can pop down and get them as soon as I'm washed and dressed.'

'That would be lovely.'

'Righty-ho, give me half an hour.'

My phone says it's 8.30 a.m., and I don't remember how I got back to the room. I'm still in most of my clothes and I'm bursting for a wee.

Being a proactive soul, I immediately go into damage-limitation mode. First, I make myself get up on distinctly wobbly legs and go to the bathroom. I sort out the wee situation and switch on the shower, then I pop two paracetamols from their foils and wash them down with the water by the bed. It's a two-litre bottle and was mostly full when I left last night. Now half of it is gone and I'm pleased about that, as it means I had a litre before sleep, though I don't remember a bloody thing. I pour more water into the toothbrush glass and drop in a Berocca, which melts quite quickly, and I chug it down pretty much in one. When I climb into the powerful stream of hot water, I realize that my head might hurt, but my belly's okay. I thank two things for that: the bland-as-bland-can-be flatbread that I ate before I left for the bar, plus the second one that I seemingly ate when I got back (the wrapper was on the floor by the bin when I came to the bathroom), and the fact that I stuck to Porn Star martinis and, as far as I know, didn't deviate. Mixing my drinks destroys me at the best of times, but after a week off it might have been the end of me.

I wash my hair, as it always seems to help me with a hangover, and make sure to lather up my whole body with my trusty mentholated shower gel, which gets the circulation going. I wrap up in the fluffy hotel bathrobe afterwards and put the hairdryer on at its strongest. The noise is hardcore, but again it's a good wake-up call, plus I deserve some discomfort after being so stupid. I remember everything pretty clearly until I started telling Raquel witchy stories, then the warm fuzziness became total oblivion just as more folk came into the bar and it got a bit full. After that, all is a blank. Booze-fear overtakes me as I try to remember what the hell I did, which route I took home, and did I say anything out of order to the person manning the hotel desk when I got back? I'm famous for coming out with outrageous stuff when I'm bladdered, so the anxiety after a big night is always pretty severe.

I drink virtually all of the remaining water as I climb into warm 'lounging' joggers and my chunky-knit sweater, which is black, ribbed and very comfortable. How glad I am now that I packed it. With my trusty flip-flops on, which I wear in lieu of slippers, and a slick of lip gloss because I really am too vain to leave the room completely bare-faced, I take myself off downstairs and am relieved that no one bats an eyelid at the desk, which means I probably didn't cause mayhem on my return last night.

The nice lady looking after the breakfasts this morning puts our coffees in takeaway cups and in a little two-cup holder, so I can carry them both with one hand. She also hands me a paper bag with croissants and other spoils in it. We've paid for bed and breakfast, but she doesn't have to be this accommodating if she doesn't want to, because I asked her so close to the end of breakfast, and so I thank her profusely.

When I enter Sheila's room she's opened the window as far as it will go (not very far, they don't want anyone jumping) and has lit another candle that she must have brought with her. It's small but mighty and smells of lavender and ylang-ylang. It absolutely doesn't surprise me that she came with the right equipment to make a sick-room smell gorgeous. She's sitting up, propped against all the pillows that came with the double bed, and is wrapped up in a teal cardigan, with the duvet over her legs. Her hair has been combed and, despite her bright-red nose, she looks suitably regal. I hand over her coffee, then sit on the end of the bed, opening the bag of pastries between us to be picked at.

'Sheila, you look like a fairy queen.'

She laughs at this.

'My head is full of cotton wool, but I must say the pills and the sleep have helped. It hasn't gone to my chest and I'm nice and comfy. And actually this coffee tastes *good*!'

I sip at mine and take a bite of a custard-and-apricot Danish, which tastes bloody divine. Sheila helps herself to a plain croissant, which is slightly warm, and takes a nibble.

'So why did you sound like you'd been put through a mangle this morning? Didn't sleep well?'

'I slept like a brick actually, but I popped out last night and it all kicked off and I ended up getting splatted on cocktails, so it was drunk sleep.'

'What? I don't know – leave you alone for five minutes and you're out partying!'

'No, it wasn't like that. I actually went to this little bar and it turned into a spook jamboree. There was this ghost woman there who cooks all the time, she fully materialized for me and we had a chat; then this lad was being a dick and got me really mad, and suddenly Mag showed up and pushed him off his chair, and he blamed me and I thought he was going to punch me.'

'Hold up. This all happened last night?'

'Yup. The owners, Raquel and Paulo, are amazing. She's another witch and cool as hell. You have to meet them. But saying that, I don't know what the heck I was jabbering on about by the end of the night, so maybe I'm barred, who knows.'

'Go back, though, a minute. Mag showed up and pushed someone off their chair? Are you sure?'

'Uh-huh. I was just thinking how much I'd like to kick him off his chair because he was really putting his girlfriend down so badly, then up Mag pops, materializes next to him, jerks his chair with her foot and *bam!* – he's on the floor, shouting blue murder, then blaming me. Luckily Paulo stepped in; he was like James Bond, but much more sartorially appealing. He's like a taller, more funky-looking Gomez Addams. And I could see Mag laughing before she disappeared. It was crazy. No wonder I got drunk.'

Sheila is looking contemplative as she chews on her pastry and sips at her coffee. I can feel the paracetamol kicking in now, and actually I feel kind of okay, only a bit tired.

'That's not usual behaviour for spirits, Tanz. You know this, right? It's powerful stuff. Poltergeist territory basically. You seem to have a link with Mag that feeds her power, and probably vice versa. I wish I knew why you're so 'charged up' at the moment – obviously you can protect yourself, but only up to a point. Remember when you were super-open last time and it turned out it was because your friend Caroline was about to pass? I mean, I'm not suggesting someone you know is about to die again – unless it's me succumbing to this cold . . .'

'Oi, don't you even joke about that.'

'Sorry. But look, you may be so tuned into higher frequencies now that this is how it is and you're going to attract stronger and stronger energies. Whatever Mag requires you to do, she needs to hurry up and properly let you in on it. All the psychic energy you're expending at the moment will make you feel energized at first, but eventually you'll get my cold. Our physical bodies need peace and rest, and you're running on fuel that wears out eventually.'

'All right, Dr Doom, it's not like I'm attracting all of this activity on purpose.'

'I know, love, I'm just trying to keep you safe.' Sheila sneezes and blows her nose, then picks up a cherry lattice pastry. She's certainly not at death's door, the way she's getting through the pastries right now. I feel my phone buzz with a text right then and pull it out of my pocket. It says 'Raquel', so at some point I obviously took her number. It says:

> **Hi Tanz, it was wonderful to meet you and hear your stories last night. Please come back soon, or let me take you for a coffee. You're spook-tacular! Rxxx**

Well, that doesn't sound like I pissed anyone off, which is great. I notice that I texted Raquel at half-past eleven last night. I have no recollection of this missive:

**Raquel, you and Paulo rock. Thank you for a wonderful time. I'm slaughtered. I called him like you told me to. I also ate a horrible sandwich and now I'm off to bed. See you soon!**

Oh wow, oh wow! Who did I call? I check and there's a twenty-three-minute call to Thor logged at 11 p.m. Oh, for fuck's sake. I can't remember anything, only a vague echo of hearing him laugh. I have no idea what was said, but so far I seem to have behaved last night, despite having the booze-fear that I did something terrible. Maybe I just called him and told him all the ghostly shenanigans from last night. He loves all of that stuff, so I probably wanted to share it. Though that wouldn't explain why Raquel told me to call him.

'What's wrong, Tanz? Your face just dropped,' Sheila says.

'I rang Thor last night and I can't remember the conversation.'

'So?'

'Well, I might have said something wrong or bad.'

'Why would you say something wrong or bad to him? You're a happy drunk, Tanz – the worst you'll have done is tell him you like him. That's allowed.'

'Yes, but . . .'

I see a text from Thor that I must have already looked at before I fell asleep. It's just emojis. A witch, a magic sparkle and hands making a love-heart. That's not terrible, is it? I show Sheila, and she shakes her head.

'I don't know what you're worried about. That's sweet,

it must have been a nice chat. Now stop driving yourself mad, will you?'

The final pastry in the bag is an almond croissant. I tear it in half, as Sheila needs the strength more than I do, and bite straight into that delicious but far-too-sweet yellow paste. I'm going to be buzzing like an Australian cicada 'til the sugar-high dies down, but hey, we take our kicks where we find them, right?

# 'THEM UPSTAIRS'

Sheila's supposed to be going home tomorrow, but I'm not sure she should be getting the train to London if she's still exhausted and full of snot. I decide to reassess the situation later on this evening and make sure she's as comfortable as possible now. Once she's eaten and had her coffee, the caffeine seems to have the opposite effect to what it should, and she loses power like someone suddenly pulled out her batteries. She drinks some water, then lies back on the pillows as if she might flake out again any moment. I ensure she takes her cold-and-flu medicine and a big fat vitamin C tablet and leave her with the *Do Not Disturb* sign on the door and a promise of lunch brought to the room, via a lovely place up the road that sells little sealed vats of hot fresh soup. It's funny how much more appealing soup becomes when we're ill. When I was younger, you knew you were sick when your mother made you a bowl of tinned tomato soup and gave it to you with a slice of white bread smeared in margarine to pull to pieces and dunk in it.

I call my mam from my room as I straighten up the bed and make it tidy enough for the chambermaid to come in. I hate the thought of the staff here thinking I'm a total slob. Some of them have already recognized me off the telly, which only adds an extra pressure, because as soon as someone recognizes you as an actress, they expect everything about you to be glamorous somehow, and they're definitely more likely to tell people if your hotel room looks like a bombsite or you get make-up all over the towels.

'Hiya, Tanz, are you all right?'

'I am. Bit tired is all, should have gone to bed earlier, but apart from that . . .' (Obviously I'm not going to tell Mam that I should have gone to bed less drunk.)

'Good. I slept all right; no more dead animals being lobbed about. But I did have a dream – just a little one – about the hangings again. And one of the faces on the women . . . it was yours. Gave me a right fright, it did. I woke up in three seconds flat and I told "them upstairs", I did. I went to the toilet, so I didn't wake your dad up, and I said, "Right, you lot, I'm not doing this any more. If you give me one more bad dream tonight, I'll give you what for." I said that and I counted to ten, then I went back to bed and slept through.'

My mind's racing, after Sheila told me she also saw my face on one of the women being hanged, but again that's classified info.

'Glad to hear it, Mam. I'm seeing ghosts and visions all over the place, as usual, so maybe they're laying off you now. Nothing in my sleep last night, though. By the way,

Sheila's up to the eyeballs in a head cold. It came on in ten minutes flat yesterday – you've never seen anything like it.'

This is more like it, for my mother. Talk about illness and you're entering her world.

'Eeeh, never. Well, I hope she hasn't passed it on. The aches and pains I've been getting recently, and the sore throats. I'm always feeling a bit fluey, so I have to keep away from germs as much as possible. Tell Sheila I hope she feels better soon. But best not bring her here again until she's better.'

'Okay, Mam, I'll lock her in the hotel room with a plague symbol painted on the door; save the room-service people from certain death.'

'No need to be funny, Tanz, I'm only saying . . .'

'I know, Mam, I'm joking. I'll give you a ring later.'

As soon as I put the phone down, I 'know' what I have to do next. I hear the whisper from Mag. I need to go back to the Nuns Moor, apparently. It plops into my head as clear as crystal, and I dress accordingly as the temperature's dropped like a bowling ball down a rubbish chute today. I opened my window to get some fresh air and was sure I could hear distant penguins, it was so chilly. After a bit of fiddling with my concealer, on a spot that's appeared at the side of my nose and has the potential to become a new head growing out of my old one, I'm presentable enough to venture out. I message Sheila to let her know I'm popping to the Moor, then I'm off.

# A CUNNING BODKIN

The Nuns Moor is utterly silent. Apart from the chill, the light is murky and the drizzle is so cold I reckon it's millimetres away from being snow. It looks like it's too Baltic even for dogs today, and as I approach the place where the gallows were all those years ago, my toes begin to go completely numb through the thick socks and trainers. I have my hands thrust deep in my pockets, but my fingers have started to go the same way. I also have a deep sense of foreboding, out of nowhere, and I'm trying to work out if it's instinct or booze-fear. My phone pings and I see I have a voicemail. It didn't ring at all, which is odd, but I probably lost signal or something. I have a listen and, to my surprise, it's Gladys. She sounds crackly still, but I can just about hear what she's saying.

'Tanz, hello, my little duck. I hope you're okay. Sorry I'm not there when you've finally come up north for a bit – sod's law, isn't it? I wanted to say: hold strong, pet. I can feel somethin's about to happen that you might not like, and I think you need to know how much you're loved. I'll speak to you soon—'

There's no goodbye – it feels like she got cut off. I wonder if she'll ring back? As I'm thinking that, the ground in front of me starts to swim before my eyes. It does occur to me that I might be about to faint, but then I realize that this haziness is morphing into another vision from the ground up. All at once I can see the gallows being erected, and the sombre, yet triumphant face of the witch finder as he stands talking to another man, one of the great lugs I saw with him last time I was here, watching those poor sods die. They're having a hushed conversation right in front of my face, as men hammer and build behind them.

The witch finder produces the thing he cut me with and smiles at the big meat-sack of a bloke with him, who shakes his head.

'*One of the old bitches told 'er family 'ow that pricker pulls up inside the shaft. The 'usband reported it. There be nothing they can do now, but you don't want word gettin' out . . .*'

His voice is heavy and his stresses on words are very strange. But I can still glean that although he's uneasy, he's probably too scared to fully voice his doubts. The pointy-faced loon smiles at him. His canines are sharper than they should be, and his front teeth are grey with rot. He looks like a mangy half-starved wolf to me, one that's gone mad. Not a beautiful majestic creature, but a facsimile of wolf-hound and hyena, with bitter juice for blood.

'*It didn't get far, Ivan. Local councillors got their spoils and we'll be out of the district tonight. Pockets jangling and away from the eyes of these fools. Anyone pipes up, they'll get a prick in the eye!'*

The witch finder starts to laugh and it really is a scary noise, high-pitched and vindictive. He even sounds like a bastard. How did people not *notice* he was unhinged? He presses a little button on the object in his hand, which looks like a wide-handled scalpel with a thick, flat needle pointing out of it, and suddenly the 'needle' disappears up inside the handle, leaving a harmless enough piece of metal that he starts to pocket. I'm so mad at him when I see this, and realize how easily the population have overlooked this cheap trick and allowed innocent people to be murdered, that without thinking I strike out and punch him hard in the arm, causing him to drop his pricker and shout in surprise. A few men look up from their work as he quickly scoops up and pockets the contraption, before holding his arm in disbelief.

Ivan looks at him fearfully. *'What be that, Wyllam? Why did you start?'*

Wyllam looks around him, eyes darting with fear and mistrust.

*'There be more witches in this region than we can hang.'*

Ivan looks terrified. *'Maybe they know the ones you're 'anging be not witches.'*

*'Halt that mouth of yours, you fool. Of course they be witches. Truth be, all of 'em are witches – these sly cows with their lies and their "ways". Once they've bred, we should hang 'em all. More peace for us. And that damned turncoat,*

*a man who wants to defend these ugly crones – only right he be dying with 'em. We're doing God's work.'*

Ivan smiles. *'Well, if it be right with God, it be right with me. But I be thinking to get a new pricker. That one is obvious, Wyllam. Folk are getting wiser, not believing so 'ard.'*

*'When we reach Hawkshead, I'll look for a craftsman who can make a cunning bodkin. One that no pryin' eye can suspect.'*

As he speaks he's still casting glances about him, obviously rattled. I'm absolutely stoked that I managed to smack Wyllam, but also scandalized by what he just said. Bullshit misogyny as always, stretching back and back in time. It's so upsetting, as I've also seen love back then too – real love – and it feels like there are two kinds of men and they're almost a different species from one another. Just like there are different kinds of women, and the spiteful, manipulative ones seem to have had a ball going along with the murder of other innocent lasses, for material gain or to wipe out a rival.

The annoyance of it makes me try again for one last clout. I decide it'll have more effect if I aim for Ivan this time, so I hold my palms up and, launching myself forward, clap him on his ears as hard as I can. Well, you've never heard a yelp like it as Ivan jumps in the air in fear, then falls on his backside. This time all the workers on the gallows stop what they're doing as Ivan continues to make terrified noises from the ground. Wyllam is absolutely infuriated by this display and crouches down by his 'friend'.

*'Get up. Get up now and don't be squawking like this.'*

Ivan turns to him and suddenly he looks only half-solid as the vision slides and I hear him, in the distance now, cry out tearfully, *'The witches be not happy with us!'*

That's when my vision goes and I pass out.

# WARMING FLASK OF TEA

There are times in life when something happens and it seems so weird, you don't at first believe your own eyes. That's what happens to me when I wake up at the Nuns Moor and I'm being propped up by someone big and solid, who has one arm around me, while their other hand is brandishing a flask, and their big, bright peepers are three inches from mine, staring intently. We're sitting on the ground and at first I think I've been transported to another vision, but then the cold bites into my bum, and a voice says, 'Thank God for that – you dropped like a sack o' spanners. You okay?'

It's Lydia, and I have no idea what she's doing here. I sit up properly, so that I'm not leaning on her, and she hands me the cup bit from her metal flask, with some kind of herbal tea in it. I've not smelled this one before. I'm used to peppermint and camomile and the usual flavours. She nods encouragingly.

'Have a bit o' this; it's fresh herbs and it'll warm you up. My nanna swore by it.'

I take a sip. It's sweet and bitter at the same time. Tastes earthy, but not terrible. I take another drink, to be sociable. I mean, Lydia did come to my aid, though I have no idea where she was to see me drop, as the place was pretty much abandoned when I arrived.

'How did you find me here, Lydia?'

I flex my fingers and my toes, bend my knees, checking that everything's okay. I fainted last time I got caught up in the vision before me. I now suspect that going to a place where I can touch 'them' uses up a lot of psychic energy, and pretty quickly my body can't do it any more and I pass out.

Lydia blows on her hands and rubs them together. 'I come here as well sometimes. I was going to lay a flower on the site of the gallows. Parked just over there and was walking here when I saw you drop. What happened?'

'I don't know. I'm wondering if I'm catching Sheila's cold. She's not well right now, and maybe I'm coming down with the same.'

I know this isn't true, but I'm really very reluctant to tell Lydia anything. She's probably a perfectly nice person, but I'm bumping into her a lot more than can be attributed to coincidence – and we all know what I think about the word 'coincidence' anyway. She could very easily be a bit of a stalker, as people often get weird when they recognize you from the telly. I always get looks and whispers when I'm out and about, especially in the North, but luckily when people approach they're usually nice and the nutters are quite thin on the ground, or maybe just shy. In this case I'm suspecting Lydia may be a nice-but-more-bold nutter.

'Well, whatever's going on, you need to be back at your warm hotel, and I don't think getting the Metro is a good idea. Let me drop you off, come on. Finish that and I'll help you up.'

I take another drink, then pour the last of it into the grass. Lydia helps me up and, to be honest, I do feel a bit queasy and my head is definitely feeling heavy suddenly. Shit, maybe I actually have caught Sheila's lurgy. Lydia puts an arm around me, like she's my best mate and we're taking a stroll together across the Moor, and soon we've come to a mucky little blue Ford Ka and she's helping me in, while my head does its best not to loll to one side. I don't know what's going on here, but if I've got what Sheila's got, it's come on even more quickly than it did with her and I'm about to fall asleep any second.

As I strap into the car seat, I try to tell Lydia the name of my hotel, or anything at all, but find that I can't. As I'm slipping between the waking world and unconsciousness, I take in piles of fast-food wrappers and the smell of spilled milkshake, sweet and curdled mixed with a sourer stench of meat that went off. Then there's a voice – a woman's voice that I know, but can't completely place.

*'Don't be scared. She can't match Tanz, the Geordie witch. We're with you . . .'*

Then there's nothing but the faint sound of a car engine running. Until that is also gone and there is sweet oblivion.

# SCOLD'S BRIDLE

I wake up with a hessian bag over my head. It's scratchy and smells of damp. My arms seem to be tied to the arms of a chair – by ropes, as far as I can tell. My ankles are secured too. I'm sitting up and I can hear someone singing in another room. Pots are clanging and the voice is quite deep for a woman and more than a tad off-key. Lydia is sounding very pleased with herself. I feel like I have another hangover. Whatever knocked me out has left a tinny taste in my mouth and made my head throb. It has to have been in that weird tea. What the *fuck* is going on? I want to cry out, but then what the hell will happen, once it's known that I'm awake? I shout out to Frank in my head and at first hear nothing.

'FRANK! I told you I was done with all the danger. What's going on?'

There's no answer immediately, and then I hear another familiar voice – not Frank, but Gladys. *'Don't you worry, pet, however bad it gets, the cavalry are here.'*

'Gladys, how are you talking to me? You're not dead, are you?'

*'We'll talk about that at a more appropriate time. Other, more important fish to fry right now. She's a total loon. We've got to get you out of here still breathin'.'*

'Fucking hell, mate. Excuse my French. Is she going to kill me?'

*'She's goin' to try, but you've got a lot of support. We're goin' to try hard to stop you from gettin' hurt too badly.'*

'Too badly? TOO BADLY? Why is this not as comforting as you probably meant it to be?'

*'Sorry, pet, there's a lot at stake here. I can't guarantee you comin' out of it without a scratch.'*

'Thanks a bunch.'

*'She's comin' in, pet. Hold steady.'*

Considering that I can hardly move, I have no choice but to hold steady. Heavy feet approach, with Lydia still humming the chorus to 'Devil Woman' by Cliff Richard, one of the most ridiculous songs ever written about a woman with a crystal ball. I honestly thought it was his best song when I was younger and that it was actually about a sexy woman he couldn't resist, then I found out that no, Cliff was just very Christian and believed that anyone having anything to do with Tarot cards and crystals was 'of the devil'. I mean, really? How judgemental is that?

I try to stay limp so that I don't look conscious, but it makes no difference. Lydia rips the bag off my head and shouts, 'SURPRISE!'

And I definitely am surprised. For a start, I'm in doily hell. I'm tied to a dining chair in a vintage-chic nightmare of pastel colours with a carefully curated style-dump of cutesy charity-shop furniture. If you think this sounds nice, it isn't. It's faux olden-days and claustrophobic. Lydia herself has now donned glasses with pointy sides and tortoiseshell frames, teamed with a long hippy dress and a denim shirt that I couldn't see under the big padded coat. You would never think this flame-lipped Amazon would kidnap anyone. Behind her there's a clock on the wall and, judging by the time I was at the Moor, I've been knocked out for a couple of hours. How?

She smiles at me, and she's lucky my legs are tied or I'd kick her knees off. This room is what I'd have as a filmset if I was portraying the living quarters of an obsessive stalker maniac. Apart from the pastel hell of lampshades, curtains and kitsch chairs, I'm sitting in front of a table that has a very corny altar on it. There's a rag doll – homemade, it looks like, in the same kind of clothes as the people I've seen in my witch-hanging visions – standing upright, so obviously with a pole or something inside to hold it up. There are also little broomsticks, black-cat ornaments and tea-light holders with moons and stars on them. All still in the chintzy style, but with a slant of Satan.

The walls are basically papered with pages from books and magazines about witch trials, witches, witch finders and gallows. A lot of the pages have aged and many of them overlap, with new articles being stuck over old ones. I can't see what's written on them, but I can see headlines, plus drawings and photos. Boy, Lydia must have been at this for a while. There are also things hanging on the walls, behind the free-standing tasselled lamp and wooden hat-stand with silky scarves hanging off it – quite extraordinary things. One in particular glares out at me, a big metal mask-like contraption with a caged structure. It's heavy and ugly and I think I know what it is, but Lydia sees me looking and tells me about it anyway, in the tone of a very superior Geordie tour guide.

'Looking at my Scold's Bridle, are you? I shouldn't have that, but I'm a resourceful lass, and I managed to nick it from a collection in Scotland. That's where it started, you see. Shutting women down by enclosing their faces in metal and pushing their tongues down so they couldn't speak. Scotland is where it began. Same place your bastard ancestor came from, to tell lies and kill my far-back aunt, a woman who never hurt anyone. They used to use these bridles to torture witches as well. Would leave them on for far longer than they were supposed to. They were supposed to be on for a few hours at most. Let a husband humiliate his wife and shut her up. But if they wanted to stop a witch casting her spells and saying her incantations, they'd wrap one of those monstrosities around her head for days at a time. Look at this!'

She picks up a printout on a side-table and thrusts it at me. It's a black-and-white photo of a woman in a mop cap, like Edna at the bar. This woman's eyes look incredibly sad and she has a different, less mask-like contraption than the one on Lydia's wall, fixed on her face and pushing into her mouth. She doesn't look particularly old, but she does look defeated.

'That was County Armagh in the year 1900. She was a prisoner, accused of being a scold. As in a woman who spoke her mind and didn't want anyone else telling her what to do. That recently, they were still torturing women like this!'

Spit flies as Lydia rants, and I notice she goes from calm and quite pleased with herself to fire and brimstone, then back to calm as she finishes speaking and stares at me, like I can do anything about this. I look back at her, keeping my demeanour as calm as possible, then ask what I think is a pretty reasonable question.

'Lydia, I find this as repulsive as you do. And I find the way women have been treated in society to be an absolute fucking bin-fire. So why am I here tied to a chair?'

'It's time for you to pay for what your family did.'

I almost laugh at this and the reply comes before I can stop myself.

'What my family did? My parents have hardly left Gateshead for forty years and my nanna's virtually wheelchair-bound. What the hell are you talking about?'

Lydia takes off her denim shirt and her meaty arms glint with some kind of glittery body lotion. The woman put on body-glow to kidnap me. Nice touch, actually. She looms over me, her lips wet, and it's hard to ignore how imposing she is. Tall and strong, with that mane of bleached hair piled up on her head. If she wasn't bloody mental, she'd be magnificent.

'Now, now, Tanz, you know that's not what I'm talking about. Your lot destroyed my family line and took away any chance of true happiness for generations to come. I'm here to redress that karma.'

'Redress that karma? I spend my whole time trying to

help . . .' I suddenly remember that Lydia has no idea about my spooky side, and I'm not sure how helpful it would be to mention it now, in case she thinks I'm lying to save myself. '. . . people. I spend a lot of time trying to help people.'

'Small fry – this is bigger than that. What we need is a ceremony. But that'll keep for a minute. Fancy a cup of tea?'

'I don't drink tea, and after what you just did, I certainly won't be drinking anything else you give me.'

She gets a glint in her eye. 'You should maybe try being less of a bitch. You're in a very vulnerable position.'

'I did notice. And you drugging me to sleep for a second time won't make my position any less vulnerable.'

'Well, don't say I didn't try to be accommodating.'

She leaves the room again, and I hear all the familiar kitchen sounds that occur when my mam's making a pot of tea. When she returns, she's got what looks like a homemade fruitcake plus a pot of tea and a cup on a tray. She places it all down on a pile of magazines by the 'altar' on her table and lights a candle that smells of cheap vanilla. It's marginally better than the smell of burnt cooking and stale cigarette smoke that preceded it, but it's still pretty awful. She then pulls a chair out, so we're facing other, a few feet apart. She pours her cuppa, drowns it in milk and cuts herself a huge piece of the cake.

'I suppose you don't want any of this, either?'

'No, thanks, I don't like fruitcake.'

She looks at me like I'm from a different planet. 'Who the hell doesn't like fruitcake?'

I resist the urge to tell her she's fruitcake enough for anyone, and instead I give my best charming little shrug, while moving my wrists in the tiniest increments to see how difficult it will be to loosen these ropes. Right now I'd say 'impossible' covers it, but if Lydia leaves the room again, I can start wriggling them, see if I can get any purchase on escaping.

'So, Tanz. You've been sent to me by my distant aunt and all of the other innocent souls who were murdered on the Town Moor, to right a wrong that blighted many lives, and *also* in the process to hopefully restore my luck.'

'How do you know I was sent for that reason?' (I'm figuring: keep her talking for as long as possible and she might become my friend. Unlikely, but it's how a few intended victims of serial killers have escaped, so worth a try.)

She lights a cigarette and I watch the smoke curling into the air, using the distraction to calm myself.

'Because you walked into "my" library. And as soon as I looked at you, I knew that I knew you. And you perched there on the chair – usually my chair – all smug about researching witches, *my* heritage, fancying yourself as a private investigator. Then, just before you got a phone call when you *had* to let me know that you had one of the good men – like I haven't been cursed so badly that men don't stick around me for more than five minutes – you let it slip that you thought you were related to the witch finder; and as soon as you said it, I knew it had to be true because I *knew* you and I disliked you on sight.'

'Lydia, I'm an actress on TV, you probably knew me through that.'

'Shut up, I don't watch normal telly, I only watch history shows. It's not off the telly, you *liar*!'

Wow! It hits me for sure now that she's definitely not to be reasoned with.

'You came to me because it's time. Time the price was paid and your family line was stopped.'

'You do know I'm a witch, right?'

'What? No, you're not – I'm the witch.'

'I come from a whole line of spooky women. That murdering pig from back then was the male line, and I hate him probably more than you do. I saw him this week and he stabbed me in the cheek.'

'What are you talking about? He died hundreds of years ago.'

'Look at my face, there. That little cut I've covered up. He did that.'

'Bloody hell, you're mad as well as a liar.'

'What has happened to you to make you feel you're cursed?'

'Not just me – my whole family line. I have never found love, I work in an office with a bunch of jackals, I've got no proper friends and things are always going wrong. Everything I want and everything I try goes to pot. Then there was my mam. Got cancer and died in pain shortly before she retired, after a lifetime of being a nurse to other people. My auntie, her sister, drank herself to death. My dad left home to be with a floozie when I was ten and never ever visited me again. Miserable, boring, knackering existence.'

'What about your mam's mam?'

'What about her?'

'Well, was she okay?'

'No, she was mental!'

Lydia stubs out her cigarette viciously in a glass ashtray on the table and the witchy rag doll falls over, so she picks it back up and sighs.

'My grandma made everyone's life miserable because she hated her own life. She was poor, her husband was an imbecile and she didn't like kids, but gave birth to three of them.'

'Wait a minute – these are the reasons you're "cursed"?'

'Why are you saying it like that? You don't get to judge. You're descended from a monster and you're doing just great.'

'Wow, you assume a lot for someone who doesn't even know me.'

I move my hands, as my wrists are hurting from the ropes and they're going numb. I'm not feeling so sure of myself now. I'm always ready with a wisecrack or a plan, but right now I have no plan and this isn't funny. We all think we know how we'll wriggle out of a life-threatening situation with a wrong 'un, but now that I've actually got a maniac in my face, she's really hard to gauge, she's bigger than me and I'm losing confidence.

'I don't need to know you. And stop moving your hands; this isn't a ridiculous film where I tied loose knots that you'll escape from. You're here to learn a lesson, then right a wrong, and it's going to hurt!'

'Oh, is it? Well then, I'd better tell you before you start with your pain jamboree that you're a fucking whiner. Do you think you're the only one who had a crazy grandma who made all her kids miserable? I'm sorry you've had so much pain, it's horrible; and losing your mam like that must have been a nightmare. But from what you've said about your mam and her siblings, they were horribly unhappy because they had an absolute nightmare for a mother. Ninety-seven per cent of people over fifty in the North-East of England could say the same. We've got bad times, pain and depression in our blood. We've come through plagues, wars, cruelty, TB epidemics and poverty. It's ingrained in us that something terrible is about to happen to us at any minute, and the only way to get through that shit is to decide you're not going to let yourself be unhappy all the time. It's a slog, but also it's a decision. If you don't like your job, change it; if you don't have friends, do stuff you enjoy in groups and eventually make some. If you want love, give love, generate love, be kind and appreciate everything that you have. It's not easy, but if you do the work, you can change everything. Your dad didn't teach you how to love and he seared abandonment into you. But that's not about being cursed; it's about life being a twat, and what you have to do is change the patterns that don't work for you. It takes effort and self-love. No one can do it for you, and it's not *my* fault you're dissatisfied.'

'Oh yes, it is. And I'm going to right the wrong.'

Lydia smiles and her leaking lipstick suddenly makes her look like John Wayne Gacy, the killer clown. My encyclopaedic knowledge of serial killers is probably not my biggest friend right now. She reaches into a pocket in her dress and pulls something out. Oh my God, it looks like the object that ghost-bastard cut my face with. I recognize the shaft. She presses something, a button or whatever, and a long, flat needle pops out. It looks tarnished and scary. She grins at me.

'Let's see if you're really a witch.'

I'm wearing warm jeans. They're stretchy and grey-black. She puts down that infernal pointy thing on the table and moves in to unfasten them. There's not a lot I can do, as my ankles are tied to the chair legs, but I start to wriggle to stop her pulling them down to reveal my old-lady big knickers, which I put on for comfort because it's cold. That's when she does something that's not ever happened in my adult life. She punches me in the stomach, jabs hard, and all the wind goes out of me. A girl at school once did that to me when I was about ten; it was horrible and I cried my eyes out. It's no less unpleasant this time, though I absolutely refuse to cry in front of this crazy cow. I press my lips together and concentrate on trying to breathe air in and out, while my eyes fill with tears and I will them to dissolve back in and not to fall.

Soon my jeans are pulled down to my knees and Lydia laughs.

'You should be glad. If there was any way of getting you to the river without being seen, this would be your ducking stool. And being tied to it hand and foot makes it quite difficult not to sink to the bottom and die.'

It's still hard to talk, but I manage to gasp out, 'That's not how ducking stools worked. You didn't just throw people in the water tied to a chair.'

When she replies, she sounds almost gleeful. 'It's how *my* ducking stool would work.'

She now picks up the pricker and looks at my legs. 'Oh, look at that cute little mark there. Looks like a cherry. Is it a birthmark?'

I nod but keep my mouth shut. Anything I say will only make it worse, I know it will.

'Exactly the kind of thing that your disgusting relative would have pointed out as a "witch mark". Then he would have stuck this in it, to see if it bled or not. If the accused bled out, then she was innocent. If she didn't bleed, she was a witch. Should we see if you bleed? If you don't, then what you just said was true: you're a witch; and if you do bleed, then you're innocent of witchcraft, but a damned liar. Either way, you will be punished.'

She leans her left hand hard on my leg so that I can't move it, then brings the pointy pricker into my eyeline. I'm now feeling a bit sick. It doesn't look sterile or anything; it's actually darkened as if it's had blood on it recently, but I think it's rust. Whatever it is, the pricker looks old and manky and I don't want it piercing my skin.

'Obviously he would have retracted this blade, so that no blood came and the innocent person would be "proven" to be a witch, but I'm going to give you a fair chance and actually stick it in.'

'Please don't, Lydia.' This comes out before I can stop myself. I've had a tetanus shot in the past year because I cut my foot on some glass, but that blade looks dangerously mucky. 'This game has to stop soon, and it's probably better if it's before you give me blood poisoning. For fuck's sake, you can't kill me – you'll be found out immediately. I saw you when I was with Sheila, twice, so you're going to be a top suspect.'

'It doesn't matter. I'm doing a job for karma, I'll be protected as I am the righteous avenger!'

I begin speaking very fast. 'You do know that a huge percentage of people in the world hate their jobs, hate how bored they feel, hate how trapped they are in their relationship or how lonely they are without a lover, hate how they don't have enough money and how they were meant for great things and it never happened, right? You're not cursed, you're just a human who longs for more.'

Lydia tuts. 'Oh, shut it.' Then she rams that manky thing into my birthmark. Not a little bit, but a good inch and a half of metal up under the skin. It hurts like a bastard and I yell louder than I ever have in my life.

'Oooowwww, fucking hell, OOOOWWWW, you stupid mad cunt!'

I don't mean to shout these words, but they come out on their own. Blood also comes out too. Not squirts of it, just a pooling of liquid. And right when I finish shouting and am looking down in disbelief at the horrible thing sticking in my leg, there's a knock at the front door.

Lydia has closed the curtains, so we can't see anyone out of the window, but evidently someone was out there close enough to hear me scream and now they're banging. She rips the pricker out of my leg and retracts the needle-like blade.

'You noisy little swine!' She slaps me hard on the head. 'You shut up or I'll kill you right now.' She grabs a silk scarf off the vintage hat-stand and shoves it in my mouth so that

I find it hard to breathe, then closes the living-room door behind her as she goes to speak to whoever is knocking insistently. Though I try really hard, there's no getting this balled-up scarf out of my mouth without the use of my hands, and I can't muster enough of a scream with it in there. My eyes are now leaking, whether I like it or not, and I feel as stupid and helpless as I ever have. My leg is sore as hell, my jeans are pulled down and Lydia's a violent nut-job that you can't reason with. I honestly don't see any way out of this, and my 'voices' are terrifyingly quiet, considering how much trouble I'm in.

'Oi, you knackers, you got me into this – where are you?'

Lydia's coming back into the room now, and she looks red in the cheeks under her trendy specs. 'I'm going to have to leave this thing in your mouth if you're going to scream like that.'

I make a noise, but can't reply, so she takes it out, then I say, 'What do you expect me to do if you're going to stab me?'

'That wasn't a stab, it was a prick. Don't we all love a little prick?'

Is she making a double-entendre while torturing me?

'That was Mrs Delaney from across the road, by the way: old, nosy and walking her dog past when you started making all that commotion. I told her it was the telly going loud when the adverts came on and that it gave me as much of a fright as it did her. Don't expect anyone to rescue you – this place is detached. That was an anomaly. For the next bit of fun, I'm putting the gag back in.'

Lydia reaches to the table where she put her pricker while she answered the door. Stops dead. Then looks at me through magnified lenses with true malice.

'Where is it?'

'What?'

'You know what.' She reaches forward and slaps my head again. Then looks at my secured hands and feet and does a three-sixty turn, looking around the room, obviously wondering if she misplaced it. These bangs to the head are starting to make me feel sick – she has very heavy hands. I'm also wondering myself where that pricker has gone. If she stabs me again I might pass out, as much from fear as anything else, because this is getting really terrifying now. I can feel my breathing getting more and more uneven, as it occurs to me that there's no getting out of this without help and I could actually die here. Fuck, what'll she do to me if I have a panic attack?

'Right, well, I must have put it down somewhere. I'll find it again for the last bit of the ritual. Let's complete this bit.'

She kneels on a cushion in front of the little table so that she's at eye-level with that cloying vanilla candle and touches the rag doll 'witch' three times, gently so that it doesn't fall over, then chants in her fulsome Geordie accent.

'I bring her to you, my ancestors, as a sacrifice, to right the wrongs her family did to mine. I set my intention as the blood is let. This rental will be swapped for my own lush house, overlooking the sea. Management will promote me before I retire, so that I get a better pension. They'll give me my own office, and I'll make everyone else do the work for two years until I leave. And Dave in Accounts will finally realize he's in love with me. So mote it be.'

This is the worst spell-making I've ever come across. I also feel bad for Lydia. She's not asking for world domination or fame, or whatever, she just wants her life to be more comfortable and to have some security and some love. I wonder if she knows that 'so mote it be' came from Aleister Crowley, and not from some witch she imagines she's related to. Speaking of which . . .

'Can I ask you something, Lydia?'

She looks round at me and pulls a face. 'Ask away, but don't think you can charm me out of finishing what I've started.'

'No, I'm actually curious. We know that the women who were hanged and burned and tortured, and all that horrible stuff, weren't witches. They were family people who were accused for all kinds of sneaky and nefarious reasons – mostly to take their stuff from them, to shut them up or to make money from killing them. So why do you now think you're a witch? I mean, your distant aunt was innocent, right, so what qualifies you?'

'I just know it, right? I *know* it in my bones. I've always been special, and it was the curse holding me back from getting recognized for who I really am.'

What she doesn't realize is that she now sounds like every murderer I've ever read about who killed because they had a grandiose sense of self. Of course I don't tell her that.

'Very few people get recognized for how "special" they are, Lydia. The world's shit.'

She stands up and goes to the far wall, then takes down a large wooden frame containing a dusty mirror and places it under the table. She carries it like it's made of balsa wood – that woman is a powerhouse. The frame has witchy-looking symbols carved into it and I suspect it's another one of her 'artefacts'. What surprises me, when she takes it down, is that it's been hanging on a large and quite vicious-looking hook, strong and thick.

'Well, that's about to change for me. Once I've sacrificed you and then the mother, I will be unstoppable. No one will know. My magic will protect me.'

'Sorry, what? Go back a minute – *the mother*?'

'Of course. It's funny how you thought you were the "big I am" detective in the library, while I managed to find out everything I needed to know in two days.'

I'm starting to panic again, and the hairs are standing up on the back of my neck. She's after my little mam as well.

'That first day I met you, you didn't see me once. I followed you from the Lit & Phil, saw you go to the graveyard, saw you go to Blakes, where I hung around in the bar across the road with my book and with my hair in my black woolly hat. Being a detective obviously involves luck as well, though, and my first bit of luck was you getting the bus home to your parents. My car was parked a few minutes from the bus stop that you waited at, and the bus took so long that I had time to get the car, then had to sit in an illegal space and wait for it to arrive and for you to get on. I followed the bus, saw you get off and watched you go to a house. I parked up around the corner and walked past, with the hood up on my big coat. A couple of glances down the stairs and straight into the bay window was all it took really. The lights were all on, the blinds weren't closed yet, and you were sitting cross-legged on a settee, with a little woman on another settee talking to you and a fat dog lying on the floor. I was pretty sure that was your family home... Got a parking ticket, mind, for being in that space waiting for your bus to come.'

I don't like her calling Zorro fat. Only I'm allowed to do that.

'You followed me around that whole time? And you threw that hare?'

'Aye, nice touch, wasn't it? I love a bit of hare anyway.'

'You frightened the life out of her.'

'Good. And it was fun showing up at 3 a.m. I'm rubbish at sleeping at the best of times and it gave me a mission. I covered my registration number with mud, then stopped outside the house and lobbed the hare out of my car window. It was a great shot!'

'What the hell is wrong with you?'

I have to admire Lydia's dedication, as she really did scare everyone. And I can tell she's loving telling her story, so I let her carry on, though I do get alarmed again when she pulls a rope out of a side-cabinet and starts shaping and knotting it into a noose.

'Nothing. But I like a bit of the theatrical, and a dead hare was very fitting, considering that innocent women were accused of turning into hares. This was offered as proof that they were witches. That's why I always have a few in my freezer. Plus, my luck held when you came back in the Lit & Phil with your friend. Of course it wasn't luck, was it? It was exactly what was meant to happen. As soon as you left, I put my big puffy coat on and my black woolly hat. With my hood up and hat on, I just had to make sure I kept far enough back – not that you two were looking anyway. You had a brolly up and you were under it together; thick as thieves. I nearly did a little dance when you went into the hotel, as that meant I knew where Sheila was staying. Plus, I got on the Metro a few carriages down and you didn't even see me following you to the Moor. I didn't dare get too close. I saw you get to where the gallows had been, then I left before you noticed me. I knew then, truly knew, that you were the one I was after. And my only problem was how to get you on your own and bring you back here for the ritual.'

'I still don't get how you were there today. Or how you had that flask of knockout juice ready.'

Lydia grins as she finishes making her noose, and I shiver as she stands and looms with it. She knows that she's scaring me, I can tell. And she's loving it. I don't think it's only fear I'm feeling. I think I may have gone into shock because of the leg stab. The blood has dried, but it really hurts and I'm pretty sure that it'll get infected.

'Lydia, is there any chance of some Savlon or TCP for my leg?'

'Don't be ridiculous, what would be the point? You won't feel anything soon.'

God, she's brutal.

'Today was a case of "be prepared", Tanz. Dib-dib-dib, et cetera. I'd already followed you and Sheila yesterday, then doubled round so that I manufactured bumping into you at the Guildhall. God knows what you two were up to – you don't half behave weirdly together. Anyway, I gave you my number, thinking I might entice you to mine, but you didn't take the bait. So then I got a flask of my special herb tea together first thing, laced it with a lot of my medicine and watched the hotel this morning. I didn't see you go in, but I suddenly saw you come out and followed you to the Metro. Instead of following you in there, I took a chance and grabbed my car and went to the same place as yesterday, parked as close as I could to the Nuns Moor. I was as shocked as anyone when you actually showed up, as it really was just a punt. I thought it would take more time before I actually got my chance to grab you, but it was like the stars aligned for me for the first time in years, which also seemed like a sign that I was finally playing life right.'

'And you took your chance when I fainted.'

'I did indeed. Ran over as fast as I could. Why did you faint incidentally?'

'I don't know.'

'One minute you were standing there like you were in a trance. The next you were keeling over.'

'Sheila's got a cold. I think I'm getting it.' I don't know what else to say. I mean, the truth would sound mental to anyone.

'See! Lucky *again* for me, or she'd have been with you. This was all meant to be. I was even blessed when we got here: no one about, and you were coming round a bit, so you walked in with your arms around me like we were best buds. I gave you another nice big dose then, because I had to pop to the shops. Tied you up and left you on the sofa, but you were out for the count for ages, hadn't moved a muscle when I got back. Gave me time to cook a nice pie while I decided properly what I was going to do with you.'

She takes the chair she was sitting on, places it against the wall under that scary-looking hook and stands on it. She threads the rope she's holding through the hook, leaving the noose end hanging, and I stare at her in disbelief.

'You really think you're going to hang me?'

'Aye. "What was done by them shall be done unto them." I made that up, but it sounds very fitting, doesn't it? An eye for an eye. Then I'll strangle the mother and put her on the fire.'

'She's not "the mother", she's my little mam. She's done absolutely nothing wrong, and you're not going to touch her.'

'Ha! We'll see about that.'

'You do realize that this isn't how it works, right?'

She climbs down from the chair and messes with her hair, which is falling out of the big clip. 'What are you jabbering about now?'

'An eye for an eye. Karmically, you have no idea what balance has been restored by fate between the hangings and now. You don't know what balance the hangings were redressing. You're not redressing anything; this is more like when you see a nation or gang of people who've been brutalized, then a couple of generations later brutalizing another nation or gang of people and claiming they're the victims and are defending themselves. The bullied become the bullies. That's you. You'll just be causing trauma and devastation for my friends and family, and my mam's. A new line of torment. And don't think you're getting me to stand on that chair, because it's not going to happen.'

'Number one, you can call me names all you like, but I'm stopping your line dead when I sacrifice you, so there'll be no offspring to upset. And number two, you don't need to stand on anything. I'm putting you under that rope while you're in your chair. The hook's very strong in the wall. Means I can hoist the other end of the rope and, when I jerk you upwards by the neck, it'll snap like a stick of rock because of the chair weight. Like a ducking stool and a hanging, all in one. Very symbolic.'

I don't doubt she'll be strong enough to do it, either. I've been clouted by Lydia several times now and there's plenty of power in those arms. But I can't let her get to my mam; and at the mere thought of my mam being in danger, I feel a protectiveness kick in. It builds up the energy in my body to a point where I don't fucking care what happens – I'll die stopping her if I have to. She's not touching the little nutcase who gave me life.

And that's when it starts.

The beating inside.

Just like when I landed in Reykjavik, which seems like a lifetime ago but was actually within the past fortnight, there is a pounding that runs deeper than my pulse. It's primal and vibrates in my solar plexus. The beat that is also echoed by the music of the Hidden Folk, my special ones, my

Alfvin. He's watching now, I can feel him. He's whispering to me, reminding me – this room is a human thing. Lydia is sadly, horribly human. She's frustrated and looking for answers to her unhappiness, but that doesn't change the fact that she is a low-frequency spirit and I'm not. Yes, I'm also human, insofar as I'm stuck in this sack of meat and bone whether I like it or not. But I'm also 'other' and, to my honour, I am 'Chosen', according to the most incredible being I've ever encountered. A being who is vibrating in this room right now, sending me courage.

Lydia seems oblivious to the seismic energy-change happening in the room and kneels again in front of her ridiculously corny altar, puts her hands in prayer at her chest and begins to chant a stream of whispered nonsense about manifesting the ancients, and all that. Exactly what you'd see in a film, but with absolutely no power behind it. Still, it buys me a few minutes of thinking time.

I listen to my gut and realize that I need to engage human-logic mode. The truth is, if I get knocked out of this vessel, it's okay; if Lydia hurts me or even kills me, it doesn't matter. But I've got more chance of reacting accordingly and staying alive if I lose all the fear and stay calm. That's when I hear Gladys, loud and clear.

*'Summon Mag, pet. I don't know why you haven't already. You saw what she did in the bar last night. That was your strength that you gave her; the reason she can do the things she can is through you. Why do you think you can touch and be touched in the witch finder's world? Why do you think Mag can summon storms for selective eyes and jerk chairs around? You have an extra power, and*

*everythin' that happened over the past few weeks – the rise in frequency, the communin' between worlds – it's all concentrated in Mag. Bring her to you now.'*

I have questions, but this isn't the time to ask them. Instead I focus my mind on Mag and mentally scream blue murder.

# HELL UNLEASHED

At first it feels like nothing happens. Lydia stands up again, smiles at me like she's a Bond villain and reaches to pick me and the chair up together. That's when we hear a crash against the wall with the hook in it that makes us both jump. Lydia halts what she's doing and straightens, looking to the site of the noise in confusion. I'm not sure what's happened, but she runs over and picks up some little shards.

'My *cat*!'

She walks back with her hand full of black porcelain, and I realize the cat figurine from the table is gone. 'Someone' just threw it at the wall. I was tied to this chair, so she can't blame me, but she looks accusingly at me anyway.

'What the hell did you—'

She stops speaking as the rag-doll witch on the table lifts into the air and floats around on a full tour of the room.

'I don't know what's going on, but STOP THAT!'

Lydia tries to grab the doll as it flies, but instead it ducks and dodges, and starts hitting her on the head and flying off again. It would be funny if I wasn't trapped and tied up, risking this maniac losing her temper any second and smacking me upside the head again with her giant gammon-mitt. The doll lands back on the table suddenly and lies there, like the show is over. Lydia turns to me, sweating, with bright-red cheeks, and growls. Actually physically makes the sound of a threatening dog.

'If that happens again, I'm going to snap your neck like a bloody twig with my bare hands. Understand this, you jumped-up little cow: you can do as many party tricks as you like. You die today, then it's your mam's turn. This place will burn down with you in it. No one will ever know you were even here, and I'll be long gone.'

'You fucking idiot, do you know how many holes there are in that plan?'

Her mouth opens and shuts as she grasps for a retort, but doesn't have one. Lydia really doesn't like to be answered back. 'Right, that's it, I'm getting the carving knife. Death by ceremonial dagger is just as magical.'

She stalks out of the room and I begin to twist and struggle against my ropes. As I do so, the witch doll jerks and moves, which brings my attention back to the table. A doily – the worst kind of crocheted monstrosity that would give me the creeps if I owned it, one that I think the cat figurine sat on – now flies off the table, revealing the 'pricker' that disappeared after Lydia stabbed me. It was under there all along.

*Holy fuck, good going, Mag!* I could swear I hear a laugh as I see a haze in front of me displacing the air. Right then Lydia marches triumphantly back in, with a great big knife, and I can't believe this shit is happening to me. She raises it with a cheeky twinkle and lets the overhead light illuminate it.

'No amount of flying dolls are going to save you now. I don't know or care how you did it, but it's still time to die,' she tells me.

It occurs to me, even as I'm in peril, that this woman must watch a lot of movies. Nothing she does seems original or new; it all looks and feels like she saw it somewhere else and copied it. I hate unoriginality, and unfortunately my mouth has a habit of jumping in before I've considered the consequences, even now.

'Jesus, Lydia, do you realize you're about as scary as a Yorkshire pudding? You need to work on your one-liners. You're not in *Blade Runner*, you're in the North-East in a boring, chintzy living room. And your lipstick's bled. Grow up!'

Oho, well, that certainly adds a bit of spice to the situation.

'Right, DIE, BITCH . . .'

She lunges towards me but, like lightning, the rag-doll witch takes up the pricker between her little felted arms, flies straight at Lydia and stabs her with force through the hand holding the knife. Lydia shrieks like a banshee as her lethal-looking knife falls to the floor, then holds her wrist, looking with disbelief at the artefact, the blade of which has entered the back of her hand and gone straight through, so that it's sticking out of her palm. We both stare at it as blood begins to drip onto the floor.

'Well, Lydia, if you really do believe the old stories, we can safely say you're not a witch.'

Lydia howls, then runs to the twee, shitty sideboard, rips open a small drawer and takes out a bottle of TCP. She obviously also knows the power of this mighty cure-all, as she does the absolute unthinkable and rips the blade back out, flings it onto the floor, then opens the bottle with some difficulty and pours the pungent motherfucker of all antiseptics onto the bleeding wound, on both sides. It must sting like a thousand wasps, but she hardly flinches, but just starts shouting in a panicked voice, 'That pricker is so unsanitary, I could get infected. Who knows where it's been – what a disgusting thing to do . . .'

'You did it to me.'

'THAT'S DIFFERENT. YOU WERE GOING TO DIE ANYWAY.'

I've had enough of her now. Completely enough. 'Mag, UNLEASH HELL!' I shout. Yes, I know, 'Gladiator', but at least I give it my full-diaphragm voice and it sounds *awesome*.

This room is rammed with little china ornaments on the surfaces, most of them with a witchy theme. One by one, they start flying through the air, but this time they're not aimed at a wall, they're aimed at Lydia's head. She starts putting her hands in the air to fend them off. Droplets of blood from her palm start flying and the whole place reeks of TCP. As she's fending off flying objects as best she can, the knife that she brought in floats up in front of my face, then sticks into the rope binding my right hand. It's obviously as sharp as it looks, because it immediately starts to cut through the fibres.

Lydia runs out of the room while the knife saws away, until finally – as it gives and the knife handle is shoved into my freed hand – she runs back in with a battle cry, brandishing an old-fashioned metal bin lid as a shield. More debris comes at her, but bounces off the metal as she tries to get to me before I can free the other hand. My right hand has pins and needles in it, so I'm not as quick as I'd like to be, and I know there is a finite number of ornaments to throw. But then Mag decides to start singing her song at full volume.

'*Sleepe, sleepe, though greife torment thy body . . .*'

And suddenly the room fills with a full-throated first line, then a big, loud bunch of humming, as the vintage-looking glass ashtray from the table floats like it's as light as a feather towards Lydia and starts hammering upon her metal shield, sprinkling fag ash everywhere, until the force of the blows is too strong for her to withstand and she throws the whole lid at it and starts ducking and diving to get away.

While this is happening, I manage to free my other hand. Now I have to untie my legs, and Lydia, seeing that I'm half undone, bellows like a rutting stag before coming at me, lifting me and the chair in a bear hug and scooting over to the noose like she's carrying a bag of washing. I have no idea how she's this mighty, but I truly believe that if she'd put her mind to it, she could have been rich and famous as a strong-woman. It's amazing what the lure of a better-paid job and a snog off Dave in Accounts will do to a woman, as she's currently a raging animal. She's blinking determined to wipe me off the planet and make her 'spell' work, despite the glass ashtray following her around the room and trying to stove her head in.

As Lydia drops me and the chair under the noose, she grabs for the tin tray that she brought her cuppa and cake on, all of which go flying, and holds it over her head so that the missile hits it and not her, then cries out in triumph as she bats it as hard as she can, sending the ashtray spinning towards her big telly in the corner. The ashtray shatters, as does the screen, which obviously wasn't the plan, as Lydia gasps in dismay.

'Right, you broke my telly, you evil shite. Now DIE!'

Grabbing the noose, she puts it over my head; then, laughing maniacally, she loops the other end of the rope around her uninjured hand to get good purchase and begins to pull. Even as this horror is unfolding, I recall Sheila and my mother both dreaming of me with a noose around my neck. I really have to start paying more attention to other spooky people's dreams. My arms are now loose, so I grab at the rope around my neck, trying to keep some space so that I can breathe and maybe even support my weight, but I already know that I'm not that physically strong and I'm probably jiggered.

As I begin to see dots dancing before my eyes and start to lift into the air, choking and flailing, a lamps flies across the room and hits Lydia in the face, but she hardly blinks, she's so concentrated on what she's doing. The last thing I hear before I black out is her chuckling, then a bang from the hallway. Then nothing.

# HEAVEN CAN WAIT

But 'nothing' is not completely true. It's dark. But not completely black. And what's happening now isn't that easy to describe, but suddenly my neck's not hurting, nothing about me is hurting, and I'm actually not really aware of my body at all. I feel light; weightless-light, but also light of spirit. Wiped clean. Plus, I'm moving. I've heard stories of going down a tunnel when you're dying, but I wasn't sure how to take it or what it meant. Now it feels to me like you're not so much rushing down a tunnel as changing vibrations, altering states, and the human part of you, which just experienced the intense dream of being on Earth, can only translate it as 'moving' through a tunnel of consciousness.

Suddenly seeing a light is absolutely correct, though, as now I can sense the darkness melting back into a glow, and the glow is becoming brighter as I accustom myself to being out of that admittedly very hardcore death-scene. Weirdly, although I was pretty determined not to succumb to dying at the hands of such an embarrassingly self-pitying moron, if it has happened and I'm here now, then it doesn't feel so bad, and actually I think I'm happy for this to be the end. As long as 'they' promise me that I can contact Sheila for a minute and get her to call the police and save my mam, who might be full of talk about illness, but definitely doesn't want to die at the hands of the bride of Frankenstein. And to think, when I met Lydia, I thought she was incredible.

The light's brighter now, and all at once I'm in the warm grass. The grass is full of daisies and there's an ancient wall in the distance bordering this field, and I know exactly where I am. Beyond that wall, through an arch, is the next field, which has an old-fashioned bandstand. There's a photo of me, aged four or five, sitting in this very spot in the sunshine, with my favourite little sundress on. I'm in Saltwell Park – the Saltwell Park of my childhood. Of course I am. It always comes back to here.

The light is so bright, it's suddenly hard to see any details more than a few feet away. I close my eyes and let the warmth of being here seep into my soul. When I open them again, the grass has gone and there really is just the most beautiful light. I can smell books, my comfort smell as a child. The smell of the library. And now there are people. People coming towards me. It's not that thing of 'seeing my life flash before me' or 'seeing everyone I ever knew' welcoming me to heaven. I can see the faces of people I don't know but do recognize, smiling at me. I feel kinship and love towards all of them, as they beam love right back at me, forming a protective circle around me, with light beaming from them all.

As I take them in, love radiating like UV from a sunbed, I pick out a few of them to study harder. There's a man from goodness-knows-what century with a dark, wise face and long hair; a Chinese man with a twinkle that makes it look like he's about to burst into laughter at any moment; an Inuit woman who radiates calm knowledge; and behind them, staying back but impossible to ignore because he's about eight feet tall with a blue light beaming out of him, is Alfvin. These aren't the dead coming to claim me, these are my guides. There are many – I've only concentrated on a few.

Alfvin moves and suddenly he's behind me and the warmth coming from him has to be healing. He's healing my human traumas from the past few years, I can feel it. He's helping me reset. Isn't this what they do when you die? Help you reset? Oh my goodness, maybe I'll be helping Sheila and my friends and family from this side now. Maybe that's my purpose. I really like this idea.

Now I feel myself rising, just like when I flew on an eagle with Alfvin in my dreams. In this moment there's nothing around me but light and warmth and him. I can't see my body, but I feel that I'm floating in blue light. Oh my goodness, that's what he's doing – he's readjusting me to his frequency. The Hidden Folk really are my people. I start to laugh with the joy of this realization and am very gratified to hear the 'cough, cough' noise from Alfvin, showing that he knows what I'm thinking and is laughing with me.

'Am I dead, Alfvin?'

*'Not yet.'*

'Yet?'

I *know* Alfvin. It's why I've been so emotional about encountering him, why my frequency has changed since I was in Reykjavik, and why I've constantly felt outside my body since I met him and his kind. They're *my* kind. He begins to hum an ancient song as my being thrums with his energy. I know this song and I hum it with him. I have never experienced a sense of belonging in this way – not as a human, not in my whole life (apart from once when I took an Ecstasy tablet and thought everyone in a rave club in Liverpool was part of my secret family. I had a terrible comedown from that experience, though, so never repeated it).

Faces now appear, here in this netherworld of light: not solid, but identifiable balls of energy. Caroline May, who I only just saw in my dreams, comes in close and gives me a burst of the purest yellow love, which feels like sunshine. Then there's Mona, who died at the hands of Creepy Dan the Creepy Murderer and became a helper, who looks to be made of all the colours of the rainbow. Her energy beams out understanding and kindness. Then I suddenly feel Frank arrive. And in this place, in this form, without my expectations and assumptions about Frank as I knew him in his lifetime, I see a stunning lilac sheen to the white light he embodies. Frank pulsates with life-force and connection to source. Suddenly I 'know' why he's such a busy lad. Frank works with those who've only recently passed in a difficult way and are in trauma or torment. He helps them to let go of any darkness they cling to. He's up to his elbows in the dirt. It makes me even more proud of him. Nobody needs to speak in this realm; whatever I'm thinking, they know, I can tell. I can't tell what they're thinking, though, which leads me to a conclusion I'm not happy with.

'Am I going to be forced back down there?'

Alfvin's 'cough, cough' makes me smile, despite my doubts. There's really no way of feeling depressed in this realm. But it doesn't change the fact that my thoughts are still very much Tanz thoughts – I'm a human among higher beings. I want to be one of them. As I think this, another light-force appears. One that is almost pure purple and therefore a channel of the third eye. A mystic and a seer, the kind of lightworker that illuminates the spiritual on Earth.

*'Hiya, pet!'*

It's Gladys. And I have questions.

'Gladys, what's going on? I only spoke to you a few days ago.'

*'I know, me little duck. But you have to understand, some things need time to unravel. You can't know everythin' that's going on every minute. I've left you somethin' at my place. Go to the cottage when you get a minute; there's no hurry, there's nobody there. Walk down the side to the garden-gate bit and you'll see there's a little birdhouse hangin' from a hook with a slide-out compartment in the bottom. Me house key's in there.'*

'You see, this is making it sound more and more like you want me to go back. So I'm going to ask one question and I want the honest answer: do I *have* to return? Because I want to stay here with all of you.'

It's Caroline's energy that gets closer again at this

moment, as Gladys replies, *'This is one of your exit points, pet. We all have a few built in. You could exit now if you wanted – just stay here. It's up to you. But you really are needed there for now. There are stories that you've not finished.'*

Caroline beams her sunshine light until it's almost blinding, and it reminds me of the dream I had the other night, and of Caroline telling me to remember eating chips with her. As soon as I fix on that memory, I'm sitting on a bench in Tynemouth and the salt from the chips is delicious on my tongue, Caroline is next to me trying not to look content, and the sunset over the sea is one of the most beautiful things I've ever seen. That sunset triggers another memory, and suddenly I'm with Milo, watching his play that I directed, stage-lights red and yellow like the Tynemouth sunset, and me glancing sideways and catching his eye and feeling so much love, then glancing to the right and there's Sheila, looking proud as punch. Then the sun is shining on my parents' back garden and I'm at their glass garden table with a Diet Coke, howling at one of my mam's ridiculous malaprops, while my dad rolls his eyes and my mam tries to look angry, but actually enjoys the fact that I'm laughing my head off and joins in. And then the light transforms to the glow from candles and a wood-burner, glistening off snowy windows as I make love in a flame-lit room with a beautiful man who understands who I am . . .

Then it's dark and I'm whooshing backwards and, *holy shit*, Caroline tricked me into going back. Just wait 'til I see her next.

# RUDE AWAKENING

I wake up to pandemonium. I'm lying on my side, not tied to a chair any more, with my throat on fire, my eyes squinted shut and what sounds like a demon losing their shit. I'm actually scared to even look, though there's something else happening that is so randomly impossible that I wonder if this is a dream anyway and I'm not actually conscious at all. A soothing hand strokes my hair away from my forehead, then cups my head, while a very familiar but absolutely shouldn't-be-here voice croons close to my ear.

'Come on, my beautiful northern witch, take a sip of water . . .'

My eyes flip open like roller blinds. And there he is, my Icelandic wizard, pushing a bottle of water to my lips and looking crestfallen. The look changes very quickly, though, when I smile up at him and croak out, 'Took your bloody time, didn't you?'

Through the open living-room door, half in and half out, I can see Lydia. Her feet are in this room, kicking and struggling, while the rest of her is in the hallway. From what it looks like, Milo is sitting on top of her abdomen and her hands are tied with a scarf from the hat-stand. Despite being bound, she's trying her damnedest to kick him off and get up, while Milo is using all of his weight to keep her down while shouting, 'How is she still conscious – is she a cyborg? I don't think she's human, Sheila. She's a fembot. CALL THE POLICE!'

Sheila, with a big red flu-nose and the warm hat on that I bought her, has the most furious face on her I've ever seen, and every time Lydia struggles to sit upright, she gets slapped across the head with a frying pan, accompanied by the words 'TRY. TO. KILL. MY. FRIEND. WOULD. YOU??'

Finally Lydia passes out, which means silence at first, but very quickly she starts snoring like a sailor, which assures us all she's not dead. Sheila and Milo count to three and turn Lydia on her side, then Milo ties scarf after scarf around her legs, including his own beloved one that looks like Tom Baker's *Doctor Who* scarf, which I know he'll want back.

I sit up and have some water. Everything hurts,; my jeans are around my knees, the cut to my birthmark stings like a bastard, and every part of me aches. Thor kisses me repeatedly on the head and face, whispering something in Icelandic that sounds like a prayer of gratitude.

Sheila comes into the living room and her face blossoms with relief when she sees me sitting up.

'She's all right, Milo.'

Milo looks round at me, then crawls on all fours to where I'm sitting and tries to catch his breath.

'I'm not made for this level of excitement, Tanz. *What the fuck?* And look at the state of this room: nothing matches, nothing works, she's obviously deranged. Also, can someone call the police, please? Lydia might wake up again and I think I'm going to faint.' He then goes a very strange colour, and Sheila runs through to the kitchen to get him a glass of water.

Usually I'd try to make the tip-off to the police anonymous, but this one's different. It's not going to go away that easily. And we need someone to come and get Lydia before she wakes up, turns into Godzilla and runs off towards my parents' house.

Sheila comes back and gets Milo to sit with his head between his knees, then takes out her phone. From the comfort of Thor's arms, I hold out my hand to her and she grabs it. The other hand I put on Milo's back and give it a rub. My throat is knackered, but the water has eased it sufficiently for me to say something.

'I have no idea what's going on or how the hell you found me, but thank you. I didn't think I was going to survive this one.' Of course I don't add that I also didn't really want to.

# THAT'S GOTTA HURT

To their credit, the police arrive pretty sharpish once they're told there's a suspect tied up in her own house after she kidnapped someone, stabbed them, then tried to hang them. There's a whole bunch of coppers outside, I can hear them, but only three come in: an older guy who's a total silver fox; a younger serious-faced bald lad; and a calm-voiced Indian woman with the most probing eyes, whose jaw drops when she sees the mess and the noose. She comes straight to me while the other two go to Lydia, who's waking back up and is foaming at the mouth with fury that she didn't manage to carry out her plan.

Thank goodness Sheila has cotton-wool balls in that Mary Poppins-like bag of hers. I got Thor to quickly photograph my leg while the police were en route, before pouring what was left in Lydia's bottle of TCP onto a ball and thoroughly soaking the wound-site, then pulling my jeans back up, so there would be a chance I could kill whatever infection might be setting in. Turned out that once the dried blood was wiped away and the cut bathed, it didn't look as bad as I thought it would. A spectacular bruise is flaring up, though. It's so nice to get a bit of dignity back, plus cover up the comfortable knickers that no one was ever supposed to see (which will now be going in the bin asap, obviously).

I'm still in a kind of stupor, partly because of shock and partly because I don't feel fully returned from that near-death 'dream', which I know with all of my heart wasn't a dream. I still have no clue how the Three Musketeers found me or what the bleedin' hell Thor is doing here, but I'm glad he is, as the questions start slamming in from the nice police lady. I explain what I can, including the drugging from the flask of herbal tea, waking up already tied to a chair hours later and the fact that Lydia believes my family did her family a great wrong.

As I talk, with Thor by my side holding my hand, both of us sitting on slightly worse-for-wear dining chairs, while Sheila and Milo sit on the sofa listening in amazement, there's a sudden monstrous roar from Lydia. She's now standing, with the scarves around her legs gone and only one cuff on. Obviously there should be two, as the police were in the process of cuffing her, ready to take her outside, but grossly miscalculated Lydia's brute strength and the level of her madness that I'm still alive, as she bulldozes her way through the door and stares at me, yelling like a loon, waving her arms. The policewoman, who's called Preeya, screams down her walkie-talkie for help as the two police-men desperately attempt to pull Lydia back when she tries to get at me, her Doc Martens stomping hither and thither as she kicks out; and the silver fox finally holds her in a bear hug from behind.

And that's when I see Lydia's face change and realize what I'm dealing with. That weak little shit who destroyed so many innocent women – his face is overlaying Lydia's. It's Wyllam who is trying to destroy me. As well as Mag being empowered by my latest energy surge, so has he been. He's been working through Lydia. Lydia's obsession with the witch trials, coupled with her constant claiming of victim status in life, has been the perfect breeding ground for the restless spirit of Wyllam to thrive. He's exploited this situation to his advantage, urging Lydia to destroy me and, in the process, destroy Mag. This whole drama isn't about me at all; it's about some awful dark feud in my family line between him and Mag that needs to be taken care of immediately before someone in the present gets killed.

That's when I stand up, and Thor joins me for extra strength, just knowing what I need as he stares intently at my profile, oozing calm. Preeya has put herself between me and Lydia, as Lydia shakes off the bear hug momentarily, whips round and lands a full head-butt on the bald lad who's been trying to get her other handcuff on. He drops hard and other police file in from the front door, crowding into the little hallway, shouting and trying to get past their fallen comrade. Now, with only the silver fox holding Lydia – less and less convincingly, it has to be said – I go for the power of that dark beat that heralds my connection with Alfvin, with 'my' people, with the power inside me that I won't be frightened of any more. I breathe in and out, letting it build and grow; then inside my head I yell like a fishwife, 'MAG, I GRANT THE POWER OF THE

ANCIENTS TO YOU. USE IT WELL AND GET HIM!'

A heat-haze appears that solidifies into a transparent woman with long hair and a battle cry on her lips. She stares at Wyllam, who is now openly displaying his smirking face over Lydia's. Lydia shakes off the two policemen and steps into the living room, the door slamming behind her. A bunch of fists start banging, but it's no good: they're outside and Thor, Sheila, Milo and I are locked in, with Preeya still shouting down the radio.

I look at Thor. 'Do you see her?'

'Clear as day. It's never boring with you, is it?'

I pull his hand and also take Preeya's arm, dragging them both to the wall furthest from the door. 'Get back, everyone.'

Milo and Sheila don't need telling twice, as they jump behind the sofa.

Mag faces Wyllam in the body that is Lydia, and Wyllam points and growls, 'You will not win this time, wench. Your witchcraft will be the end of you!'

Lydia's voice has deepened to a man's voice, and Preeya drops her walkie-talkie in shock. Mag laughs, and the room echoes with it. Preeya may not be able to see Mag, but she can certainly hear her, because suddenly she's behind the sofa with Sheila and Milo. I ramp up the energy that I know I'm projecting into Mag and see her lift her hand, palm outwards, and aim it at 'his' chest. I see Wyllam try to move and he can't. His face contorts as Mag speaks.

*'Wyllam Hooper. I stopped you before and I will stop*

*you now. I should have strangled you when you were a whelp. There never were any good in that black heart of yours. Just greed and pestilence.'*

He struggles in Lydia's body and tries to get at Mag, but he is stuck, so he howls out, 'Lies, always lies from the filthy witch!'

*'The filthy witch who was your sister. The filthy witch who saved many lives with her herbs and healing hands. The filthy witch you were jealous of. The filthy witch you tried to lie with, you unnatural cur, you abomination. You killed so many, and why? Because I would not let you inside me. Pig! Killing those women because you knew if you tried to kill me – the real witch, a gift passed from our mother – Father would chop out your worthless liver.'*

'Well, you didn't stop me for ever, did you, you daughter of Satan.'

The lamp that got thrown at Lydia's head earlier now lifts in the air and flies at Mag, but that's pointless as she's not in a human body and it passes straight through her and hits the wall two feet to the left of Thor, who, to his credit, only jumps slightly, then shakes his head.

'Terrible shot.'

Mag doesn't waver, but her body gets a little more solid and her genuine grief comes through as she says, *'No. You knew they would burn me in Scotland if I tried to stop you. They were too caught up in the lies. And in Newcastle the trials were too far gone, and you'd given money to the councillors, and the gaolers were making more than their usual, too. Again I would have been killed. But I regret it every moment, Wyllam. I watched, I saw them die and I knew what you did was evil. I should have saved those poor innocent lasses and that broken man.'*

'WHAT YOU DID TO ME WAS EVIL!'

*'I did what had to be done – you were my brother in name only. You were the worst of men. You were stopped. I am glad of this. I will do it again. You have no place here.'*

I'm getting very tired now, and I can feel the energy slipping from my limbs as today's craziness takes its toll. And that's when, with a roar of triumph, Lydia suddenly regains movement and grabs a dining chair. I think she's going to attack me, but instead she runs to the window, rips the curtain open and smashes the bay window with a huge clatter.

'I WILL DESTROY THE MOTHER!'

She jumps through the smashed window, probably cutting her hand to pieces as she holds the windowsill to vault out. We all scamper to watch, as Preeya shouts out to her colleagues. Two policemen outside make to tackle Lydia, but she grabs them and knocks their heads together like conkers. Both of them pass out. I'm just thinking she might get away and go for my mam when I hear a weird noise, then another one, like the cracking of an electrical fault. Lydia stops dead, then pitches forward and twitches on the ground.

Thor gives a sharp intake of breath and shakes his head. 'Two Tasers at once. That's gotta hurt!'

While every single officer that Lydia didn't manage to knock out surrounds her and gets ready to take her away, I hear Mag's voice loud and clear in my head: *'Pick that up. We will banish him for ever.'*

I look at the floor and am surprised to see the discarded pricker at my feet. I know it's evidence and I know this is a crime scene, but while everything's going crazy, no one is going to notice me retracting and then pocketing that strange bloody artefact, after picking it up from the glass- and porcelain-strewn carpet. Mag knows what she's doing, and now that I've discovered she's my far-flung witch-sister, I'm going to trust what she asks me to do.

Only Thor notices what I'm up to and, as he looks at me inquisitively, I wink and give a quiet 'Shhh'. Outside the window, the street explodes with flashing lights and shouts; grown men try to wrestle a maniac in a hippy dress into a waiting police van, and a little old lady with a dog moves around animatedly, probably to get someone's attention and tell them about the screams she heard earlier.

Inside, I look around at my best friends, who appeared as if by magic and saved me from the jaws of death: Milo, who has his hands over his mouth as he watches Lydia fight like a wildcat not to be put in the police van; and Sheila, who nods at me and seems to be suppressing a smile at the spooky lunacy of it all. As far as I can tell, she's completely unruffled, the absolute warrior. Then of course there's Thor, who I've not even properly said hello to yet, and who has flown in from Iceland out of the blue – and, for all I flippin' know, on the back of an eagle. I smile at him, happily bamboozled, and put my lips against his.

For the few seconds that I leave them there, I get that feeling again – the one I thought maybe I made up in my head. The feeling of being home.

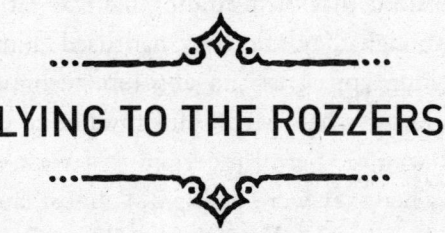

# LYING TO THE ROZZERS

Holy shit, dealing with the police and getting checked by the ambulance crew and all that sure takes a lot of time. It seemed to go on for ever. Luckily for me, there was more than one witness to everything that went on today. Preeya came and told me, just before we set off back to the hotel, that plenty of the neighbours were used to Lydia being a difficult and grumpy woman, but they never saw her with visitors, so it was very much noticed by the whole street when she half-carried me into her place. Plus, Mrs Delaney across the road really wasn't satisfied with the whole 'TV adverts came on loud' nonsense, because apparently she'd come halfway up the path earwigging and had then called the police, saying she'd heard screams. There wasn't enough basis for the fuzz to come out then, but that's why they came speeding when we called them, as they'd already had a call about that address earlier.

The rest was a blur. Milo and Sheila kept staring at me in shocked relief, and I could only imagine how scary it was for them to come in and see me tied to a chair and being hoisted up by a noose. In the bits I heard of their statements, I realized that them finding me was rather hard to explain, although they said they had used 'Find My', the phone-tracking app. I am an absolute technophobe and don't even know what that is, plus my phone is total rubbish. But I was 100 per cent certain that wasn't how they found me, when they were saying it. I almost laughed, even in my knackered state, that all of them – including Thor – were lying like absolute rugs to the rozzers.

My coat was in the hallway, hanging over the banister, with my phone in the pocket and my bag underneath, I was told as I was handed them by an apologetic officer who'd trampled all over my coat. Everything was fine and in working order, though, so that's one less thing to worry about, as we fall into my room at 11 p.m. Before I can even drop onto the bed, Thor is running a bath for me. Milo has gone, after hugging me expansively, saying that he'll come and see me for a debrief once he's had some sleep. (I heard him on the phone to his lad, to whom he was going for late supper and cuddles, which makes me very happy.) As he was leaving, he and Thor shared a prolonged man-grapple and Thor said, 'I knew her friends would be amazing, but what you did was incredible, restraining that monster. You're a hero.'

Milo swallowed hard at that, wiped an eye like he had something in it, then mouthed at me behind Thor's back, 'He's a keeper.'

Sheila looks like she's gone ten rounds with Mike Tyson as she flops on the bed next to me. Her cold has come back with a vengeance, so I hand her two of the strongest cold-and-flu pills in existence, four of which I keep in my bag at all times. Thor has ordered food and two bottles of red wine to the room. The wine comes first, and he pours us all a big glass each. Sheila stares up at him as he busies himself making three espressos with the little machine and checking on the bath. Once it's run (and boiling hot, so we can leave it awhile) he makes everyone down the coffee, welcomes room service who bring three toasted-cheese sandwiches with chips, and then sits in the little armchair, close enough to be able to hold my hand whenever required.

Sheila looks at him with something akin to awe.

'Thor, I have to say, you were incredible today. I don't think Tanz would be here now if it wasn't for you.' Then, to my surprise, she bursts into tears. Sheila's not usually a tearful person, so I'm shocked.

I give her a side-hug and she hiccups.

'Your poor neck, Tanz – look at those bruises. And your leg. I'm so sorry I wasn't with you; it's my fault that happened. You were on your own because of me getting this stupid cold.'

'Are you kidding, Sheila? You can't blame yourself because you got *ill*.'

I look at Thor for back-up and see that he's tearing up as well. He tries to hold them in, but it's a struggle, and his voice is rather strained when he says, 'I could have lost you.'

I take a large bite of my toastie, chew it and then, realizing I don't have a huge amount of saliva right now, I help it along with a gulp of wine, which is now going down a treat after tasting like poison for a week.

'Sheila, it will forever be emblazoned on my brain: waking up from near-death and seeing you rhythmically whacking Lydia over the bonce with a pan. I wish your Pan could have seen it. Lydia wouldn't stay down, would she?'

Tears turn to laughter and Sheila eats a few bites, then cocks her head and says, 'Wait a minute, those pills are kicking in and my nose is drying up. That's amazing.'

'Aren't you knackered, woman? I'd love to know how you all found me, but it can wait 'til tomorrow.'

'No, I think I can last long enough to tell a bit about today, especially with those pills taking the edge off. Them and the wine have given me a second wind, and who knows how long it will last? You game, Thor?'

'Yes, might be a nice way to wind down, after all that excitement. Then I'll have to insist that Tanz gets in the bath, to help relax the shock that she'll be holding in her muscles.'

'May I just say, Thor – your English is fantastic. You put me to shame.'

'Oh, thank you.'

'All right, you two, so come on: what happened? Why are you even here, Thor? And how did you know there was anything wrong, Sheila?'

'Okay, you first, Thor. He's the one who showed up at the hotel about half an hour after you texted and said you'd gone off to the Moor.'

'Yes. After our chat on the phone last night, I decided to throw caution to the wind and come and see you. I booked the first flight. I wanted to see you so badly.'

'Thor . . . I . . .'

'Don't remember what you said – I know, Sheila told me.'

I shoot her a scandalized 'how could you' look and she laughs. Thor grins.

'It doesn't matter, we can talk another time about our conversation last night; all that matters is that it brought me here. And when I landed, I got a cab – I can't believe how close it is here to the airport and how cheap the cab was.'

'Thor, you're going to find a lot of things cheaper here compared to Reykjavik, so get used to it. Now get on with it. I want to know how you guys *knew*.'

'You are so impatient.' He leans forward and kisses my hand.

No one but me knows how much this warm physicality is making my life feel better, after such a hardcore day.

'The thing is, on the flight something very strange happened. I'd made arrangements after I spoke to you and it was last-minute, so I was up late. Once I took off this morning, I felt the weariness descending, so I put my little cushion against the window and fell asleep. It was quite comfortable and an hour's power-nap is all I need to feel refreshed, so I was glad I'd bagged the window seat. In this case, though, I immediately launched into a dream that was so vivid I'm pretty sure it wasn't a dream at all. I could hear them, Tanz – the music, the beat – and I could smell the fires too.'

I know what he means immediately. 'The Hidden Ones?'

'It was him. Your Alfvin. I was sitting on a rock in that cave that we visited together and he was sitting opposite me. He said, *"Chosen needs you. She's in danger."* He was calm and focused and he reached out and touched my arm. And when he did, I could see – I could actually see – a big tall blonde woman with mad eyes. *"Tell her friend,"* Alfvin said. *"The seer, go and find her. Chosen will be with this woman that I show you. The seer is wise and good, she knows her. You'll find her."*'

'Oh my GOD, Sheila, you're the seer! Of course you are.'

Sitting on the bed next to me, she shifts the pillow behind her so that she can sit up taller, and raises her glass. 'My reputation precedes me, even in Iceland!'

I look back to Thor. His soft beard is neatly trimmed and his dimples are perfect. His eyes have little amber speckles that stand out in the light from the bedside lamp. He's beautiful.

'So this troubled me obviously and, when I landed, as I said, I found a cab and went to the hotel. I had planned to surprise you and go to your Bougie Bar with you later on, but I already knew something was very wrong. I knew what your room number was, and I asked the nice lady at the desk if I could call your room, and then Sheila's. Luckily Sheila was in, and awake. She invited me up and I told her what Alfvin had just reported to me. And like he said, Sheila knew straight away who the tall blonde woman with the mad eyes was. We tried calling you, and of course there was no reply. From the timeline you've given today, you must have been on the Moor then.'

'Dammit. My phone's always on silent when I wake up, and today I was so knackered I forgot to put the ringer back on.'

'Well, either way, you texted Sheila and said you were going there, so she kindly got up, despite being unwell, and came with me to search for you. It's not like we could call the police, as you weren't even "missing" yet, and I'm pretty sure dreams about ancient hidden people don't count as proof that someone's in trouble, as far as law enforcement is concerned.'

Sheila nods at this. 'Thor, you wouldn't believe how many times we've "known" things were happening but we couldn't call for back-up from the police because we have no concrete evidence.'

'Oh, I would believe it. Since I met Tanz, I'd pretty much believe anything.'

'Well, like Thor said, we went looking for you and when we got to the Nuns Moor we went to the spot where the gallows was built and there was something there, wasn't there, Thor?'

'Yes, like a message. A card from Bougie Bar. I was shocked. Did you drop it on purpose?'

'No! I had a vision again. I don't know if Sheila told you, but we've seen some incredible stuff together. And this time I could actually touch the witch finder and his mate, Ivan. I clapped Ivan on the ears and he nearly shat himself, then unfortunately I passed out. Used too much energy probably. The card must have fallen out of my coat pocket.'

Sheila begins to giggle her head off. 'You bugger – must have scared the life out of him.'

'I did, the arsehole.'

'Well, that card was the message for me and Sheila that

you'd been there recently. Sheila said it had been raining on and off since she got here and the card wasn't yet soaked through, so it couldn't have been there for that long.'

'Good work – you two are amazing detectives.'

'Yes, like Columbo!'

I love that Thor names one of my absolute favourites.

'Thing is, though, Tanz, we still couldn't prove you were missing at all. What if you'd gone to get some lunch for me from town and would just turn up at the hotel? What if Lydia was dangerous, but it was a warning to Thor to get you away from her – and not that anything bad had actually happened yet?'

'Sheila's right, but I knew,' Thor goes on. 'Alfvin was very emphatic on the plane. So we came back to the hotel just in case, and established that you'd not returned. That's when Sheila called Milo, in case you were visiting him.'

'And of course as soon as I told him, Milo freaked out. He'd got back from Manchester last night, woke up late today because he went to bed late, and said he'd had the weirdest dream about you. You were saying goodbye. You told him that you'd decided you didn't want to be "here" any more.'

Oh my God, I knew that boy was a wizard. I'm saying nothing and try to keep a poker-face, but Thor cocks an eyebrow at me, before moving on with the story.

'Sheila told me Milo was on his way to the hotel, as he also felt there was something very wrong. I have to say, you've got some amazingly caring friends. I'm very impressed.'

I can tell from Sheila's face that this moves her, and she

blows him a kiss. Wow, today has obviously been quite the bonding experience for them.

'Once Milo arrived, we had a debrief in the bar. I'd been told who the woman was – Sheila knew who I was describing, and her first name. We also knew that Lydia had a major interest in the witch trials.'

'Yup, and as I told the boys, you'd actually bumped into her first in the Lit & Phil and then we'd both seen her there the second time, so we decided that was the place to start looking for you both.'

Thor nods eagerly. 'And what a beautiful building. But of course I couldn't check it out properly because we were on a mission. We quickly established that Lydia wasn't there, so we went to the desk and asked the head librarian if she knew her and she actually said, "Lydia Donaldson, with the bright blonde beehive, loves reading about witches?" And we said yes, like she was someone we knew well. Now we had her surname, and next we asked if the librarian possibly had an address for her. The lady said no, she absolutely couldn't give out any details; then Sheila said thank you and made us walk to the other side of the library and down some stairs. Next thing I know, she's standing there, whispering to no one.'

'But it wasn't really no one,' Sheila tells me, 'it was the tiny sparrow lady who'd warned me that you needed protection. I could feel her trying to catch my attention, so I went over, away from prying ears, and told her you were now in danger and that we suspected you were with Lydia somewhere. She said that she'd always steered clear of Lydia's energy as it was "off", and that I should go to the special reading room "over there" and check out the book on the desk. I did as I was told and found that it was a signing-out book for taking certain publications upstairs or out of the library. I looked through it and a few pages back there was the name Lydia Donaldson from about a month ago. It had her street name and postcode, no door number, but that was enough. Milo was so chuffed he was jumping up and down like we'd won a trophy, and he asked where the little ghost lady was standing so that he could say thank you to her face, which he did. It was very sweet.'

Thor's voice now gets rather strained, obviously reflecting his impatience at trying to get to me after that.

'We went to the train station to find a cab and it took longer than we hoped, and then it was twenty minutes to get to the right street because the traffic was terrible. And there we hit the next wall.'

Sheila nods at him and pours everyone more wine. 'We had no idea how we were going to find the actual house, Tanz. There's only so much you can do with instinct and gut feelings, and even at four o'clock the sky was so dingy that it was pretty much night-time. We walked up and down, didn't we, Thor? Milo was looking through windows with the curtains still open, hoping to see you, or a hulking great woman with a pile of blonde hair. But there was nothing, and lots of houses had their curtains closed.'

'So how did you find me then?'

Sheila points at Thor. 'Him.'

Thor nods enthusiastically. 'Alfvin. I heard your little bell as we walked past a totally anonymous house, same as all the other ones. Or it seemed to be the same as all the other ones, until I looked closer, and for a second caught a glimpse of a tall figure standing in the shadows by the window. I went up the path for a closer look and the figure disappeared, but the door had a little light hanging over it and, when I got closer, I could see this small lantern had a black cat and a broomstick painted on it. Then I heard someone shouting. I couldn't really miss it, because one of the windows over the bay had been left open. Whoever was in there had drawn the curtains and not noticed the window was open. The voice inside shouted, "Right, you broke my telly, you evil shite. Now DIE."'

'I was at the end of the path with Milo and even I heard it, it was so loud. No wonder that lady heard you screaming,' Sheila goes on.

'Anyway, I just knew then that my northern witch was in there and in trouble, so I tried shoving the front door and nothing happened. Then Milo and Sheila ran up to help and, after pushing and shoving and trying to use our shoulders, we counted to three and all kicked the door as hard as we could. That's when the latch splintered open – and the rest, as I think you Brits say, is history.'

Sheila yawns expansively, right on cue, and Thor stands and puts out his hand to help her up.

'Everything else can keep until tomorrow. You saved the day today, Sheila, but now you must rest.'

'Sheila, aren't you supposed to be leaving tomorrow?'

'I am, but I'll call downstairs and see if they can extend both of our stays for twenty-four hours. I think the police may want more information, plus I also want a major lie-in. I'm completely bushed.'

I try to stand, but can hardly move.

Sheila blows me a kiss. 'Don't get up, I'll see you for brunch tomorrow. Sleep well.'

Thor grabs her into a hug. 'You are a wonder.'

She smiles sleepily. 'So are you.'

When the door closes behind her, he locks it.

'Thor, you may have to carry me to the bath – I can't move anything.'

He climbs onto the bed and wraps me in a full-body hug.

'It should be perfect by now, but let me check. Then I will happily carry you in there, my fine maiden, and we can get some heat into those muscles, and some ointment on that cut, and some arnica cream on that neck bruising. I'm here to serve.'

How I adore this spooky little Viking right now.

# BADASS MAG

The field is dark and there's a bonfire burning bright. I'm close enough to be warmed by it, despite the chilly air, and I watch, transfixed, as it crackles and shoots small red flames into the air. The smoke smells sweet. A woman is standing close by and is carrying a basket. She throws herbs and roots on there, which makes it smell good and also makes me a tad light-headed. She turns and smiles at me. It's Mag, looking different. Her face is more relaxed, and the grief that I always sense isn't hanging so hard on her. She takes my hand and starts leading me around the fire, where we encounter women both old and young standing expectantly, shawls pulled tightly around them to stay warm. They look poor, but they're clean, and there's expectation in the air.

As we walk, these women kindly offer us hot chestnuts and small chunks of bread with lard, and they all taste delicious. Mag speaks as we stroll, draping her arm companionably in mine.

'*This was Wyllam's big mistake. After Newcastle he*

came here to spread his canker, his death and misery to more women, and any man who should disagree with him. He came to Hawkshead to panic Cumbria with talk of witches and make himself a pretty packet. But I got here first, and I told the women. Around here they'd had a hard time, and the women and men had worked side by side to get through the plague and endure the lack of food and the misery. They were united. I told 'em, afore Wyllam got here, that he would have a pricker that didn't prick, that he murdered for money, and that he tried to rape his own sister and would rape any of the women who took his fancy and who he could get alone. Afore he could get rid of the pricker, or ask a craftsman to fashion a new one, they took it from him and saw it were true. I told 'em about the supposed witch who gushed blood when she were hanged after Wyllam said she bled not.'

An old lady approaches. She hands Mag something wrapped in a cloth. '*My Thomas got the cursed thing for ye. I telled him ye'd know what to do with it.*'

'And that I do. Thank you, Rebecca.'

'*There's a light yonder. They come.*'

Women begin to whisper expectantly, and there's the sound of horses as a cart approaches with a bunch of men walking by it. Mag holds my arm tighter, a look of sorrowful resolve on her face.

'*What happens next, he brought to himsel'.*'

A man is dragged off the cart by a gang of around ten village men. It's Wyllam, naked from the waist up. He's snarling at them, but I can feel the fear radiating off him from here. His back is covered in welts, and I'm pretty sure he must have been whipped. This makes me feel very sad. I hate violence, but they were terrible times and people had been frightened to death by men like him and killed en masse. I can see why folk would feel Wyllam needed some kind of punishment in return.

Ivan isn't there with him and, before I can ask where he is, Mag leans in and whispers, *'Ivan ran off, after Newcastle. Went to church to beg forgiveness. Said that God struck him down for his sins. But it weren't God who clapped 'im round the ears, was it?'*

She begins to chuckle and I try to smile, but the whole atmosphere here is suddenly more subdued and dark, so it's difficult to get in a laughing mood. One of the men from the village steps forward, and he is built like a farm shed. Tall and wide, with a rough beard and shaggy hair. A tasty unit.

The witch finder is brought forward to the shed-with-a-beard by the two men holding him, and he really is too puny to do much about it. Not so smug now, as the women gather closer to the fire. Many of their faces are illuminated. They don't look greedy or fevered, it has to be said; they are mostly serious and, from what I've read and seen of those times, I can imagine why. Women, after plagues and occupations and mad kings, and being murdered in their hundreds at the behest of psychopaths – everyone must have been exhausted by it all.

A collective whisper picks up, and at first I don't know what it means, but then I see that Mag is leading it. She must have taught them some kind of incantation, because they're in sync, but I have no idea what they're saying. The men holding Wyllam look quite scared at the power of this collective chant, and Wyllam himself is howling and shouting and flailing away, just like Lydia was in her house when she couldn't get at me. He's not the most dignified man, and the women chant louder, bolstered by the fact that he's got to be crazy, the way he's flinging himself about. He's presented to the shed-man, who comes in from behind and wraps his forearm around Wyllam's neck. Mag steps away from me and in front of Wyllam, as the shed-man begins to apply pressure to his hyoid bone. I know exactly what that is because I've watched more true-crime shows than anyone else in the world.

Mag raises her arms and, with impressive projection, cries out to the whole crowd, *'Wyllam, son of Edmund Hooper, you are not of the dignity or honour to bear that good man's name. You have shamed my family and been a blight on the innocent. Much blood has been shed, and it stops here. Death-for-death is not the way, but this is a necessary sacrifice. Repent as thou diest.'*

Gasping and with furious bulging eyes, Wyllam pushes out the last words he can: *'YOU WILL NOT BE RID OF ME, MAG, YOU SORCERESS. I WILL BE AVENGED. MY DEATH BEGETS DEATH!'*

Before anything else can come out of his mouth, the shed-man gives a twisted tug and breaks Wyllam's neck. The men in attendance mount him on a pole and, with a bit of manoeuvring and the help of ropes, he is inserted into the fire. The men then step back again, looking relieved as much as anything; and now it's just a gathering of women, some crying, some hugging each other – glad, I'll wager, to see at least one of the huge dangers in their lives alleviated for now. Then the humming begins, and I know the song because I've heard Mag sing the first line a million times. I wonder if she even knows the rest. They all begin to hum in unison and, as the fire completely consumes Wyllam, Mag leans into my ear and whispers, *'Close your eyes.'*

I do as I'm told and for a few moments all goes quiet.

Then she says, *'Open'* and I'm standing in the graveyard at St Andrew's Church as it was in those days. Birds are singing and the sun has come up. There is Mag, digging a fresh hole over the mass grave, with dew still on the ground. She is quietly mouthing words to herself. I hear her voice in my head, like she's in two places at once.

*'My mistake. I was a wench filled with guilt. I felt I should have tried to save them. But when I got to Newcastle, they were already pricked and tortured and it were all too far gone. Wyllam could easily have accused me too and had my tongue torn out. I hoped by burying the pricker with them, covered in purifying salt, that I might set them free from the shackles of their miserable end.'*

The Mag who is on the ground takes the witch pricker, still wrapped in the cloth, unwraps it momentarily to liberally sprinkle what must be salt on it, then rewraps it and begins to cover it with soil.

*'This is what undone me and brought his darkness back. The bones were dug up when the church were being renovated. They found the pricker. It was on display for a long while. Wyllam got into Lydia and she stole it three days ago. No one expected it to be taken, so it weren't really guarded. It must be burned and cleansed. Then our line will be*

*purged of Wyllam for ever. If I had my way, it would be thrown to the bottom of the sea 'n' all, where salt would keep it pure and it couldn't be taken by no thieving madwoman.'*

Suddenly the vision fades and I'm simply standing in light, with Mag's voice in my head and her energy surrounding me with warmth. Her smell is unbelievably comforting.

*'I'm sorry you had to be in so much danger today. I did what I could. You are my sister and I love you. You are a changer, a healer, a woman of light. You move between time – not even I could do that. When you saw them hanged the other day, you went there, you reached back to them, and with thy healing love you changed it. I watched you do it. I seen you change how they felt at the end, with my own eyes. I buried the pricker with them, trying to do that, but failed. You did it with love instead. This blessing will wash down through their ancestral lines, as it will through ours. I don't know how you do those things. I am proud we are of the same blood.'*

'Mag, you were a real witch at a time when it was truly dangerous – that's worth a lot.'

Her voice sounds proud. *'Indeed, indeed. Few of the women who were murdered were true witches. We are a rare breed – teachers and learners. Though they got the midwives and the healers, which still aches my heart.'*

'You are a special being, Mag. Can you rest now?'

*'When the pricker be burned and cleansed by a true wise woman, I will be peaceful. It were the energy from you that brought me here. I was needed. I hope I did enough.'*

'Are you kidding? You were absolutely magnificent. What a powerhouse.'

Her energy gets even warmer. *'I didn't know if you would overcome him. Wyllam was the worst of weak, ugly-hearted men, and he left that behind on this Earth, but he got inside a strong woman. That were the big danger. He is out of her, now that you are strong, and she don't have the pricker; and as soon as that be gone for good, then so will he be.'*

'As soon as I can, I'll do it.'

*'Thank you, my sister. I will be with you.'*

'Be free of guilt, Mag; you did all you could. That warm love for the innocent dead, I now channel it into you. You deserve peace, and you deserve to be proud of everything you did.'

I hold my hands out and she materializes enough that I can see her, then she holds my hands tightly in return. I feel them heat up like furnaces in my palms as electricity surges into her, and then Mag begins to laugh, a tinkling, unburdened thing. She stares in my eyes as I hear her voice in my head.

*'I have a parting gift for you, my sister. Matthew Hopkins, the vile Witchfinder General, another liar, cur and hater of women. He were the one who gave my brother ideas. He were lyin' low after his last hangings, he knew times were a-changin'. After Wyllam were dispatched, young Mag weren't completely satisfied. Other liars were still abroad. Soon I found out where he lived – he'd sloped off to the country, livin' in a prosperous village. Divined it from my own special 'elpers. He were having babbies with*

his healthy, beautiful-lookin' young wife after leaving so many without mothers. Him with his eyes too close together and his shrivelled, nasty mind. Well, I couldn't have that, could I? So I sent him a gift; signed it from the local parish councillor. Sent some to that bastard too, truth be told, but he didn't drink it after he found out about Matthew dyin'. It were my own damson wine, Tanz. Special recipe, aged long enough to burst with the flavour of the fruits I grew. Strong and too tasty to notice the hemlock in it. Also grown by me. No one knew who sent the poison or the letter about the innocent witches. Didn't expect a poor woman to be able to write, did they? And no one dared talk or write about Matthew dying in case they were next. I'm glad I done it, and probably I should be in hell.'

I know I shouldn't be glad about a poisoning, but fuck me: Mag was a bit of a rockstar. Obviously as mad as a coot after everything she went through, but still. An absolute legend.

'Mag, you shouldn't be in hell, you should have a medal. A great big shiny medal with "Badass Avenging Witch" on it. I might have one made anyway, in your honour. I bloody love you.'

I hear her laugh one more time as the light begins to fade.

Total badass.

# ANOTHER WITCH PRICKER

When I wake up there's a chink of winter light sneaking through the imperfectly closed curtains, and I'm looking straight into the sleeping face of Thor. Considering the day we had yesterday, he looks surprisingly peaceful; and after that dream with Mag, I feel much more refreshed than I would dare expect. Thor's beard is a little shorter than in Iceland and, being careful not to wake him, I raise my hand to touch it, noting the threads of red and grey in the soft brown hairs, like a tawny owl. Next I admire his long lashes and his well-shaped lips as I slowly reach below the duvet and savour the softness of the skin of his back. As I tenderly stroke across his shoulder, he stirs and opens his eyes. It's amazing how quick to smile he is when he sees me; it's like he snaps from asleep to awake in three seconds flat. He lifts his hand to touch my bruised neck.

'How are you, beautiful witch?'

Just hearing his voice, plus feeling the kindness in his

touch, makes my chin wobble, and only with a monumental effort do I make it stop.

'I'm aching everywhere, but I'm fine. I think the TCP saved my cut, because it's sore, but it's not itching.'

Thor pulls me into his arms and I nestle into his neck. His skin is so warm to the touch, and his musky, clean smell is like medicine.

'I hope you don't mind that I showed up in Newcastle,' he says.

'Are you bloody mad? I would actually be dead if you hadn't.'

'No, you wouldn't, your guides would have found another way to save you.'

'You really are a one-off, you know. You show up, all guns blazing after talking to elves in a dream, you bond with my friends immediately, you knock in a door as a mentalist is trying to hang me, you completely accept a ghost throwing a lamp at you, you handle the police like a pro, and then you make me feel safe enough to sleep after a really-not-very-fun near-death experience. Plus, you don't tell on me when you see me stealing from the crime scene.'

'Most of that was simply instinct and love. Apart from the last bit, and that was me being curious as to what could be so important that you had to take it.'

'Give me a tick to clean my teeth – my breath smells like a cesspit – and then I'll show you . . .'

I get out of bed in my vest and shorts, and Thor inhales sharply. I look in the mirror over the hotel desk, and in even in the gloomy light I can see how knocked about I am.

I turn on the little lamp to get a better look and inspect the purple, yellow and black bruises around my neck; the other massive bruise around the pricker stab-wound, which is black and green and slightly raised, but doesn't yet seem to be infected; plus lots of smaller bruises and cuts all over me, from rolling in broken glass and pottery on the floor with my jeans pulled down.

'Jesus, Tanz, look what she did to you.'

'It wasn't her – it was an evil fucker called Wyllam. I'll explain all when I've had some paracetamol and my first coffee.'

I pop into the bathroom and clean my teeth and, when I come back out, Thor is making us both an espresso. Even in my bashed-up state, the close proximity of this delicious wizard, with his chest-rug, his cheeky twinkle, his gentle voice and his very warm skin, starts to make me feel naughty. I think it might be the first traces of survivor's euphoria. He's only wearing boxers, and as he passes me the espresso cup, then makes one for himself, there's an electric crackle in the air as his energy links in with mine. I reach for my jeans – another item of clothing I intend never to wear again – and take out the witch pricker.

'This is what I picked up. It's a retractable skinny little knife. It's got Lydia's and my blood on it, and I have a lot to tell you, Thor. But I need to take care of something else first.'

I put the pricker down on the little table by the window and begin to close the space between us. Nothing else needs to be said as he shoots back his coffee, places down his now-empty cup and moves towards me. In seconds we are face to face, and I pull him to me so that I can feel his skin against mine, and I crush my lips against his. Considering how bashed up I am, it's incredible how much I want him right now. Romantically slow, getting-to-know-you-even-better sex will definitely have its place at some point, but right now I need to devour him, and so I do, and his response is the thing of dreams. Not ghost dreams, but sex dreams.

Yes, this is definitely a big improvement on yesterday.

Huge, in fact.

# IRISH DANCING NEXT DOOR

Brunch ends up being in Blakes, as the hotel couldn't accommodate us for another night, so we have our little cases and they've let us put them in a cupboard by the kitchen. All three of us order more food than we need, including a pile of toast and loads of coffee, plus a mug of builder's tea for Sheila. She looks much better today and has some colour in her cheeks, as well as a nose that isn't running any more.

'I woke up a different woman this morning, so I went out and bought more of those pills you gave me. They're superb. Not much point staying in bed anyway, as the couple next door were making a right racket.'

For a second I don't get it, then my jaw drops '*Sheila!* No, we weren't.'

Thor chokes on his latte and then can't stop chuckling.

Sheila winks. 'I'm bloody joking. Sort of.'

Thor grins at me, his dimples breaking out in full force, and begins to butter his toast. 'Maybe the couple next door were playing video games?'

'Yeah, maybe. Sounded more like they were Irish dancing, from where I was sitting.'

I eat some scrambled eggs and wait for my cheeks to stop burning.

'So, Sheila, I'm about to book myself and Tanz into another hotel. Would you like a room too?'

'Actually, no, thank you. Fate's been playing silly buggers again and my friend has returned early from Jamaica. He was meant to be away for much longer than this, but for some reason he needed to get back to London and I got a text this morning saying he's landed!'

'I know why Pan's back, Sheils. Why don't you just admit that you can't get enough of each other?'

She takes a sip of her tea and shrugs. 'I think you're mistaking me for someone with a heart. Anyway, before I start looking at train timetables, I wondered if you need me for anything else here. The police will have to interview me by phone, if they want anything else, but what about you?'

'Oh no. I have one last thing to sort out, and that doesn't need an extra witch.'

'You going to tell?'

So while we eat and Thor fiddles with a booking app on his phone, I explain about the nasty pointy pricker that needs to be burned in order to cleanse it, and how it has to be me who does it, and that I'll sort it asap. That I want to say some words over it, plus wrap it in salt again. I tell Sheila that Mag wanted it to be dropped to the bottom of the sea, but I think it would be a nice touch to drop it into a deep part of the River Tyne from one of the bridges.

'This was where Wyllam last used that thing to kill

people, so this is where I think it should stay. It only went wrong before because Mag buried it where it could be found. Also I'm not sure it did go "wrong". This was something that needed addressing, and now it has been.'

'I think you're right. Is that all – nothing else to sort out?'

For a second or two I see a humour-filled round face with gigantic glasses on, sitting opposite me, eating a cake. She looks directly into my eyes, nods and then disappears. My heart gives a little jump. My Gladys. What the hell will I find at her cottage?

'That's all.'

'Okay. Well, there's a train I can get in forty-five minutes, so that's perfect. I'll message Milo and apologize for not seeing him today, I'm sure he'll understand.'

'Oh God, of course he will. He's not replied to my text yet, so I reckon he'll still be in bed. Yesterday was a lot. You okay, Thor?'

Thor, whose head has been furrowed in concentration, suddenly puts down his phone and digs into his sausage and bacon with a look of satisfaction on his face. 'I got the booking I hoped for. Once we've seen Sheila to the station, we can go and claim our room.'

'You going to tell me where we're staying?'

'No.'

Sheila waggles her eyebrows at me. 'International man of mystery.'

'Isn't he just.'

# CATATONIC STATE

Holy shit, I'm staying in the HILTON.

Here's the thing: Thor isn't a millionaire, he's not super-rich at all, but he works hard and his parents brought him up in a nicely middle-class environment. Also, he's a man who knows a lot about a lot, is a tour guide and knows exactly how to get plenty of perks on booking sites. So here we are, in the swanky Newcastle Hilton, which he got at a reasonable rate, so I don't feel so bad letting him pay, which he insists on doing. And there's a free bottle of fizz waiting, a box of chocolates and some fruit (has he told them we're just married or something, the little scamp?). This is my favourite hotel in this part of the North, because of the views over the river, but I usually only have the chance to stay here when I've done a particularly well-paid job. Thor did good and got a room on the right side of the hotel to have an amazing view of several of the bridges, the quayside opposite and the river flowing by. Tonight, with all the lights on, it'll be simply breathtaking.

We're sitting at a small round table with two chairs, right

next to the window, drinking our herbal teas and absorbing the information that Preeya, the lovely police lady, recently imparted. I think it's only right to say at this point that people always tell me more than they should anyway, including members of law enforcement, probably because I'm so damned charming, but in Preeya's case there's a very good extra reason. She was in the room yesterday when ghost shizz was kicking off and has had to carefully cherry-pick what to say in her statement about that. Lydia's voice deepened and changed accent, and the person 'Lydia' was shouting at (I'm sure Preeya will have said she was shouting at thin air or arguing with herself) appeared, at the very least, as a heat-haze to most of the rest of us. Also, even Preeya saw Lydia's face change when Wyllam fully got hold of her. It was one of the only times I've seen a face transmogrify like that and it was freaky as hell to me, so fuck knows how scary it was to a layman. We're the only other people in the world who witnessed the lunacy that went on, and I think that forms a bond that lends itself to sharing confidences.

From what Preeya said in her phone call, which came in just after Sheila had given us one of her queenly waves and buggered off to platform three to get back to her own bed and (probably) the delicious man waiting in it, it's all been a bit manic since Lydia was taken into custody. First of all, Preeya asked me, in the timid voice of a cornered mouse, if I'd heard 'the voice' speaking back to Lydia when she 'suddenly sounded like a man'. Seeing no need to lie at this point, I told Preeya that the voice she was hearing was actually attached to a spirit form that only some of us could see, but we all heard; and that her name is Mag and she's a throwback to the time of the Newcastle witch trials. On hearing this, Preeya relaxed, safe in the knowledge that if she's mad, I'm mad as well, and said that Lydia had undergone quite the transformation last night. Her arrival at the police station had been punctuated by more kicking, screaming, hitting anyone who came close and generally getting herself into more and more trouble, as far as the law is concerned. Having already seen her head-butt one poor sod to the ground, then knock another two officers' heads together to the same effect, I can't say I'm surprised that Lydia carried on in the same vein. In the end she was locked in a cell for the safety of herself and others, awaiting an assessment officer to determine whether she was mentally fit to be there or whether she should be taken to a secure psychiatric hospital.

Preeya said she called the duty officer, also a friend of hers, to see what was going on with Lydia a few minutes after we all left in an Uber to go back to the hotel after our ridiculous night. Apparently, within half an hour of our leaving, Lydia was on the floor of the cell, rocking and muttering, 'She took it back, she took it back.' Then she lay down on the prison bed, went deadly silent and refused to move or speak again. And as far as Preeya knew, Lydia was still in the same catatonic state right now.

As I sip my tea, I mull over the meaning of all this, and decide that if Thor's come all this way on love and a hunch, the least I can do is make sure he knows everything.

'Thor, I had another dream last night. And I have to tell you first, before I go any further, this advanced-level connection with ghosts and family lines, and being told stuff through dreams, has accelerated like a speeding bullet since I met you and Alfvin and Birta and spent time in Iceland. I mean, I was spooky before, but this is outrageous and I'm really not sure it's sustainable. For a start, I faint when it gets too powerful and I actually make physical contact with them, and that can't be right, can it?'

Thor strokes my leg with a stockinged foot and shakes his head. 'No, if it's depleting you, then you need to find a way to protect yourself so it doesn't get so dangerous.'

'*Yes*. Exactly that. Anyway, that aside, it has been extremely intense recently. Last night was hopefully as bad as it gets, and now . . . well, as I was saying to Sheila earlier, this little mission is not quite over yet. The pricker – that thing Lydia stabbed me with – it's the very same object that Wyllam the witch finder used to "prove" that innocent people were witches. He'd find a mark on their naked body, humiliating them by stripping them, then pretend to stab them in their "witch's mark", but would actually retract the blade so that blood didn't flow.'

'Those poor women. It was only women, right?'

'Almost exclusively, but if any man posed a threat to the witch pricker's authority or was too sympathetic to the "witches", then he would be killed too. Here, it was fourteen women and one man, who was accused by a woman who was almost certainly mentally ill and probably had an obsession with him, despite being married.'

Thor shakes his head sadly. 'Brutal times.'

'Yup. Anyway, Wyllam caused a lot more deaths than just the ones here; he wreaked havoc in Scotland too, and

Mag – the woman we saw last night who was furious with him – truly was a witch and was also his sister. He had a sexual thing for her, plus jealousy that she was so loved by their parents. He actually tried to rape her, but Mag fought him off and threatened to tell their dad, who would have killed him. Instead Wyllam left home and, following in the footsteps of Matthew Hopkins, the self-named Witchfinder General, started a business in murdering women for money. The misogynistic little shit would name young lasses who took his fancy, as well as all the older women. They were often freed when he was told the lasses were too young and pretty to be witches, by councillors and justices of the peace who were just as misogynistic as Wyllam was; but before that he got the chance to strip, humiliate and abuse them, which I'm sure sexually gratified him no end.'

'And all because of a twisted relationship with his sister?'

'Oh, it's amazing how many atrocities in this world seem to come down to such a basic premise. Honestly, serial killers are often very obvious creatures.'

'So what did Mag say in your dream?'

I try not to smile too much here. Some of what she said I will keep to myself for the time being – a warm secret to remind me that not all bastards get away with their sins, especially with glorious loons like Mag around, refusing to take their shit.

'The pricker – Mag buried it with the poor innocents who were hanged in Newcastle. It was her way of trying to right the wrong. Unfortunately, that part of the grounds was dug up during a renovation. The bones of several of those who were hanged were discovered, and the pricker was also found. It ended up in some museum display. Mag didn't say where. What seems to have happened is that the whole witch-trials thing was suddenly reignited by my energy, as was a massive unresolved incident in my family line. My sudden surge in power gave extra energy to Mag's spirit and also reignited Wyllam's curse. His dark force found a vessel in the form of Lydia, who was absolutely obsessed with the witch trials and the "wrong" that was done to her. Personally, I don't think it was anything to do with her relative's hanging that brought misfortune to her family. Shit happens – everyone lives through difficulty. It's more likely that a midlife crisis about lack of achievement cued up a mental-health episode. Anyway Wyllam managed to get Lydia to nick the pricker. And when she did, that was it. He was able to fully take over proceedings with her.'

'Okay, so far, so much like a horror movie!'

'I know, right, but that's the thing: we're coming to the denouement of the movie now. When we left last night, I took the pricker. I knew I shouldn't, but I also felt I had to. And within a short time of us leaving, Lydia powered down in her cell. The furious force that had her beating people up and spitting and screaming just stopped. He lost power, and she lost energy. And now we have to finish it – that's what I was telling Sheila about. It's not complicated, but it would be nice to have some company.'

'Cool. So what's the plan?'

'There's somewhere we need to drive to and, I must warn you, I think I might get a little emotional when we get there. But what's new? And I feel it's better to go when it's nearer twilight.'

A wicked smile crosses Thor's face. 'In which case, we have plenty of time.' He stands and holds out his hand to me. 'I need to kiss your bruises better. All of them. And maybe give you a prolonged shot of healing.'

I don't know how he does it, but Thor knows exactly what to say to speed me from nought to sixty in ten seconds flat. I stand and am pulled to him, then lifted, which is a novel thing, so that he can lay me on the nicely plumped white duvet, then lower himself next to me and slowly kiss away all thoughts. I cannot stress sufficiently the difference it makes to be kissed by someone you absolutely know understands you, and who also wants to eat you alive, even when you're bruised and cut from head to toe.

As our clothes and inhibitions fall to the floor, I feel that extra drumbeat underneath my heart, pulsing and vibrating with hot life, and for this moment at least I truly understand why sticking around on this planet for a little longer than I wanted to definitely has its perks.

# MINXY MAM

When my little mam sees the friend that I'm bringing into her home is in actual fact a man – a cheeky-faced beardy man with twinkly eyes, no less – she's as close to coquettish as I've ever seen her. She smooths down her pale-blue velour tracksuit and white fleecy cardigan with the sensual hands of a horse-masseuse and switches her kettle on with a girlish giggle.

'Eeeh, well, Tanz, when you said you were popping over with company, I thought you were bringing Sheila. Who might this be?'

'Sheila's gone back to London, Mam, as she only booked her hotel room for three days and she was feeling much better today, so she was well enough to travel. And this is Thor. We met in Reykjavik. He saved me when I was trapped in the snowy cabin.'

'Hello, Thor. Nice to meet you.'

'Nice to meet you too. You have a lovely home, and the garden is beautiful.'

She glances out of the window and nods. 'Tanz's dad

does the garden – he's a dab hand with a trowel and a paintbrush, I have to say. Would you like a cup of tea, Thor?'

Obviously I don't exist now.

'Yes, please: milk, no sugar.'

'A man who knows what he wants. Excellent.'

Holy shit, I have never seen Mam like this with anyone, ever. None of my exes, none of my friends and definitely not my dad. 'Are you okay, Mam?'

'I'm perfectly fine, thank you very much. So how come you're here, Thor? Tanz didn't say you were coming over.'

She begins to fill the pot and I turn to Thor, shrugging in amazement, as she all but sashays to the cupboard to get the biscuit barrel.

'I wasn't meant to be here. I came to surprise her, because we had a nice chat on the phone and I missed her too much to stay away.'

'Aw, that's nice. Isn't that nice, Tanz?'

'It's lovely, but I missed Thor's arrival yesterday because I got kidnapped, and if it wasn't for him being a spooky sod, Sheila talking to a friendly ghost and Milo sitting on a raving lunatic, I'd probably be dead now.'

I wasn't going to tell her this, but Mam's weird behaviour has made me want to snap her back to her senses.

'You *what*?'

'Sit down, Mam. We've got a lot to tell you.'

# HE'S A WIZARD

We're half an hour in and the biscuit-barrel contents have been seriously depleted by the time Dad enters from his latest shift in the shed and Zorro wags his way in behind him, both of them with cold, fresh air clinging to them like nature's incense. Thor looks up at Dad and I don't even know what the look is that passes between them, but Thor stands and holds out his hand. 'Hello, I'm Thor, I'm in love with your daughter. She's a Geordie spitfire.'

I don't know if it's the accent, the twinkle, the surprise or the fact that my dad can tell a genuine person from a hundred miles off, but he doesn't simply laugh, he absolutely howls. And Thor joins in. Zorro doesn't know what to do and starts to bark. My mam isn't used to not being the centre of attention in her own home and watches the men in confusion, while I inexplicably well up, because seeing my dad laugh joyously makes me so happy.

When he's finished laughing and has calmed down the dog, who really can't deal with so much action in his territory, Dad does the absolute unthinkable and pulls up an extra two seats (foldaway chairs from the shed) and has a cup of tea with us (I go for a weak Nescafé Gold).

'So, Thor, what do you think of Gateshead?' My dad is dunking a Gypsy Cream. Like father, like daughter.

'I love it, from what I've seen of it. We're staying at the Hilton, which is on the Gateshead side of the river, I believe.'

'It is. Pricy, though.'

Thor winks. 'Not when you have connections.'

'You speak English brilliantly, lad, and I would never guess your accent. I can hardly speak English myself, and I was born here.'

'That's not true – your accent is very lyrical.'

Mam spots an 'in' here, as the attention has been elsewhere for too long.

'Thor, what you were saying about the witch finder before. How did you know that Tanz was in trouble?' She looks at me. 'Tanz, show your dad your neck.'

I'm wearing a turtle-necked Icelandic sweater that Thor brought with him. I pull it down a bit and my dad gasps. 'What the hell happened?'

'Oh, it was only a nutter, Dad. She's safely behind bars now.'

Thor pipes up here, 'I don't know how she does it, but Tanz came over to Iceland and she tuned me into something that I didn't realize I had in me. A sense of what may happen before it does – that's the best way to put it. And I knew she needed help before I even landed. Your daughter is extraordinary.'

'Oi, my head won't fit through the door in a minute. Look, one of the main reasons for us coming here right now is to tell you something that I think will make you both happy. Those dreams Mam's been having about the witch trials and everything, which coincided with mine, should be a thing of the past from now on. I've found out how to put it all to rest for good, but most of the work's already done. No more dead hares in the garden and no more restless, wakeful nights, Dad, with Mam seeing bad stuff. Well, for now, anyway.'

Mam looks at me, then down at her tea. 'That's not the news that would make us most happy.'

'Sorry, Mam – what?'

Dad immediately swerves the subject. 'In all fairness, Tanz, your mam's had restless nights with weird dreams since I first met her. She just blames you now.'

'Hey, don't say that. I had it all under control before the shenanigans with Tanz started.'

Dad looks at Mam and smiles kindly. 'I've had to listen to you talking in your sleep for years. This stuff isn't new.' He takes her hand momentarily, which is something I don't ever remember seeing. The closest they ever got to that when I was little was Mam linking Dad's arm.

She gives his hand the tiniest squeeze, then returns it to her cup of tea.

'Tonight, Mam, the last link to that awful past will be gone. And I already know there'll be no more synchronized hanging dreams.'

'Well, try not to get yourself killed while you're doing

it.' And suddenly my mam's crying and I have no idea what's going on.

My dad looks worried, then Thor jumps up, squats at her feet, puts his hands on her knees and looks straight into her eyes.

'Seeing Tanz with all those bruises and marks made me feel the same. But just so you know: she's incredibly protected. Her guides need her alive and well – she's such an amazing bridge between different worlds. And while I'm around, I will protect her in any way I can.'

'Thank you, Thor. Tanz doesn't always appreciate that this stuff put my own mam through a lot; it's not something I was brought up to appreciate. It was to be feared and avoided.'

Thor takes a couple of tissues out of his pocket and gives her one. Mam dabs at her eyes and he pats her knee, before retaking his seat.

'Well, Tanz is very skilled in these special arts and she has protection from energies that you wouldn't even believe. I've seen it: your daughter is looked after.'

My dad stands up. 'Thor, it's been a pleasure to meet you, I'll tell you that, and I think our Tanz is safer by knowing you. She's gone out with some right Charlies in the past.'

Oh my God, I have no idea what's got into my parents today. But if nothing else, it's nice to see them not hate my . . . well, my boyfriend, I suppose. I've not chosen anyone who treated me well in the past, so this is a revelation, seeing them chat away with Thor. Almost to the point where I feel uncomfortable.

Dad goes off to his shed again to 'finish a project'. And Mam looks much more relaxed than she did the day that hare landed in her rockery.

Thor hugs Mam, and she hugs him back.

'Thank you, Thor, you've helped put my mind at rest. You're a lovely lad. He's a lovely lad, isn't he, Tanz?'

'Yes, Mam, he's a wizard.'

# COTTAGE BY THE SEA

By the time we're back in my car, the light is fading and it's time for the last part of my northern mission. I can hardly believe what just went on. There wasn't one thing Thor did that was false or contrived. He's just a laid-back, beautiful soul, and my mam and dad adored him. He looks at me as I put the car in gear.

'Your parents are sweet. Different life from you, so it must be scary for them – your adventures.'

'Yeah, you're right. But my mam knows a lot more than you think. She doesn't like it – she doesn't like having what I have – but she gave it to me, Thor. She's scared of it, but it was her gift first. And she gets upset, but actually she's known pretty much everything I was up to since this stuff all kicked off. Her dreams and visions are off the scale.'

'Remember you have to be gentle with her. She's not like you. She hasn't travelled and she's only really been with your father. She's not worldly.'

As I pull out, I pat Thor's knee. This lad is emotionally mature. That's a first for me. I need to be careful, as I've rejected good men for less. And I don't want to be doing that again.

'What was that look between you and my dad by the way? When he first came in?'

Thor doesn't answer immediately; he thinks before he can properly put it into words. 'Your father is not very English. He may seem it, but underneath he has the deep thoughts of a Norse man. I think there's a lot he doesn't vocalize. He understands more than he lets on. I like him.'

'Well, he obviously felt the same about you on sight – like he recognized something in you immediately. It was strange.'

'Isn't everything in your life strange?'

'Pretty much.'

I drive on in silence, just happy to have Thor in the car, and he looks about him, taking in the landscape as we pass into the fields and countryside around Gateshead.

'It's beautiful here.'

'I suppose it is. I sometimes forget. It takes seeing it through someone else's eyes to remember again.'

We're on the way to a village near Blyth, which is a seaside town, but not in any kind of romantic way. It used to be a mining town and, when that industry died, the place fell on hard times. Depression was high, as well as drug use. But then, like all places filled with such depravation, there is also a high incidence of creativity, and I used to know a lot of eccentric but very artistically talented young people at the rock clubs in Newcastle who came from Blyth.

I tell Thor a little bit about it until we get nearer to

Gladys's cottage, when I start to feel scared. Thor, being Thor, feels the change in energy from about six miles off.

'Are you okay, Tanz?'

'I am, but I'm going to tell you something, by way of warning. A lovely friend of mine lives at the place we're going to now. I had an amazing experience with her not that long ago. She's a healer and a funny, beautiful soul. She's helped keep me sane at times when the spooky stuff was freaking me out, and she's always been nothing but kind and strong. Now something's happened and it may be quite dark. Something tells me I'll know as soon as I get inside her cottage. You can stay in the car if you like, but I know – from looking out of her kitchen window as she made a cuppa the few times I visited – that she has a little firepit out in the garden that she lights in the evening, especially in autumn, she said, and watches the flames while playing with her crystals. She told me about fire and how it purifies the soul. If it's still there, it would be the perfect place to purify the witch pricker too, and to soak up Gladys's energy.'

'But you don't know if she'll be there?'

'Oh, she'll be there all right. I just don't know in what form.'

'Okay, it takes a bit to creep me out, but I have to admit, when you say it like that, it sounds a little scary.'

'Yes, it does. How about you let me find the key and go in first? Then I'll come and get you out of the car when I know what's what.'

'Are you sure?'

'It's probably for the best.'

Thor leans over and kisses me gently, before I get out of the car and take in a lungful of cold sea air. There are no lights on in the cottage. I look to the little side-path that Gladys told me to go down. I can see the birdhouse from here.

*Okay. Here goes nothing.*

# LOVE LETTER

The key is exactly where Gladys said it would be. I stand at the front door for a good minute before putting it in the lock and going in.

The first thing I notice is the lack of a smell. No one's dead in here. In fact as I turn the lights on and walk through the living room towards the kitchen, I realize it's not only the smell of death that's absent. A massive number of Gladys's crystals have gone, as have all the plants. The furniture is still here, but the crystals and plants that crowded every surface have left the building, apart from a few of her biggest and most magnificent examples, including a huge amethyst cave and a giant labradorite crystal ball. I check the little bathroom, which is spotless and unused. Gladys wasn't a houseworky kind of lass, so the sterile look of the place is as worrying as anything else. When I go into her bedroom, which overlooks the garden, the bed is made and everything is tidy. Her spare room is the same. It's like something, or someone, came along and sucked Gladys and her whole personality out of the place.

Back in the living room, I glance at the tiny telephone table near the TV. The landline telephone's gone, but the telly's still there. A great big box of a thing that was probably made in 1985. And there's an envelope. As I get closer, I see it's addressed to me, with a stamp on it. I wonder why she didn't post it?

I walk over to look at it and momentarily I don't want to pick it up, as this is all so odd. But then my nosy side absolutely gets the better of me and I sit in the threadbare armchair that I've sat in every time I've been here and open up the envelope, noting that it's dated the day before I flew to Reykjavik, so this has been waiting for me for more than ten days:

*Dear Tanz,*

*If you're reading this letter in my living room, then my little experiment worked. If it's arrived at your place via the mail, well then, someone else came in here before you did and either I've been burgled by a petty criminal who's nice enough to post my mail or everything we ever believed in was a right load of bunkum!*

*As you'll see at the cottage, I've spent the past week packing up my crystals and giving them away to all the New Age places and charity shops in a twenty-mile radius, plus leaving the plants outside people's houses in the middle of the night, because I didn't want them to die here, unwatered. (The crystals that I've kept are for you.) I've also put my clothes into old suitcases in the wardrobe and cleaned the place the best I can, even though I bloody hate cleaning. I have to admit, mind, that once I started, it was very therapeutic: cleaning up my life and not leaving it for someone else to sort out.*

*Two months ago I finally went to the doctor's. I was losing weight at a rate of knots, which is unheard of, what with my metabolism being like a snail on a broken escalator, plus my tummy was like a swollen little drum. That's when I found out I had the big C. (I thought I'd developed some kind of reaction to Viennese Whirls, because I'd got into the habit of eating a packet every night while watching my old musicals.) But don't you be thinking I'm going to talk about the ins and outs of finding out that I've got an incurable and ridiculously fast-moving cancer; let's just say it was too late to be getting all flustered about it, getting thin isn't all it's cracked up to be, and I certainly wasn't going to let them blast me with all those horrible chemicals in the last weeks of my life. So I got to work sorting out all my bits.*

*The place is now legally yours. Do what you want with it. There's no sentimental value for me and while you'll not exactly make millions from it in this area, it'll still be a nice little sum. And while you've got it, the garden's lovely when you need a bit of peace. It gets the sun in the morning.*

*I just want to add: it was one of the great pleasures of the past twenty years – after losing my son and then my husband – to meet you, Tanz. You're a chaotic, clever, magical miracle who makes the world a better place and you enhanced my life immeasurably. You also let me know that my little Andrew is waiting for me, and you have no idea how much easier that made it for me to take this decision. Please don't look for my body, pet. I went somewhere hidden away that always brought me comfort and peace. I took every bit of morphine with me that I managed to get my hands on. They think I've been taking it at home every day for the past week. Silly sausages – I've saved it up. The chances of anyone ever finding me are pretty slim, and I want it that way. I want to sink back into nature like I came from it. No one needs to cry for me. I lived the life I wanted to and now I'm ready to see my Andrew and maybe even Giancarlo, if the universe wills it (he talks to me all the time anyway, so I can't see why he won't be there to tell me how much his back hurts as I fly out into the stars).*

*As soon as I'm out of this sack of skin and bone, I'm going to make sure you hear from me – it'll be my first mission. To show you it's all true, everything we talked about, and hopefully make it easier when you next experience loss. Just so that you know: being seriously ill did not stop me having as much cake as I wanted. I will take my last breath chewing on a Wagon Wheel.*

*You are very loved.*
*Gladys xxx*

Thor lets himself in, as I didn't lock the door behind me. I've been in the chair crying for the past ten minutes and my eyes are like wet ping-pong balls, but I'm trying really hard to pull myself together, and I hug him, then hand him the letter and pop to the kitchen for a handful of kitchen roll to mop up my face. As I stand there, looking out on the beautifully kept little garden with its bench, its swing seat and its firepit, I see Gladys, of course I do. She's standing there in the light from the solar lamps that come on by themselves, holding little Andrew, exactly as I saw him in my dream that time, in his red T-shirt and white shorts with frogs on them. He told me then that I was to tell his 'mamma' that when he saw her, he would hug her as hard as ever he could; and there he is now, arms wound around Gladys's neck and little legs around her ribcage, as she smiles and waves at me through the window. Andrew, with his curls and big, big eyes, turns his head towards me for a minute, flashes his bright-white milk-teeth and waves too, before he buries his face back in his mother's neck. Then they disappear like they were never there and I sink to the floor.

Thor comes to join me, having read the letter, and simply sits beside me and rocks me in his arms while I let it all out.

# NEVER GOODBYE

There were still quite a lot of fire-logs in the cupboard by the sink and three cigarette lighters, probably there for the job of lighting the touchpapers. And now the little firepit is roaring with flames and we're drinking a glass of red wine each that Thor ran and got from the corner shop down the street. My face is still swollen, but hopefully I look a little less like a toad. I've retrieved the pricker from my bag and it feels cold and heavy in my hand. Amazing that such a small thing could help bring so much devastation to people's lives. Just shows how dangerous belief can be. I didn't have a square of linen to wrap it in, but seeing as I'm not going to bury it, I don't think that matters.

We add another log to make the fire even hotter. These logs are made of compressed sawdust and paraffin and, boy, do they flare up when you light them. Thor and I hold hands while I make a witch's prayer, to finally neutralize this awful symbol of suppression and cruelty for good.

'I call on all the women who went before me and will

come after me, in my family line and in all family lines affected by the witch pricker and by the witch finder who wielded it. I ask you to help me purify this tool of all the bad feeling and cruelty that it represents. Let it inflict no more harm. I ask that it is cleansed of all bad energy, purified by fire and is never allowed to cause misery again. I thank you for this opportunity to right these wrongs and hope you will join with me in protecting all of our sisters from similar future suffering. With all love, we cast this evil into the fire.'

I look at Thor and nod, and he places the pricker on a flat stick that he found in the garden for the job and pushes it to the centre of the blaze. We leave it there and sip from our glasses, resolved to stay here until the flames die down and we can fish the pricker out again and pour a jug of water with salt in it over the hot metal.

'Are you okay, Tanz?'

'I am. I'd already guessed Gladys wasn't with us any more. I just couldn't understand how I'd spoken with her on the phone and everything. She even left a voicemail. But it never sounded right. Voices go crackly on old-fashioned landlines, not on iPhones. Obviously I've checked my phone and there's no trace of her calls or her voice message. She was already gone by then and was just using that method to speak to me until I found out the truth. My friend Caroline spoke to me on the phone after she died too. Spooky stuff is wild.'

'That's crazy.'

I sip at my wine, and then something occurs to me.

'Bloody hell, Thor. I've just realized. The way my energy

went through the roof in the past few weeks and the vibration rose, and it seemed like everything behind the veil was closer... It was *Gladys*. When someone close to you is near death or actually dies, everything gets magnified. That letter was addressed the day before I flew to Iceland. Oh my goodness, that's how the portal between worlds was open so wide for me. Gladys, it was you!'

Both of us see what happens next. I know this because Thor gives a little gasp of wonder. As usual, he's awed instead of scared. Behind the fire, which is already less fierce, a little woman with thick glasses and the biggest smile ever, with fire glinting off her lenses, materializes near the tiny potting shed – half-transparent and looking very pleased with herself.

*'It certainly was, pet. I went over easily – it was my time. And straight away I got to work. You wouldn't believe how bright your light is from that side.'*

'You were brilliant, Gladys. Thank you for guiding me through it. I was clueless.'

*'No, you bloody weren't. And don't think you've got rid of me. I'm still here, still your pal. Now don't forget Blyth West Pier.'*

Then she fades out again. And Thor looks at me with wonder shining in his amber-specked eyes.

'Gladys spoke to us! I really heard her. Did I just meet your friend from the other side?'

I've got tears running down my face again, not from grief, but from gratitude. 'You certainly did. And so did I. Oh my God, she looks so well! Being a ghost suits her.'

Thor laughs and kisses my cheek.

'Shit, I've realized what she meant, Thor, about the pier. When we've fished the pricker back out – whatever state it's in – I think we should lock up, walk to Blyth West Pier and drop it off the end. I forgot there was a pier here. That way the pricker stays in the North, but Mag gets her wish and it'll be in the salty depths. Then we can go back to our lovely hotel and cuddle up.'

'Music to my ears.'

I can't seem to stop talking, because suddenly I'm inspired and grateful to be on this planet with all my gifts and this beautiful man. 'And tomorrow you can meet my lovely old nanna, and later we can go to Bougie Bar and see Raquel and Paulo. Raquel said I'd met my match – my wizard. I remember that bit now. She would absolutely love to meet you! And if Gladys has given you her blessing by flashing up like a little Geordie good-luck charm to say hello, she must obviously like you as well. So that's it, you're in trouble now.'

I pause for breath and Thor puts a hand on my cheek, not seeming to mind that I currently look like a bloated puffer fish.

'Good. I like being in trouble with you.'

Then he kisses me as only a Viking wizard can.

# ACKNOWLEDGEMENTS

As always, I'd like to thank Lucy, Kinza and everyone at Pan Macmillan for being fantastic – the whole team is wonderful. I'd also like to again acknowledge the fabulous audio work of Adrian Cecil, who makes every recording an absolute pleasure. Thank you to David and Bev, who didn't turf me out when the rent was hard to come by; and thank you to my son, who grew up suddenly and became a beautiful man. Thank you to my parents, who've helped me through some real rough patches, plus provided comedy gold over the years that I've nicked and put into the books. Thank you to all of my pals, who have provided much-needed chats and laughs over the past year. Thank you to Jill H, for being more determined than I am to make sure these stories are seen as well as read; you're a diamond. And as for you, Tom Lenk, thank you for being the best cheerleader ever. You rock.

# WHEN THE DEAD CALL . . .

Discover the full Accidental Medium series!